LAS VEGAS NIGHT

By Stephen Leather

Table of Contents

CHAPTER 1

When the two men finally found the box, they had no idea of its significance, and were never to find out that they had overlooked a far more important discovery. The year was 1885 and Flinders Petrie and James Quibell were prominent Egyptologists from England. They had made the long journey to the West Bank of the Nile, opposite the modern city of Luxor, where once the city of Thebes had stood. They planned to excavate beneath the *Ramesseum*, the memorial temple to the longest-lived Pharaoh of all. Ramesses II.

Their excavation was destined not to produce a trove of ancient treasure, as the tomb had been robbed many centuries before, but the lowest part had been left untouched. At the bottom of the tomb's shaft, four metres down, Quibell and Petrie found a heap of debris that covered a small space of half a square metre in the wall. In this space was a wooden box, covered in white plaster, with a crudely-painted jackal on the lid. Inside the box were papyri, reed pens, ivory wands, a wooden female figure, an ivory figure of a boy carrying a calf, tiny beads, and seeds.

The two men recognised it as a Magician's Box, probably used by a specialist in childbirth, judging by the engravings of women and children on the wands. The tomb was, thereafter, known as the Magician's tomb, though Quibell's map to it was so poorly drawn that nobody has managed to find it since. The contents of the box were distributed to museums in Manchester, Cambridge, Pennsylvania and Berlin. The box itself was lost. With the exception of Petrie and Quibell, no living man had seen that chamber for centuries, apart from the native boy who accompanied them, carrying their food and water.

His name was Achmed, and he was twelve years old, happy to earn a few *piastres* for such light work. Neither of the older men noticed him wander away to the other side of the shaft, as they were inspecting the box. There, he cleared away some more rubble, and, as he had been told he would, he found a smaller niche cut into the wall, and inside it, a purse of goatskin, remarkably well-preserved. His eyes fixed on Petrie and Quirrell, he slipped the purse swiftly inside the folds of his robe, and moved away from there.

That night, when the Egyptologists and their party were sleeping soundly after celebrating their find, Achmed carefully and silently sneaked away from the camp and walked in the direction of the Nile. He had barely travelled five hundred metres when a figure on a horse appeared silently out of the moonlight and loomed above him.

"You have it?" asked the rider.

Achmed trembled at the authority in the voice.

"Yes, my Lord, it was as you said."

"And you have not opened it?"

"No, my Lord, I would not dare."

The figure dismounted, unrecognisable beneath the flowing white robe and scarf wound about his face and head.

"Give it to me."

"It is yours, my Lord. And I was promised a reward?"

Achmed's eyes shone at the thought of what he could buy with the promised gold.

"Yes indeed, your reward. Die now, and live forever." The wicked, curved blade appeared in the rider's hand faster than the eye could follow, and Achmed had no time to make a sound, before his head was struck cleanly from his shoulders. The rider remounted and disappeared into the desert, without a backward glance.

In the morning, the archaeologists noticed the boy's absence, but thought little of it. They probably assumed he had returned to his people, and mounted no search for him. The scavengers of the desert made short work of his body, and soon there remained no trace of it. The purse of Baufra had claimed another victim.

CHAPTER 2

Salman Bin-Saheed waited until he reached home before examining his prize. His house was much larger and more richly decorated than the average peasant abode, as befitted his wealth and status. He handed his mount's bridle to one of his servants, walked through the arch of the main entrance and into the spacious courtyard. He went up the stone steps on the left and entered his personal chamber.

The room was painted in rich ochre, the walls and round pillars decorated with paintings of gods and scenes from ancient life. The shelves were of brown marble, and a brown upholstered divan couch lay in the middle of the room. Tables and chairs of mahogany were dotted around the room, many of them bearing small statues, of black cats, gold sphinxes and the ibis, the sacred bird of Egypt.

He lay on the divan, then rang a small bell on the table by his head. A servant shuffled in, dressed in the traditional long shirt, the *galabeya*, his head covered by a skullcap or *taqiyah*. He inclined his head to his master, but did not speak.

"Mohammed, light the lamps, then bring me my sherbet and my hookah."

The servant bowed his head again, and left the room.

Ten minutes later, the master of the house took a sip of sherbet, a long contented draw on the flavoured tobacco in his water pipe, and finally opened his new possession. His eyes widened with pleasure. The old goatskin leather of the purse was almost perfectly preserved, soft and supple to the touch, as if it had been kept oiled for centuries. He opened the top, and proceeded to remove the contents.

First came the three papyri. Thousands of years old, yet, unbelievably, still intact and readable to anyone who understood the old system of writing. They would take many months of painstaking work to decipher, but he knew he was equal to the task. Then came half a dozen reed pens, probably the same as had been used to write

3

the papyri. Of limited use now, but still, a valuable link to the past. A shaft of bronze, some eight inches long, covered in what looked like human hair.

"A serpent wand," he muttered. "Perhaps useful for parlour tricks."

And finally the great prize itself. A flat, crescent-shaped wand of ivory, covered with ornate carvings. A crocodile, a frog, a cat, an ibis and a snake, a sun disk with legs, and a winged griffin. There were also representations of the god Set and the goddess Tawarett but the largest and most prominent carving was of Anubis, jackal-headed god of the dead.

A sigh of satisfaction escaped his lips. "Aah. The wand of Baufra. At last. With this, the power of life and death shall be mine." He shuddered with pleasure.

CHAPTER 3

Jack Nightingale had more experience of violent death than any man ought to carry around with him. It was not something he ever dwelt on, at least not consciously. When he was working on a case, he pushed past horrors out of his mind to concentrate on the job at hand, but it was in the down times that they came back to haunt him, especially during nights of fitful sleep.

It started with the couple he thought of as his parents, though he now knew he was adopted. The Nightingales had been killed in a stupid road accident, crushed by a lorry at traffic lights. He hadn't been there to see them die, but his sleeping mind always produced a picture of the accident. He had witnessed the lorry driver throw himself off a high balcony some years later. Then his real father. Ainsley Gosling, the satanist, who had blown out his own brains with a shotgun, rather than confront the awful reality of selling his children's souls. His birth mother, who had torn out her own throat in horror at what had been done to her son. The images were relentless.

Nightingale tossed and turned, his sheets drenched with sweat as he saw, once again, the young girl Sophie throw herself off a balcony to escape the abuse inflicted on her by her father.

"No, Sophie. No, don't jump, love," he muttered in his sleep.

But she always jumped. Some nights he managed to catch her by her feet and held her close, sobbing at her that she would be alright now. Other nights he watched helplessly as her tiny frame lay smashed on the pavement.

His aunt and uncle. He hadn't seen them die, but he'd been the one to discover the bodies, her brutally butchered, him hanged. He couldn't save them, still didn't know who had killed them or why.

Robbie, his closest friend on the force, mown down by a taxi crossing the road for no reason at all. His father's chauffeur, his head torn from his body by the chain he'd looped round his own head before driving off. Jenny McLean's gamekeeper, who blasted himself with a shotgun in front of Nightingale. The man Mitchell and his bodyguards, torn to pieces and blasted into Hell. Marcus Fairchild, whose murder Nightingale had helped to set up. It never stopped, a parade of dead bodies that seemed to follow him around London, ending with the clone of himself that he'd personally killed in order to arrange his escape from England.

The dream went faster now. The victims of the Apostles in San Francisco, the young people possessed by demons in New York and their victims. The dead children in Memphis, Joshua Wainwright's whole family slaughtered. Most recently the young athletes whose lives were robbed from them in New Orleans.

He couldn't count the trail of death that followed behind him, and as he tossed and turned he saw newer faces in his dream, stretching out in front of him. A middle-aged man clutching his heart, an old woman, a surprised look on her face holding her stomach, an old man, blood streaming from the gash in his chest. A little man in a dark suit, bleeding to death in the street from bullet wounds. A woman smashed and broken on a sidewalk. A young, brunette woman frantically swimming as huge jaws opened behind her to show rows of yellow teeth.

"Faster, faster," muttered Nightingale, but he knew she'd die if he couldn't save her. But what could he do? He was too far away.

Nightingale woke up with a jolt, the girl and the teeth vanished. He mopped his brow with the bedsheet, and noticed that his hand was trembling.

He reached for the bedside table, found his cigarettes, lit one and blew smoke up at the ceiling as he tried to make sense of his dream. The memories he understood, they were burned indelibly into his psyche. But what about the other visions, the deaths that he hadn't witnessed. Were they to come?

CHAPTER 4

The Cabin stood dozens of miles from any other habitation, almost in the centre of the Bald Mountain Wilderness in Eastern Nevada. The trees which had grown there originally had all been cut down, some of them used in its construction, and the rest cleared away so there was an uninterrupted clear view for two hundred and fifty metres all around.

The nearest town of any size was the old copper mining centre of Ely. In contrast to the neon city of Las Vegas, two hundred and forty miles south, Ely was one of the coldest places in the contiguous United States, with snow falling for nine months of the year, and temperatures frequently dropping below minus thirty degrees at night. Not that Ely interested any of the current residents of The Cabin, since none of them had taken the usual route to Bald Mountain, which involved driving west from Ely and then hiking to their final destination. They had arrived in two helicopters, three weeks previously, under cover of darkness.

There were nine of them altogether. Eight federal agents, dressed alike in jeans, hiking boots and warm black hunting jackets, plus The Package. The eight agents were heavily armed, each one carrying a high powered pistol and with Heckler and Koch assault rifles always within reach. The Cabin was ringed with well-hidden remotely operated anti-aircraft guns, ready to deal with any unauthorised helicopter determined enough to ignore the no-fly zone which extended for twenty miles around The Cabin.

The Cabin itself was quite a piece of work. Every part necessary for its internal construction had been flown in by helicopter, and the site was miles from any hiking trail or place of interest, so there was very little chance of civilians casually stumbling across it. From the outside, it looked like a typical hunter's cabin, built of logs, with wooden window frames and front and rear doors and a log roof. Anyone authorised to look inside would notice at once that this was no ordinary construction. The walls were lined with steel, and the windows armoured. Nothing short of a tank shell would be likely to breach the walls. Perhaps a dozen men with rocket launchers might have forced their way inside, but there was no way for them to get there unseen by either the watchers in the woods or the drones which flew overhead. In the unlikely event that The Cabin was attacked by anything its defences were unable to handle, a flight of F-35A Lightning fighter aircraft could be summoned up almost immediately from the nearby Nellis Airbase. It had never been necessary. The Cabin's best defences were its anonymity and complete secrecy.

From the outside, The Cabin appeared to have one floor, and at first glance inside this would be confirmed. The main area was used as a living space, with cheap but adequate sofas and armchairs, a large-screen TV and a music system, which was rarely used. At the far end of the room was a fridge, a microwave and a sink, alongside some cupboards for food and plate storage.

Leading off the living area were four doors. Two led to bedrooms, generally occupied by the two agents who were off-shift at any time. The third led to a bathroom, with a power shower and toilet. The fourth looked, at first glance, as if it might be another bedroom, but in fact it hid a steel door, which could only be opened by a special code on a keypad. Behind the door, concrete steps led down to The Cabin's greatest secret - The Bunker.

The Bunker ran the whole length of The Cabin, but was on two levels. At the bottom of the steps was another thick steel door, which could be used to isolate the subterranean section from the building upstairs. Behind the door, there was another living area, six more bedrooms, a fully-equipped kitchen, two more bathrooms and, on the lower floor, a storeroom with enough tinned, frozen and microwaveable food to last a dozen men for months. The lower floor also contained the communications centre, with state-of-the art computers, as well as radios and a hot line to headquarters in Washington. At one end of the lower level was yet another steel door, but this one could be opened from either side, by anyone knowing the correct keycode. This was where The Package was stored at night.

The contents of that room was always referred to as "The Package" by the men in the Cabin, and in all communications with the outside world. In the seven years since The Cabin had been completed, there had been twelve different Packages.

This particular package was five feet eight inches tall, with a scrawny build and an unhealthy pallor that suggested he spent most of his life sitting indoors. There was still some brown in his badly-cut short hair, but it was mixed with a good deal of grey, and a yellowing forelock which matched the nicotine stains on the fingers of his right hand. None of the FBI men smoked, or were permitted to drink on duty, but these restrictions didn't apply to The Package. It was important to keep him happy, so The Cabin's ventilation system ran most of every day to expel the fumes of fifty cigarettes, and most of a fifth of Chivas Regal. To be fair, there was precious little else for Enzo Florentino to do during his stay at The Cabin. He was no great reader, the TV didn't interest him much, and he was denied his usual, rather unpleasant, pleasures. Even the FBI had its limits when it came to keeping him happy. Apart from smoking and drinking, he passed most of his days playing poker against a computer program on the laptop that had been provided for him. Its internet access had been disabled. Nobody was going to trace him that way.

Enzo Florentino was just starting his third week in The Cabin, and was very definitely getting bored out here. He pushed away the remains of his chilli and rice, topped up his glass from the latest bottle of whisky, lit another cigarette and stared over at the heavy-set young man opposite.

"Any news?" he asked.

The young man shook his crew-cut head. "Nothing that I've heard. There's talk of them swearing in a jury pretty soon, so maybe you won't have much longer to wait."

"And that's when the fun starts,"said Enzo Florentino. "You guys need to get me in and out of that courtroom for me to say my piece. Then what?"

"You'll be well protected, we've done this kind of thing dozens of times before. And after the trial, you disappear."

Florentino gave a humourless sneer. "For sure, I do...one way or another."

"You know what I mean, Witness Protection. New city, new name new ID, maybe a few changes in your appearance. Like I say, we've done it dozens of times."

"And how many of those dozens are still alive?"

The young man looked at his shoes and said nothing.

"Somebody'll talk," said Florentino. "With five mil on my head, somebody'll talk, and they'll find me."

"If you think that, why did you agree to testify?"

Florentino shrugged. "What choice did you bastards give me? Sing or I'd be looking at forty years in Federal prison. I don't have forty years left in me."

"Rock and a hard place, eh? Still, we're all glad you decided to do your duty as a citizen."

"My ass."

"Yeah, that's right, it's your ass that's at stake here, so just let us do our job."

"Some job you've got, stuck out here in Nowheresville for months at a time, babysitting some witness. Is that what you signed on for when you joined the Bureau?"

The younger man sighed. "I can't say it was the main attraction, but it's not like I've spent my whole career in this place. Soon enough, I'll get posted somewhere else."

"You should have tried a different line of work."

"Really," said the agent," so I could wind up like you, looking over my shoulder for the rest of my life?"

"It has its compensations." Florentino slowly and deliberately pushed back his left sleeve to expose the gold Rolex Daytona, which had cost at least a year's worth of the young man's salary. Maybe after the trial he'd need something less noticeable - it was always the small mistakes that killed you. "Looks like it's getting near my bedtime, nothing worth staying awake for. Wanna come tuck me in?"

"I can live without that, but we'll walk you to your room as usual." He looked over at his colleague. "Dave?"

A similarly thick-set young man, with an identical haircut, stood up from an armchair in the corner. Florentino raised his eyebrows, but said nothing. He thought he'd been talking to Dave, but maybe it was

10

John, or Steve What the hell, they all looked the same, apart from Paul the black guy. They all dressed the same and talked the same and he wasn't here to make friends.

He got up from the table, turned and walked down the steps, through the storeroom and stopped at the door of the Package room, the two federal agents behind and on either side of him, their pistols drawn. Florentino had given up wondering why, he guessed it was the way they'd been trained. Steve...or was it Dave...keyed the number of the day into the pad, then stood aside for Florentino to enter. He walked inside, closed the door behind him and heard the click of the magnetic lock. He knew the two agents would sit outside his door for the next four hours, until they changed shift. That was no concern of his, he planned to put them out of his mind and enjoy ten hours of sleep.

The room was comfortable without any hint of luxury. It was reminiscent of any bedroom in one of the cheaper hotel chains. A door to the right led to a toilet and shower-room. Florentino brushed his teeth, used the toilet and changed into the pyjamas they had provided for him. He lay on the bed and smoked his final cigarette of the day, carefully crushed it out in the ashtray on the bedside table, and drifted off to sleep.

If there had been any justice in the world, his dreams would have been filled with the anguished faces of people whose lives he'd helped to ruin, but Enzo Florentino never had developed a conscience, and his sleeping hours were generally calm and undisturbed, even on his last night alive.

CHAPTER 5

Around two hundred and fifty miles away, final preparations were being made for the ritual. The crystal ball had been cleansed with salt, the wand was free from all impurities. The old woman sat silent in her chair, ready to receive instructions. The man sitting opposite her was dark, just around medium height, with deep blue eyes, dressed in a rich, blue, silk robe and wearing a blue turban. He took one last draw on his hookah, then carefully hung the mouthpiece on the hook of the pipe. He exhaled the sweet tobacco smoke, steepled his fingertips, closed his eyes and began to breathe slowly and deeply.

Eventually he opened his eyes, and smiled at his assistant. "Everything is ready?"

The blonde woman nodded. She was in her twenties, curvy like a forties movie star, her hair soft and wavy, her makeup thickly applied.

"Yes. Khamsin. Everything has been prepared."

"Good. Let us begin."

He spoke in a soft, clear voice, giving his instructions precisely When he finished, the old lady in the chair nodded. He moulded a crude figure of a man from the bowl of Nile clay in front of him. His assistant passed him the items she had obtained from Enzo Florentino's house, two cigarette ends from an unemptied ashtray, and he pressed them into the back of the figure, and passed it across to the old woman. She held it in her left hand, with her right she took the carved ivory wand from him and pointed it at the crystal ball, as she had been commanded.

The old woman repeated the incantation she had been taught, pointing the wand at the crystal ball as she spoke the final words.

For just a fraction of a second, so quickly that it might never have happened, the figure of a man, his face the muzzle of some animal seemed to flicker from the end of the wand and race towards the crystal ball.

There was a bright flash of golden light and a loud cracking sound, and the old woman slumped back in her chair, her eyes closed, her breathing laboured.

The man parted his thin lips in a smile of triumph, and reached for his hookah again.

"It is done," he said. He gestured at his assistant. "Help her. Then send her away."

CHAPTER 6

In the mountains near Ely, Enzo Florentino jerked awake, feeling a sudden presence in his room. He opened his eyes and despite the darkness, thought he saw the flash of a strange figure approaching him, with the shadowy head of some animal. He felt a crushing pain in his chest, and his eyes closed again forever.

CHAPTER 7

The lights were always on in The Bunker, so nobody had any external clue as to the time. The Federal agent on the left-hand side of the door leading to the Package room glanced at his watch, and was surprised to find that it was 8.35 am. He looked across at his colleague.

"The bastard's a little late this morning. Usually out and wanting breakfast smack on 8.15."

"It's not a crime to oversleep."

"Not compared to his other crimes, but it's unusual and..."

The agent nodded."...and unusual spells trouble."

"Probably not, but nobody ever got fired for making sure." He rose from his chair and knocked on the door.

"Mr Florentino? You okay? Breakfast time."

Ten seconds passed before he tried again. "Guess we'd better take a look," he said when there was still no answer. He keyed in the code, and opened the door. He grimaced when he saw Florentino, dead or close to it. "Shit!" he shouted. "Get The Chief, fast."

The second agent took one look into the room, then pushed the red alarm button just outside the door. Instantly the whole Cabin was filled with a loud buzzing. Inside a minute the mission commander had arrived at the Package room, still buttoning his shirt. By now the first agent was kneeling on the bed and had started CPR.

"What the f..."

"He's dead."

"How? Any wounds?"

"Nothing I can see, no response to the CPR so far."

"And there won't be, he's stone cold. Face is in *rigor*. Been dead hours."

15

"Shit. They'll have our arses for this."

"They're not going to be happy, that's for sure, and the legal guys will throw a fit. But it was our job to keep him safe, not guarantee him immortality. Guy was getting up there in years, smoked like a chimney, drank like a fish. You two stay here, I'll call it in."

Events moved very quickly from then on. Inside an hour a full medical team arrived by helicopter from Nellis Airbase, quickly ascertained that Enzo Florentino was indeed dead, but the cause would need to be determined by a full autopsy. Nobody was offering any guesses at this stage. Shortly afterwards, two more helicopters landed, bringing a new team of federal agents and crime scene specialists. The original team of agents were extensively questioned on the spot, and then transferred to Regional Headquarters, where a full debriefing could be held. Florentino's mortal remains were loaded onto the medical helicopter and flown away.

It would be nearly twenty-four hours before the news of Florentino's death became public. One of the first people to find out was an expensive criminal lawyer named Adam Markowitz, who promptly filed a writ of *habeas corpus* on behalf of his client Luca 'Lucky' Marino, to have his pretrial detention terminated, since the main witness for the People would not now be giving evidence against him. Two days later, Marino was a free man once again.

CHAPTER 8

Luca 'Lucky' Marino sat at the head of the oval, mahogany conference table and gazed around at the other occupants of the room. The table had chairs for eighteen, but had rarely seen more than twelve people round it. Today there were ten, in addition to Marino himself. Seven of them were middle-aged white men, most of them carrying a few surplus pounds, which their expensive suits couldn't quite disguise. Those that had kept their hair were generally turning grey, but there were a couple of them with suspiciously dark, thick and immobile coiffures. One was a couple of decades younger than the rest, he sat on Marino's right, and there was a clear family resemblance. Marino, at seventy-one, was the oldest in the room, but he was fit and strong and had the constitution of a man half his age.

Two young men, large and blank-faced stood behind Marino, their eyes constantly scanning the room. The blond-haired one on the left kept patting his left pectoral area, as if to reassure himself that his gun was still in place. The one on the right, the one with the shaved head, seemed more sure of his weapon, and stayed motionless. The seven older men were also accompanied by bodyguards, but Marino's rule was that they should wait in the room outside, where two more of his heavies could watch them.

Marino mentally counted them, all present, as they should be. He glanced up at the screen, which showed four views of other offices, one man in each. Reno, Lake Tahoe, Carson City and Laughlin, four of the major gambling centres in Nevada. The first three were four hundred or so miles away from Las Vegas. Laughlin was a lot nearer, at just under a hundred, but Marino's managers were busy men, and he generally didn't ask them to travel, unless their physical presence was vital, which might be a bad sign for them. Not today. The only one missing from the last general meeting was Enzo Florentino, and nobody wanted to be the first to mention his name.

Marino broke the ice. "Thank you all for coming, gentlemen, it's good to be back with you again after my little...absence. As you are, doubtless, aware, the DA no longer has a witness against me and our organisation, so things may continue as before. Yes, Max?"

Massimo "Max" Zabatino, a burly man with the auburn toupée, was sitting two seats down on the left and he had raised a finger. Zabatino was a money man, tasked with keeping track of the Mob money that was laundered through the company's casinos.

"I was just wondering whether we'll be taking any new measures to ensure that these regrettable events don't recur?"

"That would be a good question, Max, and the answer is yes. I have increased levels of supervision, and our accounts department will henceforth be under the direct supervision of my son, Francesco." He nodded at the man sitting on his right. Francesco "Frankie" Marino nodded back. "He will report regularly to me," said Marino. "Any further questions?"

He looked around the table, but nobody responded, so he looked up at the screen, and his eyes widened. The four images of his out-of-city managers had been minimised and pushed to the corners, and, in the middle, taking up the majority of the screen, appeared the face of a young woman. She was unrecognisable, with a green silk turban hiding her hair, and giant sunglasses shading the top half of her face, but Marino was sure he had never seen her before. The other men followed his gaze, and turned to look at the screen.

"Who the f..." started Federico "Bambi" Brambilla, but Marino silenced him with an upraised hand. Bambi was one of Marino's most enthusiastic enforcers. He had heavy gold rings on all his fingers, which he used as makeshift knuckledusters when needed.

"Who are you?" said Marino, glaring at the woman on the screen. "Why are you interrupting us? And *how* are you interrupting us?"

The woman's lips parted and she started to speak, in a flat, lifeless tone, devoid of all inflection.

"Good morning, Mr Marino. How is not important, it is sufficient that it is happening. You will remember a similar interruption some weeks ago."

"But that was an older woman. At least, she looked older."

18

"My principal has many helpers. I am just one of them. It is time to discuss payment."

"Payment for what exactly?" sneered Marino,

"You were contacted, and an offer was made to you. For ten million dollars, my principal would guarantee that there would be no evidence against you, and you would not face trial. This has now come to pass, and payment is required."

Marino looked around the table at the disbelieving faces, then glared back at the screen. "But nobody took that seriously. There was a contract out on Florentino, but nobody could get near him. And besides..."

"Besides what?"

"The man died of a heart attack in his bed. You're not getting money out of me for that, it was pure dumb luck."

"The agreement was that there would be no evidence against you, and you would not face trial. You valued that at ten million dollars. I strongly suggest you pay. We had a deal. And you dishonour that deal at your peril."

It was the youngest man who spoke first.

"Turn her off, Dad," said Francesco, "she's just some scam artist trying to chisel us out of money for nothing."

Marino nodded. "Sorry, lady," said Marino, "nothing doing. I didn't get where I am today by losing money to con artists."

The woman gazed off to her left, as if she were listening to someone, but nothing was audible on the screen. "My principal sincerely urges you to reconsider, you will regret the consequences if you do not."

"I'm not interested in threats either, lady, you tell your principal to..."

"Enough. This discussion is ended. You will be contacted again in three days, by which time you may well have changed your mind."

The image of the woman was gone, and the images of the four managers again filled the screen.

"You care to bet on that. Lady?" sneered Marino. He shook his head. "In bocca al Lupo," he muttered. Italian for "In the mouth of the wolf", a phrase which meant "Good Luck."

CHAPTER 9

The case review meeting was short, and, to Paul Hart's relief, relatively painless for him. The Director was frustrated and angry, but he made no attempt to pass on any blame to Hart or the rest of the FBI security team.

"You've read the coroner's report, Paul, this one's nobody's fault. Heart attack, and a massive one. No suspicious circumstances. Coroner says it was almost as if his heart arteries had been squeezed shut."

"Is that possible?" said Hart.

"Not without smashing open his chest, and there wasn't a mark on him. Maybe a little poetic licence from the Doc. Either way, there's nothing you or any of the guys could have done. Doc says he'd have died instantly, even if he'd been in an ICU at the time."

"Shit timing though. If he could have held on for another month, we'd have had Marino in Federal Prison."

"Just one of those things, Paul. The guy was basically a walking time-bomb. According to this, he lived off cigarettes, whisky and TV dinners, and the only exercise he took was to wind his watch."

Hart didn't bother informing his chief that Florentino's Rolex would have been self-winding. He just shook his head. "No, he was sure holding a lot of tickets, but it's such dumb luck that it had to happen now."

"You can't legislate for fate, Paul. It's not the first time it's happened to us, and I'm sure it won't be the last. Remember the Minelli case?"

"Yeah, a stroke. Right on the witness stand. Kuznetsov walked free."

"We can't win them all, Paul."

"I guess not, but it sticks in my craw to see Marino walking round a free man."

"His time will come. For guys like him, it always does, sooner or later."

Paul Hart strongly disagreed, but saw no point in saying so. The FBI had tried its best, but failed. Hart was going to have to look elsewhere if Marino was ever going to get the retribution he so richly deserved.

CHAPTER 10

The celebration was mostly a family affair, with just a few close friends and associates invited to the Marino mansion. It happened that Luca Marino's release from custody coincided with his forty-first wedding anniversary, so a small catered party in the evening had seemed the way to go.

The meal and dessert had been served, and the hired-in waiters were bringing around coffee and brandy, when Francesco Marino rose to his feet and tapped his glass with his knife.

"If I could have your attention please everyone."

He looked round the room as every face turned in his direction. His sisters, Gabriella and Mia and their husbands, younger brother Luigi and his wife, his parents' oldest friends, his aunts and uncles, one or two business associates of his father.

"I'd like to propose a toast, if I may. It's great to have Dad back with us, but tonight I'd like us to drink to the strongest and happiest marriage I know. If you'll all raise your glasses with me, and drink to their health and happiness for many more years. Mom and Dad, Luca and Sofia."

Everyone round the tables raised their glasses and echoed,

"Luca and Sofia."

Luca Marino rose to his feet to respond. He looked around him and smiled. All the people he most cared for were in the room together. .

"I'd like to thank you all for that, and especially you, Frankie. It's so good to see you all here..."

He broke off, staring at his eldest son. The man's face had gone as white as a sheet. "Frankie, what is it, you look like you've just seen a ghost..."

23

Francesco's eyes widened in horror, but he said nothing as he clutched his chest and slumped forwards on his chair, his head smashing into the table.

CHAPTER 11

Jack Nightingale had been in so many American airports in the last few years that he'd begun to think they were completely indistinguishable, but Harry Reid International airport was the first one he'd ever flown into after a breathtaking view of the Grand Canyon from the plane. It was also the only one he'd ever seen with rows of slot machines in the arrivals area. He smiled to himself "When in Rome…" He fished out a quarter from his pocket, fed it into the nearest machine and pulled the handle. Plum, lemon, bar. "Mug's game," said Nightingale.

He headed for the exit, trundling his carry-on case behind him. As soon as he walked through the doors of the airport, the heat hit him, and he pulled off his raincoat and suit jacket as he headed to the TAXI line. There were quite a few people in front of him, but empty taxis were pulling up every few seconds, so, mercifully, he didn't need to stand around waiting for more than a couple of minutes before he was enjoying the air-conditioning in the back of Hank's yellow cab.

"Tropicana Hotel, please."

"Your first visit here?"

"Does it show?"

"Anyone that knows Vegas wouldn't bring a raincoat in summer. Gets hotter than Hell here."

"What's the Tropicana like?" asked Nightingale.

"Pretty basic hotel and casino, you won't find the best shows or the best food on there, but it's pretty close to all the other Strip hotels. You should be comfortable enough. Second oldest hotel in Vegas…even James Bond stayed there in the seventies."

Nightingale nodded, he was no expert on films, but he vaguely remembered Sean Connery in Las Vegas and Jill St John in a bikini.

The ride was surprisingly short, around ten minutes to cover three miles, despite heavy traffic. The taxi had pulled up outside his hotel, a long white concrete canopy over the ground floor reception area, and two twenty-storey towers behind it. A heavy-set man in a white shirt trimmed with blue opened the door and took Nightingale's small case. "Let me get that for you, sir."

"I can mana..." started Nightingale, but the doorman was already marching the twenty yards to the hotel entrance. Nightingale paid Hank, then followed his bag.

"Here you go, Sir," said the man, whose badge identified him as Steve. "I'll hand your case over to Carl here, he works the inside, I work the outside, it's a separate system."

In other words, thought Nightingale, I need to tip two guys to move my hand luggage forty yards. He'd been in the United States long enough to know that tipping was pretty much a national religion, so he handed over a few bills to each of them.

The next obstacle was the line at reception but, this wasn't a particularly busy period, and there were three clerks on duty. Five minutes later, Nightingale ended up in front of Tammy, a blonde woman in her twenties. Her smile showed off her excellent dental work. "Mr Nightingale? Yes...I have you in a smoking Club Suite on the sixth floor of the tower."

A suite? It appeared he was in favour with Joshua Wainwright's secretary, the lovely Valerie. And he could smoke in the room? At last, civilisation.

"That sounds fine. You did say a smoking room?"

"Yes sir, you may smoke in your room and in the casino area. Your reservation has been pre-paid for two weeks, I'll just need a credit card to cover your Resort Fee now."

"What's a Resort Fee?"

"It's a small fee to cover wi-fi access, use of the fitness centre, entertainment in the lounges and free local telephone calls."

"How small a fee?"

"Thirty-seven dollars a night, plus tax."

Nightingale sighed. "I've never heard of that before. Is it a new idea?"

"I think it's pretty recent, but you'll find it's standard in all Las Vegas hotels now. So, if I could take your card..."

If he'd still been in London, and still on a police inspector's salary, Nightingale would have walked out in disgust. But, he reminded himself it wasn't his money, and he pushed one of Joshua Wainwright's credit cards across the counter. Wainwright had summoned Nightingale to Las Vegas - AKA Sin City - and he would be footing the bill as well as calling the shots.

CHAPTER 12

Luca Marino sat behind the mahogany desk in his study at home, his head slumped in his hands. He was alone in the room, his wife was upstairs in bed heavily sedated, and the staff knew better than to disturb him when his study door was closed, especially at a time like this. His bodyguard had been doubled, with two heavies in a car parked out on the driveway, and two more just inside the front door of the mansion.

He heard a soft fizzing sound and looked up. The giant screen of the TV on the opposite wall had sprung into life, though he hadn't touched the remote. The man on the screen was black, with a heavy beard, most of his face hidden by reflective sunglasses, and there was a black fedora pulled low over his forehead. "Good afternoon, Mr Marino. You know whom I represent, and you were advised that you would be contacted again today. Are you ready to discuss payment now?"

"Damn you to hell, not now you bastard, my son, Frankie is..."

"Indeed so, Mr Marino, my condolences on his demise. It must have been quite a shock...for you. Now, as to the payment outstanding."

"My son is dead. You think I want to talk about money at a time like this?"

"Indeed he is dead, Mr Marino. Sudden heart failure, apparently. Just like the late Mr Florentino."

Marino frowned at the screen. "Are you trying to tell me that you..."

"Mr Marino, my principal wishes to remind you that you still have another son, and two daughters. It would be regrettable if something were to happen to them too."

Marino's eyes widened, and he slammed his hand down on the desk.

"Don't you threaten them, don't you dare threaten them. I'll have you killed for this."

"That would appear very unlikely, Mr Marino, you have no idea who or where I am, much less who is my principal. You made a bargain, Mr Marino, though it seems you never intended to keep it. But keep it you will. Now, will you pay, or must another funeral be arranged? You Italians have an expression, I believe. 'Hai voluto la bicicletta? E adesso pedala!' I am told that the translation is - 'You wanted the bike? Now you've got to ride it.' Is that correct?"

Marino nodded.

"Then it is time for you to ride the bike, Mr Marino."

Marino's shoulders slumped. "Alright, damn you. I'll pay. Just leave my family alone."

"The right decision, under the circumstances. Now, take careful note of these instructions, which are to be carried out exactly. On this occasion, my principal requires to be paid in Bitcoin…"

CHAPTER 13

Nightingale was beginning to think that Las Vegas might suit him. He'd decided to stay close to base on his first night, and had taken dinner at the hotel's Red Lotus restaurant. The honey walnut shrimp was a new experience for him, and he'd thoroughly enjoyed, it. Afterwards he strolled through the expanse of the Tropicana's ground-floor casino, watching people lose their money.

There were old ladies sitting by slot machines, feeding in quarters from the buckets they'd brought with them, barely looking at the reels as they spun round and took their stake. Overweight men in tasteless leisure wear, divided their attention between the craps table and the cocktail waitress's chests. It was a little early for the night shift, but there were still plenty of pretty girls pretending to pay attention to men old enough to be their fathers. Everyone looked to be strictly small-time, no doubt the real high rollers did their gambling away from the public gaze, in the private rooms of the more upmarket establishments.

As usual in a new city, Nightingale had no idea what he was there for, until Wainwright deigned to give him some instructions. In the absence of anything else to do, he decided to check out the action at the roulette table, even if he didn't plan to participate much. He wasn't about to join in any card games as a novice, and he had no idea of the complex rules of craps.

Nightingale had never seen the attraction in games of chance. His occasional games of poker with friends back in England came under the heading of games of skill, to his mind. He wasn't trusting to luck, and the stakes had been pretty small.

Still, there was nothing much to do other than gamble, and Wainwright's credit cards were pretty inexhaustible, so he bought himself two hundred dollars in chips and headed for the least busy roulette table. He took a chair halfway down the table and watched a few spins, with no real idea what he was looking for. As an economics graduate, even from twenty years ago, he knew enough about probabilities to know that there was no real system for beating a roulette wheel, especially the new models with three zeroes. but he was still counting the times red and black showed up. A waitress in a short black cocktail dress and black tights appeared at his elbow. "What can I get you, Sir?" she purred.

"A Corona with a slice of lime please. No glass."

He tossed a ten dollar chip onto 21 and another onto Black.

The ball span and rattled to a halt. "Red, 32, Even and High," announced the croupier, raking in the losing bets, Nightingale's included.

"Mug's game," he muttered.

"Your drink, sir," said a voice at his elbow.

Nightingale knew regular players drank free, and he also knew that waitresses lived off their tips, so he placed ten dollars on her tray.

"Very generous of you, Nightingale."

His jaw dropped, and he swung round in his seat to look at her. The black cocktail dress was made of a PVC bag, the tights were opaque and had holes in them. Her black hair hung in a spiked purple fringe, almost down to her eyes. Those eyes, so dark they were almost black, with the pupils blending into the irises. Dead eyes, not a spark of human warmth. A wicked smile curled at the corners of her mouth.

"Proserpine?"

She smiled, showing perfectly white, pointed, teeth. "You don't sound sure, Nightingale. I haven't changed that much, and it hasn't been that long."

"What are you doing here? Though Vegas is probably where you'd expect to find a Princess from Hell."

"Oh yes, I do lots of work here. But at the moment I'm just granting one of your smaller wishes. One Corona, drink up, it's not poisoned."

Nightingale took a sip. It didn't seem to be poisoned.

She gave him a sly grin. "I do wonder what dear old Mrs Steadman would have to say about you being here in Sin City, Nightingale. I don't think she'd approve. Very censorious, that one."

"We can probably leave her out of this," said Nightingale.

"You do rather have her on a pedestal, don't you, Nightingale? You really should learn to see through outward appearances. It'll be the death of you some day."

She turned away from him as a fat bald man put his hand on Proserpine's arm, and started talking. Too loud, he'd obviously had a few already.

Nightingale winced. This wouldn't end well.

"And how about fetching me a bourbon, little lady," said the fat man.

Nightingale thought about intervening, but he was too slow. Proserpine gave the man a quizzical look, then smiled. "You don't want another bourbon, Henry. Your stomach hurts. You feel very ill, you need to go home."

"How do you know my n..."

The man was cut off, and doubled over, clutching his ample stomach in both hands, sweating in agony. Still bent almost double, he hurried away in the direction of the restrooms.

"You're in a merciful mood today," said Nightingale. "I've known you kill people for less."

She smiled. "What makes you think he's going to live, Nightingale?"

Nightingale shuddered, but kept quiet. Nothing he could say would change Proserpine's plans for Henry. "So where's the pooch?" He asked, trying to change the subject. It was rare to see Proserpine without the black and white sheepdog by her side.

She frowned. "Be careful. Nightingale. He doesn't like you much, so watch your tongue. This city isn't exactly dog friendly, but he'll be here if I need him."

Nightingale shuddered again, he'd seen what Proserpine's 'pet' was capable of, and didn't need a repeat performance. "Can all these people see and hear you?"

"Not any more Nightingale. We don't want any unnecessary attention from the masses. I never pegged you as a gambler. Try eighteen."

"OK. I'm not gambling, it's a mug's game. Just passing some time."

"Eighteen, red, even, high," shouted the croupier.

"Well done, Nightingale, you've made 350 dollars. Put it all on six. Why do you say it's a mug's game?"

"You've seen this city. Every brick of it was financed by losers' bets. You can't beat the house."

"Six, black, even, low."

"That's just over twelve thousand dollars Nightingale. Not bad for a mug's game."

"Sure, and I'd keep right on winning, if I had your ability to see time both ways, future and past."

"It would be easy enough to share with you, all you need to do is make a deal. Try thirty one. All of it."

The croupier looked up at the ceiling as Nightingale placed his huge bet, and clearly received some kind of signal, as he nodded acceptance.

"It's a pretty poor offer, Proserpine," said Nightingale. "Winning as much money as I could ever want, in exchange for my soul. And I know how valuable that soul is to you."

"It's only valuable while you're still alive to sell it. Still, as you wish, Nightingale. Easy come, easy go."

"Zero," said the croupier as the ball came to a halt.

Proserpine grinned. "Oh dear, Nightingale, you've lost all that money."

"It was never mine to begin with. Now, let's get back to my original question, what are you doing here? Come to thank me for saving you in New Orleans?"

"Hardly, that stupid conjuring trick couldn't have held me for very long, and getting me out of it was just a way of saving yourself. Still, maybe I do owe you a favour."

"One I don't have to pay for? Nothing nasty hiding in the small print?"

"Maybe. You'll have to wait and see. Here's a little present for you."

She reached behind her neck, unfastened the silver chain she wore and passed it across to Nightingale. In the middle hung a silver *ankh*, the Egyptian symbol for life, a cross, but with a teardrop-shaped loop instead of the top vertical bar. Nightingale noticed that it matched her earrings, but was bigger, about the size of his thumb.

"Well, thanks, but I'm not really the jewellery type."

Her smile hardened. "You ever know me to do something without a good reason?"

"Not without what seemed a good reason to you, anyway."

"Close enough. Now, take it, put it on, and keep it on, until I come to claim it back."

"And when will that be?" asked Nightingale.

"Why spoil the surprise?"

"But why?"

"Take it from me, Nightingale, you'll be glad you did. Old diseases demand old cures."

"Old as in Ancient Egypt? That is where the *ankh* comes from, isn't it? Why do I need an ancient Egyptian charm?"

" Are you cleverer than you look, Nightingale? Or was that just a lucky guess? Perhaps you should try roulette again too, if you're that lucky."

Nightingale fingered the *ankh*. "The thing with luck is knowing when not to push it," he said.

"Very profound. Just wear it, twenty-four seven. You'll thank me Oh, and one more thing, Nightingale. Don't even think of trying to summon me if you end up in trouble, I really got rather tired of being stuck in a pentagram back in New Orleans."

"I'll try to remember that."

"See that you do. You know how I get when my wishes are ignored. Now can I get you another beer?

"Not for me thanks, I've changed my plans, I think I've seen enough of roulette for one night. Anyway, what's your lucky number?"

"I don't have one."

"See, I would have said six, six, six."

"Six, six, six is very overrated," said Proserpine. "Be lucky." She blew him a kiss and walked away.

CHAPTER 14

Francesco Marino's funeral had taken place the previous day, but the eight men around the table were still dressed in black suits and black ties. This time, the four out-of-town managers were not joining the meeting, and the giant screen had been turned off and unplugged. The wifi connection to that area of the building had been disabled. In the centre of the conference table sat a small grey metal box with a series of stubby antennae protruding from the top. Those present had been instructed to leave their cellphones outside, but the box would prevent any signal from being received in the room. Operating the jammer was a Federal offence, punishable by a fine of $112,000 and a year's imprisonment, but nobody round the table expected to be arrested.

The room was silent, as everyone waited for Marino to speak. He looked at them one by one, maintaining eye contact for a second or two. "As you can see, certain precautions have been taken. They should ensure that we are not interrupted, and may discuss matters without fear of being heard. The room is routinely swept for listening devices, but has been practically taken apart in the last twenty-four hours to ensure our privacy. The people we are dealing with seem to have some advanced communication technology at their disposal."

He looked around the room. There were a few nods, but nobody gave any sign of wishing to speak so he continued.

"To recap, gentlemen. You are all conversant with what took place in this room three days ago, when that woman attempted to extort money from us for the death of Enzo Florentino. Yes, Bambi?"

Brambilla had raised a finger. "The docs are still calling that natural causes?" he said quietly.

Marino nodded. "Our information suggests so. A massive heart attack, with no suspicious circumstances, though I am sure, in view of the timing, they would dearly love to prove foul play and bring charges against me."

"And do we know different?"

"Not with any degree of certainty. All we know is that a woman interrupted our meeting, by some technological means that has not been satisfactorily explained, to demand a large fee for having caused Florentino's death. We declined to pay, whereupon she made certain threats, and promised to contact us again in three days. Three days later…" Nobody spoke, nobody met his gaze as he looked round the table. "…three days later, my eldest son also suffered a massive heart attack and died. Unlike Florentino, he was a young, fit man, with no health problems, who neither smoked or drank. I was contacted again, by a different person, a man this time, but clearly part of the same organisation. He repeated the demand for payment, this time coupled with specific threats against other members of my family. This time I decided to pay."

There was a short murmur of conversation around the table, and Marino silenced it with an upraised hand. "Now, the question arises of our next move. There are two assumptions we can choose from. First of all, that someone, unknown to us, has the power, the technology, to kill from a distance and mimic the effects of a heart attack. In this case, they did us a great service in removing Florentino, and they would be well worth their fee. Unfortunately we had no proof of their involvement, and they chose to use their power again, killing my son as proof. I cannot permit this to go unavenged."

"But what are we talking about, Lucky?" said a big bruiser of man who everyone called Slugger because of his fondness for breaking limbs with a baseball bat. "Some kind of untraceable poison? Microwaves or something?"

"I don't know, Slugger, I'm not a fucking scientist, but it would need to be something very new and complex. Otherwise the police pathologists would have found something and they didn't."

"You said there were two options?"

"I did, Slugger. The other, more prosaic assumption on which we could proceed is that the death of Florentino was just a fortunate coincidence, from which these people sought to benefit."

Bambi raised his finger again. "Yes, Bambi?"

"Proceeding on that assumption, it still wouldn't explain Frankie's death. The woman called that to the day, it would be incredible if it was just a coincidence."

"This is true. The death of Florentino by itself we could pass over, but I can see no alternative explanation for the death of my son. One way or another, these people caused it, and they must be made to pay."

"That's not going to be easy," said Brambilla. "We have very little to go on. A heavily disguised older woman, an unrecognisable younger woman, and the third..."

"A black man, probably under fifty. Again, disguised."

"It's nothing to go on, Lucky. We don't have a clue who's behind this, or how they operate. And it's not like we can go to the police."

"Hardly, Bambi. But I intend to make it my life's work to avenge my son, and see his murderers die in agony."

"But where do we start? It's impossible."

"Then maybe we start with people who deal with the impossible. There's a man I know of who has something of a reputation in that area." Marino looked around the table. "Wainwright is the guy's name," he growled. "Joshua Wainwright. Comes out of Texas."

The men all looked blankly at him.

"I never heard of him,"said Slugger.

"Most people never have," said Marino. "The guy's richer than God, though nobody seems to know how he got that way. No inheritance, he's not connected as far as I know. Keeps a very low profile, must have some people paid just to keep him out of the news."

"So what about him?" asked Slugger.

"He seems to make a speciality out of unusual cases."

"What is he, a detective?"

"Not as far as I know. He's got a reputation as a collector of occult books, and I've heard he's been involved with tracking down some devil worshippers and a few other weirdos."

"Ah, come on Lucky,"said Bambi, adjusting the cuffs of his made-to-measure shirt. "Who believes in that kind of stuff?"

"I never said I believed in it, but some of these guys who practise it do, and get up to some seriously weird stuff because of it."

"You think this mystery 'principal' guy uses voodoo people?"

"Nah, but it could be a cover for what they're really doing, maybe some poison or something."

"So what makes you think this Wainwright can help?"

Marino took a sip from his water glass before replying. "Any of you guys ever hear about Tony Jefferson, out of New Orleans? Top man down there."

There were a few nods, a blank look or two.

"Well, this Jefferson guy was getting his boys knocked off, and there was talk of some kind of a voodoo connection. Some Doctor Something. Apparently Jefferson called on Wainwright, who sent a guy down to look into it all."

"And the guy got results?"asked Brambilla.

"Well," said Marino, "Nobody's quite sure about all that. For sure, the killings stopped, I heard the voodoo doctor guy was found with his throat slit. Trouble is, Jefferson disappeared around the same time, so I can hardly ask for a reference. But I think it's worth trying to get in touch with Wainwright, see if he has any ideas. At the moment, I need all the help I can get."

CHAPTER 15

Jolyon Winston paced up and down his office, his face blotchy, his jaw set, his breathing laboured. Every minute or so, he ran his hands through his thick white hair and swore again.

The man on the sofa watching him was younger, maybe mid-thirties, dressed in a very expensive dark grey suit, an immaculate white shirt and the tie of an exclusive gentleman's club whose long waiting list he'd been able to jump on the recommendation of his father and uncle, the senior partners in his law firm. His name was Thomas Baxter and he had inherited Jolyon Winston as a client on his father's retirement, and he heartily wished he hadn't. The elder Baxter had handled Winston's first two divorces, and his son would happily have handed the third case over to him if it had been at all possible. There was no way to win it, and Baxter was likely to get the blame. Winston was a vindictive man, and would take his loss badly. He was a nasty piece of work, though his life probably hadn't been helped by being given a ridiculous first name. Baxter assumed that the parents had been going for a posh version of Julian, and he could imagine the teasing the man had gone through as a small boy. But no matter what an unpleasant person he was, Baxter dreaded losing the man's corporate work, it would be almost impossible to replace.

"So that bitch is going to walk away with 75 million dollars," Winston hissed. "And there's not a damned thing you can do about it?"

"Jolyon, I kept you out of jail, didn't I? You broke her nose, two teeth and left her arm a mass of bruises. The battery charge went away, but as soon as she shows the photos and the medical report, sympathy for you will go through the floor."

"She can't prove I did that...could have been anybody."

"She doesn't need to prove it, you're not on trial here, and there'll be no jury, thank God. It's just one more thing to put the judge on her side, and, probably, increase her payout."

"And there's nothing we can do?"

"There is. We can increase our settlement offer, say to twenty mil, and see if she bites."

"You think she will?"

Baxter pursed his lips, and exhaled heavily. "If she were my client, I'd advise her not to. She's got a cast-iron case, and at a conservative estimate, you're worth 150 mil more this morning than when you married her. The law says she's entitled to half of that."

Winston cursed and practically stamped his feet. "Gold-digging bitch, she was just a showgirl when I married her."

Baxter had seen photos of Delia Winston in her singing and dancing days, She'd been quite something, and Winston surely hadn't been led by his head when he married her. Why Baxter Senior hadn't insisted on a pre-nup was beyond comprehension.

"And it makes no difference that she's been fucking half the men in the city?"

Baxter shrugged. "It would make no difference if it was all of them. This is a "no fault" state for divorce, so her adultery won't help your case. Professional diplomacy stopped him from adding, "and your adultery won't help matters."

"What if I had the bitch killed?" sneered Winston.

"Jolyon, you shouldn't talk like that. Anything you tell me as your attorney is a privileged communication, which I can't be forced to disclose, but if you repeat that to anyone else you're likely to end up in jail. Anyway, the short answer is that if she was killed, you'd be number one suspect, and looking at life in prison."

"But it would stop the divorce?"

"Well, of course, dead people can't divorce, you'd be a widower and the case wouldn't exist. But, come on, you could lose what she's asking for and not even notice it was gone."

"I might not notice it in my wallet, but I'd sure as hell notice it in my head. Nobody screws Jolyon Winston."

Baxter put away his files and closed his briefcase. He could think of one woman who'd done a very efficient job of screwing Jolyon Winston. "So, what are my instructions?"

41

"Offer the bitch the 20 mil." said Winston. "If she won't take it, tell her I'll see her in court."

Baxter nodded, picked up his case and walked to the door. Winston slumped onto the sofa, his head in his hands. He was still in that position four minutes later, when the giant TV screen opposite him flickered into life.

"Good Morning, Mr Winston," said the woman.

Winston looked up at the face which filled the screen. What he could see of the woman suggested that she was pretty old, there were lines round her mouth, and traces of hair on her upper lip. The top half of her face was hidden behind large dark glasses, and her long jet-black hair was an obvious wig.

Winston stood up from the sofa, and his cheeks reddened. "What the hell is this?" he yelled, "Who are you?"

Much to his surprise, the woman seemed to be able to hear him, and answered in a calm, almost sleepy voice. "Perhaps the answer to a prayer Mr Winston."

"I'm not the praying kind, lady."

"A figure of speech, Mr Winston. I understand you are having some marital difficulties."

"You and anyone else who follows the news, it's hardly a secret."

"No, indeed. I am empowered to offer you a bargain Mr Winston, one which will solve your divorce problem. Permanently."

"Oh yeah. And how would you plan to do that? My lawyer says there's no way out, short of shooting her, and you don't look like a hit man to me."

"The how is unimportant, Mr Winston, but, I assure you there will be no shooting. My...my principal is prepared to guarantee that the divorce will not take place, in exchange for the sum of five million dollars."

"How big a fool do I look, you expect me to pay five mil and then just hope for the best? You got oil wells to sell? Maybe a bridge in Brooklyn?"

The woman turned to her left and seemed to be listening to someone, but Winston heard nothing. "My principal understands your reticence, but payment will be by results," said the woman. "You need pay nothing, until you are completely sure that the divorce will not take place."

"Oh yeah? And if someone shoots my wife, and the Feds catch me handing over five mil, then I hope you'll bring me cake in prison."

Again she looked as if she were listening to someone off-screen. "There will be no shooting, nothing to connect you to any crime. As for payment, you will invest in Bitcoin, After a suitable interval, you will transfer the value requested to an anonymous numbered wallet. You may even make a profit while waiting."

"And what if I don't pay?"

"That would be very unwise, my principal would insist. The consequences of non-payment might be unpleasant for you and those close to you."

"And what if I say this is all baloney, and you can go to Hell?"

"You are entitled to do so, You may reject this offer, and you will never be contacted again, or harmed, provided you do not disclose this conversation to the authorities. If you accept, the bargain is made, and payment will be expected upon results."

"Do I sign something?"

"That would hardly be feasible, would it?"

"Do I get to think about it?"

"Certainly. Give your answer tomorrow, Be alone here between two and three, you will be contacted."

Winston said nothing, just clenched his fists.

"And, Mr Winston, don't waste your time trying to trace this signal. It will elude the ingenuity of any communications expert you could find."

The screen went blank.

CHAPTER 16

Nightingale sat at the bar, a bottle of Corona in front of him, and an ashtray filling up gradually to his right. From time to time, he fed a dollar bill into the poker machine embedded in the bar in front of him, and had managed to win enough for his next Corona. His cellphone buzzed with an incoming message. He glanced at it. His master's voice. The summons he had been waiting for. He pressed the PAY button on the poker machine to cash in his winnings, A small curl of paper appeared from a slot at the bottom. Nightingale held it up to the barman. "I can pay with this?"

The barman glanced at it. "Sure thing, I'll get you some change."

"Keep it. How do I get to the MGM Grand from here? Taxi?"

"No need, just go up a level to the walkway exit and stroll across. Take you three minutes. All the Strip hotels are connected and easy to get to. See you again soon, I hope?"

Nightingale nodded, crushed out his latest Marlboro and headed out. The evening heat was immediately noticeable after the air-conditioning of the casino, and Nightingale was glad he'd left his jacket in his room. The walkway was busy, and, as he crossed, he paused to take in the endless sea of twinkling lights that was the Las Vegas Strip, with hotels and casinos stretching as far as he could see, the street blocked with slow-moving traffic.

The walkway led him to the MGM Grand, a huge green rectangle, with its name picked out in yellow lights at the top. Once inside, he ignored the elevators as usual and took the stairs up eight floors, which left him feeling breathless, and wondering if a few visits to the Tropicana fitness centre might be a good idea. He found the room and knocked.

"Come on in, Jack."

The door opened to reveal the man who was paying Nightingale's bills. Joshua Wainwright still looked to be in his early thirties, though the occasional streak of grey in his hair, and the lines round his eyes hadn't been there when Nightingale first knew him. Both of them had seen enough to put years on anyone, and Nightingale wondered whether he should check his shaving mirror more often. Wainwright had been a billionaire in those days, and Nightingale assumed he still was one, though he'd heard the young Texan complain about deals which had gone badly for him lately. They'd both made powerful enemies in the last few years.

Wainwright certainly had enough money to make sure he still dressed well. His dark suit was immaculately cut, his white shirt dazzling, and his black lizard skin cowboy boots gleamed like mirrors. Nightingale looked down at his own black shirt and Chinos. "I feel under-dressed," he said. "You never said we'd be formal."

"We ain't," said Wainwright, "the suit's not for you, I'm coming from seeing some people and going on to some others."

"Well, if you don't want to be seen with me..."

"I don't, but it's nothing to do with your dress style. This room is booked in the name of Atkins for the night. As far as anyone else is concerned, I'm in a suite at the Bellagio, and I made damned sure nobody saw me leave."

"You being followed?"

"No idea, but it's best to plan for what people could do, rather than what they're likely to."

Nightingale nodded.

"Anyways, where's my good old Texan hospitality? Take the weight off your feet, this is a smoking room, what will you have to drink?"

Nightingale sank onto the sofa and lit a Marlboro. "Just a cup of coffee will be fine, I've had two beers this evening, and, if you're about to dump something nasty on me, I'd prefer to have my wits about me."

"Whatever you say."

Wainwright made the coffee, passed it across then sat in the armchair opposite, poured himself a large measure of Glenlivet from his own bottle on the table. "We humble billionaires can't afford minibar prices, I always travel with my own supply," he said.

"Very wise," said Nightingale.

Wainwright lit one of his foot-long cigars with a gold lighter. "I reckon Las Vegas will be the last city in the USA to ban smoking completely, but it'll happen one day. Let's enjoy it while we can, Jack."

"We're a persecuted minority, that's for sure."

"Yeah, they'll be back to Prohibition next. Good flight?"

Nightingale raised an eyebrow in surprise, it wasn't like Wainwright to waste time on small talk. Maybe he was waiting for someone else to arrive.

"The usual, except Valerie booked me in an empty row, which was nice of her. By the way, did they change the name of the airport?"

"Yeah, it had been McCarran for fifty odd years, then they decided that Senator McCarran had been a fascist and a jew-hater, so they changed the name to Harry Reid Airport."

"And who was Harry?"

"Another old Nevada senator who wasn't a fascist or a jew-hater. Allegedly."

"I hope he's grateful for the honour."

"I'd be surprised. The man was 82 and died two weeks after they changed the name."

"Bad timing."

"I guess. You British don't name your airports after politicians?"

"Not that I ever heard of. There'd be riots if they renamed Heathrow as Boris Johnson International. The only two I know that are named after people are John Lennon Airport in Liverpool, and Robin Hood up north somewhere."

"Named after an outlaw eh? Perhaps Chicago could call their airport Al Capone International."

The two men smoked for a few minutes more in silence. Nightingale knew Wainwright would break it when he was good and ready, and wasn't about to start questioning him. Eventually the silence was broken by a knock on the door. Wainwright stood up. He walked across and opened it slowly. "Come on in, Paul. This is Jack Nightingale, my...personal assistant. Jack, meet Senior Special Agent Paul Hart of the FBI. Paul and I go way back, though we don't get chance to catch up that often. We headed off in different directions."

Nightingale was definitely surprised to be introduced to an FBI agent, but he made an effort not to show it, and just smiled. Hart was tall, black and looked to be in very good shape. Presumably FBI agents had fitness targets to maintain, just as Nightingale had needed to in the Metropolitan Police. Hart's vivid red Hawaiian shirt and yellow slacks were surely not FBI issue, but then meeting a leading satanist probably wasn't in his job description either. Hart nodded at Nightingale. "Good to meet you, Mr Nightingale."

"Same here, make it Jack Any friend of Joshua's..."

"I'd be careful with that idea," said Hart, "I've heard about some of Joshua's friends."

Wainwright smiled. "Pretty risky talk for a man who's come looking for a favour. Now why don't you take a seat, try a little something from the minibar, and let's get to it. I assume you don't have much time."

"True enough, I'm pretty sure I'm not being tailed, but I'd hate to have to explain this meeting to my Assistant Director. I'd be unemployed for sure, probably followed by a long spell in Federal prison."

"So you haven't come to give me your foolproof roulette system?"

"I wish, Joshua."

"Do you want a drink? I'm on whisky, Jack's on coffee."

"I'll just take a club soda."

Wainwright fetched him a club soda and the three men sat down. "So you got my juices going on the phone, I'm ready to hear the full story now."

Hart took a deep breath. Wainwright sensed his hesitancy. "You know anything you tell me stays in this room, same goes with Jack. I'd trust him with my life. In fact I already have, a time or two."

"I know I can trust you, Joshua," said Hart, "But what I'm about to do goes against every regulation and years of training. I'm not even sure if you can help, or if what I'm thinking makes any kind of sense, it seems impossible."

"I've believed as many as six impossible things before breakfast," said Nightingale.

Hart grinned. "Alice in Wonderland, eh? Read it to my daughter. That's a world in which this might make some sense. You ever heard of Enzo Florentino?"

Nightingale shook his head but Wainwright nodded. "State witness against Luca 'Lucky' Marino. Allegedly knew where the bodies were buried and where the money went. Died just at the wrong time, and the trial couldn't go ahead without him."

"You keep up," said Hart.

"Never hurts to be informed."

"Who's Luca Marino?" asked Nightingale. "And why do they call him Lucky?"

"Big fish," said Hart. "On the surface a highly respected businessman with a multitude of interests. Casinos, hotels, real estate. Behind all that, he's a hood. Drugs, girls, unlicensed gambling, protection, extortion, you name it. The nickname Lucky came when he was a teenager and kept getting arrested. Witnesses would always have a change of heart before his cases got to court. He always claimed it was luck, but obviously his propensity for violence is a more likely explanation.'"

"And this Florentino, he was murdered?" asked Nightingale.

Hart pursed his lips. "The Docs say no. Massive heart attack, though they can't really point to any immediate cause."

"Where did it happen? Could he have been got at?"

"Not a chance in a thousand, Jack. He was being held at our safest safe house away up north in the back of beyond, nobody could get near him."

"What about the guys who were guarding him? Were they reliable? Could one of them have slipped something into his food?"

"I really don't think so, everyone there watches everyone else. All of them long-term and highly trusted agents. And besides he wasn't poisoned. Unless you believe in some untraceable drug that someone happened to have with them."

"So he had a genuine heart attack," said Nightingale. "Very convenient for this Luca Marino, very inconvenient for you. And for him. But, as they say, shit happens."

"Yeah, it does. But shit's been happening too damned often for my liking."

The other two said nothing, and waited for Hart to continue.

"I hope you guys have good memories, I couldn't risk bringing any files, and there's no way I can copy them without it being known. Anyway, almost all the information is in the public domain, so you can look it up afterwards. I'd rather you didn't make notes here...just in case."

"Ivan Sidoroff, Russian defector. Marco Vukic, bagman for the Andrettis. Shirley Tyrell, witness to the murder of Little Thursday, the rapper. Hyung Park, witness to the execution of a Tong boss, Xiao Hong. Al Malone, star witness in the Hawthorne racketeering case. All of them with vital information in their heads, which could have brought down some very big people. All of them under our tightest protection. And all of them dead in the last six months."

"Suspicious deaths?" asked Nightingale.

"Not in the legal sense. Heart attacks, all of them. But none of them any history of heart problems."

"How old were they?"

"All between forty-one and sixty-five. Not young, but statistically they had years left in them."

"Lies, damned lies and statistics."

"Yeah, I heard that one too," said Hart. "But six vital witnesses dead in six months, at just the right time is too big a coincidence for me."

"But coincidences happen all the time,"said Nightingale, and, as they say, correlation isn't causation. You run a search through a computer, it might throw up a pattern, but that doesn't make it relevant. For example, probably all those people had driver's licences, but that would have no bearing on their deaths. If you ran a search of all the bald men in the USA who died of cancer last year, or left-handed women with dementia, you'd get a horrifying figure, but that doesn't mean a connection. Could be you've just been unlucky lately, and the bad guys have been very lucky."

"And, of course, that was the official line," said Hart. "But, there's more."

CHAPTER 17

"It really isn't a lot to go on, Mr Winston," said Sergeant Jose Garcia as he looked down at his notebook. "Strange woman on a TV screen, she could be anywhere, maybe even another country. You're sure you've never seen this woman before?"

"She'd disguised her appearance, but nothing about her face or voice was familiar to me. She sounded American."

"And you turned her offer down?" asked the detective.

"No, I played for time. Obviously I wouldn't agree to anything which might result in harm to my wife. She said she'd contact me again for my final decision, which, I figured, gave me time to contact the police, and maybe you guys could trace her call."

Garcia looked across at his companion, Officer Camila Martinez, who shrugged her shoulders. "Maybe it's possible," she said, "we'd need to talk with an expert on internet communications. But I'm not sure we should worry too much about this. Probably just some crank."

"A very well informed and technologically savvy crank," said Winston.

"Not necessarily," said Garcia. Most kids these days seem to be accomplished hackers, and your...er...marital difficulties have been widely reported. Could be just some grifter trying to get some money out of you."

"It's not much of a story though if it is a grifter. What do you guys plan to do about it?"

Normally the sergeant would have just filed the report and recommended no further action, but Jolyon Winston was stinking rich and wielded a whole lot of influence in this city, and he had no wish to explain his inactivity to his Captain.

"Well, sir, I can get someone from our technical department to check over your communication system, I can arrange for a man to be here all day tomorrow and try to trace any incoming calls. If you think it's wise, I can arrange for protection for your wife..."

"Let her organise her own protection, I just need to make sure that I'm not implicated in anything. Anything happens to her, I'm the guy with the motive. But send along that technical guy would you, I'm sure you're right, that it's just a shake-down, but nobody puts the screws on Jolyon Winston."

"As you wish, Mr Winston. I'll get it organised as soon as I get back to the station."

"You married, Sergeant Garcia?"

"Engaged.'

"Do you want some advice?" Garcia didn't reply, but Winston didn't care whether the sergeant wanted advice or not. "Run like the wind, sergeant," Winston snarled. "Run like the fucking wind."

CHAPTER 18

The man in the blue turban turned away from the mirror in front of him, and made a gesture with his hand. The image in the mirror clouded and disappeared, reflecting no light now.

The blonde woman behind him placed her hand on his shoulder, and he turned to face her.

"The Dark Mirror tells you what you wanted to know?"

"I think so, but I am still a novice in its use, and I dare not look into it for long. There are stories of those who have been sucked inside one, into a world of hideous creatures and eternal torments. But this time, it has told me what I suspected."

"The man Winston is not suitable for our purposes?"

"No, I fear not."

"A shame, he is extremely wealthy."

Yes...but...perhaps..."

"Perhaps what?"

Perhaps we should try to look at this situation from another angle We may yet be able to make a handsome profit. Do you catch my drift?"

"I think so," said the woman, "but we will need another intermediary."

"Fortunately there is no shortage of them."

CHAPTER 19

Nightingale lit another cigarette, as he waited for Hart to continue. Wainwright was about a third of the way through his cigar.

"Two things have come up," said the FBI agent. 'First we have a man inside Marino's organisation who occasionally sends information our way. I'm not going to name him, there's no way you can ever talk to him, and he's not important enough or brave enough to give evidence against Marino. He has quite a story to tell. It seems that after Enzo Florentino was taken into protective custody, but before Marino was arrested, he was contacted by some guy, unknown and unrecognisable, via some kind of conference call to Marino's office. The guy claimed to be talking on behalf of someone else, offered to hit Florentino for ten million bucks,"

"Those were his exact words?"

"Not quite, Jack, Apparently it was more along the lines of guaranteeing that Florentino would never give evidence in exchange for that fee."

"And Marino bought it?" said Wainwright.

"Not really. Said something to the effect that it would be cheap at ten mil, but there was no way this guy could pull it off, the FBI had Florentino stitched up tight."

"So he didn't make the deal?"

"Well, maybe he did and maybe he didn't. He kinda said he'd be happy to pay, but it was impossible. I guess he had the guy marked down as a hustler."

"But Florentino did die, right?."

"He surely did, and as soon as Marino was back in business, he was contacted again."

"Same guy?" said Nightingale.

"No, some woman, heavily disguised, claimed to represent the same principal. Wanted the money, said they'd kept up their end of the bargain and offed Florentino."

"Marino paid?"

"He did not, Jack. He said Florentino's death was down to natural causes, and he wasn't about to be scammed out of ten mil by some con artist. He may have added in some colourful adjectives. Seems his son, Frankie Marino, was pretty much against paying, and that was a big influence on the old man."

"And the woman wasn't pleased?"

"I guess not. She made some vague threats about Marino being sorry if he didn't pay, and promised to contact him in three days."

"And after three days?"

"Inside three days, Frankie Marino, aged thirty-seven, was dead from a sudden and unexpected heart attack. Keeled over into the trifle at a celebration dinner at his parents' place."

"That's a little scary."

"That's what Marino thought too, especially after they threatened his other kids. My information is that he paid up after that."

"That sounds a little too convenient to be a coincidence, Was Frankie autopsied?"

"Sure he was. No sign of foul play, no injuries, no poison, no drugs. Classic heart attack. But absolutely no history of heart problems. Kid was as fit as they come. Apart from being dead."

Nightingale blew smoke up at the ceiling. "You mentioned two things..."

"Yeah. The other's a little different. Guy called Jolyon Winston. Rich as hell. He was going through a messy divorce, and his wife was about to walk away with a huge chunk of his money. He claimed he was contacted by some black guy he'd never seen before, again via a TV screen. More talk of a mysterious principal, and an offer to make sure the divorce never took place, in exchange for five mil."

"And you know this, how?"

"Horse's mouth, Jack. Winston loves money, doesn't want to lose it but he values his freedom, and he's no killer. He went to the Police with his story."

"And what was their reaction?"

"I don't think they really took it seriously, but money talks in this town, so they went through the motions. They checked out his office, determined that the TV hadn't been tampered with, couldn't do much with a description of a black man with his features hidden. They placed some recording gear in Winston's office, and told him to let them know if he was contacted again. Offered to go back the next day and listen in."

"And was he contacted again?"

"No, and he won't be. Jolyon Winston died of a heart attack yesterday."

CHAPTER 20

Delia Winston lay back in bed and spooned some more chocolate ice-cream into her mouth. Jolyon had never liked her eating in bed, but his wishes no longer mattered. Soon she would be a spectacularly wealthy woman, and her figure would no longer need to be her fortune. She could cut down the gym sessions, maybe let her body recover from the punishing years of dancing and as a rich man's prize possession. From now on she'd make her own decisions about money, food, drink and, especially, who she slept with. And it wouldn't be some old guy who needed thirty minutes work and blue pills to get it up.

The television was showing some talent contest or other, but she was more interested in the bowl of ice-cream and the half-empty pitcher of margaritas on her bedside table.

The screen flickered, and the panel of judges was replaced by the face of what looked to be a middle-aged white man, as much as she could tell behind the dark glasses, baseball cap and bushy black beard. It looked fake, but who knew?

"Mrs Winston? My principal sends condolences on your loss."

Delia smiled cynically. "Well thank you, but it's no great loss to me. I'll look good in black."

"As was agreed, the divorce will not now, of course, be happening."

"Can't divorce a dead man. My lawyer says Bernie's will was never changed, so I get my share, along with his kids."

"Quite. There is now the question of payment."

"Sure. But like I told the other guy, I won't have it until the will is settled."

"Of course, my principal understands the system perfectly. Once the will has been settled, you will be contacted again to arrange payment."

The man's face vanished from the screen, and the talent show panel reappeared.

"Sure," Delia muttered to herself, "you can contact me, if you can find me. I plan to be far away by then. What's mine I'll keep."

She might not have felt so confident had she realised that, but for his stupidity in contacting the police, it would have been Jolyon Winston being consoled for his loss, and being required to make payment for the death of his wife.

CHAPTER 21

Nightingale blew smoke up at the ceiling. "So it's confirmed that Winston definitely died of a heart attack?" he asked.

"According to the local boys," said Hart. "We had no jurisdiction to take over the case, it was just natural causes. Once he died, case closed, nothing to go on. I guess if the coroner finds anything unusual, they can open the case again, but my money says he won't."

"But such convenient timing. How come you got to hear about it if it's not your case?"

"They have these things called computers, Jack. Jolyon Winston was a big deal, and his death sent up a few red flags that we picked up on. That report to the police the day before rang plenty of bells."

"What kind of investigation did the cops undertake?"

"Probably more than they would have done for you or me. They checked over his office pretty thoroughly, established the TV hadn't been tampered with in any way, had no description to go on, so let it lie. As to Winston's death, well, that kind of closed the case for them. Once the docs call it natural, there's no crime to investigate."

"They don't know about the possible connection to Marino and the others?" asked Nightingale.

"No, and I can't tell them. For a start, the 'connection' currently only exists in my head. Nobody in authority is linking a few inconvenient natural deaths."

"So why are you?"

"I don't believe in too many coincidences, Jack. Someone's predicted at least two of these deaths, which, since I don't believe in fortune tellers, I take to mean that they caused them. But I can't explain how, much less who. Until I have an explanation that makes sense, my Deputy Director is going to call it 'A Series of Unfortunate Events' like the book title.

Nightingale nodded. He hadn't heard of the book, much less read it, but it didn't seem important to say so.

Wainwright flicked ash into the crystal ashtray in front of him. "So what do you want from me, Paul? I'm no policeman and there's just one of me, what makes you think I'd get anywhere when you guys and your whole organisation can't?"

"I don't claim to understand you, Joshua, but I've followed your career and I do know there's something different about you. Something that wasn't there when we were kids in Texas, but is there now. I wouldn't know how to explain it, and it might even be dangerous to try, but it's surely there, and besides..."

"Besides what?"

"As I said, I've been following your career lately."

"I hope it's been instructive."

"Not hardly, you're a hard man to keep track of. But rumours are that you've been seen in some places where some pretty heavy shit was going down. Odd thing is, there's hardly any mention of you in the department files, no suspicion has ever been attached to you for anything. But there's all kind of rumours about you, and some pretty odd stuff has gone down when you've been in the vicinity. The mysterious Mr Nightingale's name keeps coming up too ."

Wainwright's smile melted away. "Is that an accusation, Paul?"

Hart shook his head. "Far from it. If there's any truth in the rumours, seems you were on the side of the angels."

The smile was back. "Oh, hardly that. Paul. I don't have much to do with angels."

"Well, anyhow, that's the why of it, and I know it's pretty thin stuff. As to what I want, I want these people stopped, whoever they are."

"I have no powers of arrest, Paul. I'm just a citizen."

"I doubt it would help to arrest them. Whatever method they're using is foolproof, and I can't see ever getting a conviction. I just want them stopped."

"I'm not an assassin either."

Hart lowered his voice. "But I guess you know some people who are."

Wainwright stood up.

"I think maybe you have me wrong, Paul. I'm not Tom Cruise available for impossible missions, and I don't hire out to the Government, not that I guess you were planning to pay. Best I can do, for old time's sake, is to keep my ear to the ground, and let you know if I hear anything. And this meeting never happened. For either of us."

Hart nodded. If he was disappointed, it didn't show on his face. "I guess that's all I could have hoped for, Joshua. Thanks for listening."

Hart fist-bumped Wainwright and Nightingale and showed himself out.

"You were pretty brusque with him," said Nightingale after Hart had closed the door.

"I don't like people to get too close. Paul's an old friend, but he doesn't have idea one about the side of my life that you've seen, Jack. And I'd like it to stay that way. The last thing we need is to attract attention. We don't want to be showing up on any FBI files or 'Most Wanted' lists, do we? In our world, anonymity is a powerful weapon."

"So we're not interested in this?" asked Nightingale.

Wainwright grinned. "Well now, I didn't exactly say that, did I? The way I see it, we either have a mighty big series of coincidences, or something pretty nasty is going on, and we're dealing with someone very powerful."

"Someone who can cause heart attacks at a distance? That sounds pretty dangerous. Ever heard of anything like it before?"

"We both have, Jack. Remember New Orleans? The good Doctor Amede? A voodoo priest can put the fix on someone, using a mouse or a doll. But usually the victim wastes away. This seems much more immediate. And voodoo works a whole lot better if the victim knows he's been cursed and believes in its effectiveness."

"So how could it be done?"

"Beats me, it's not something I'd ever try to check out. Visiting death on people can rebound on you, I'm told."

61

"Interesting." Nightingale paused and bought himself some time lighting another cigarette.

"Something on your mind, Jack?"

"Could be. Little while ago, an old acquaintance paid me a visit. Here, in Sin City. As usual when I least expected to see her."

"You don't mean Proserpine?"

Nightingale grinned. "Oh, but I do, and best not to mention her name too often, she doesn't like it." He blew a tight plume of smoke at the ceiling. As he watched, the smoke formed itself into a black *ankh*, just like the one he was wearing under his shirt. As he frowned, the *ankh* disappeared. Had he imagined it?

Wainwright's voice snapped him back to reality. "And what did she want from you?"

"I don't know that she wanted anything," said Nightingale," she claimed she was doing me a favour."

"I didn't have her pegged as the obliging kind."

"Me neither."

"Whatever she said, did she give you permission to share it?"

"Didn't ask."

Wainwright stroked his chin. "Then maybe keep it to yourself for a while, she'd be a bad person to piss off."

"I guess you're right."

Wainwright wagged a warning finger at him. "Jack, if you really knew as much about her as I do, you'd be terrified by her."

"I generally feel pretty shaky when she's around, but it seems she's on my side this time."

"She'll never be on anyone's side but her own. You can't trust a Princess of Hell."

"I'm not planning on relying on her, but maybe she gave me a hint."

"About this?" Wainwright grimaced.

62

"I didn't know there was a *this* at the time. But it could be, I suppose."

"How does it tie in?" asked Wainwright.

"I'm not sure it does, she's not one for laying out the full story. Just one little thing though, might there be some connection to Ancient Egypt here?"

A look of surprise crossed Wainwright's brow. "Now where in hell did you get that idea from?"

"Hell, exactly. Does it ring any bells?"

"I couldn't say just yet, Jack. But maybe I have a little hunch that's worth pursuing. A loose end I've been meaning to check out. Something I've had my eye on for quite a while, but had no evidence. "

"Sounds mysterious, are you planning to tell me about it?"

"Better yet, I can show you." He crushed out his cigar in an ashtray and stood up. "Come on, let's go."

"Where?"

"We're in Vegas. Let's go take in a show."

CHAPTER 22

Wainwright knew all about Nightingale's little foibles, but didn't plan on sharing them, so the young Texan took the elevator down to the lobby and waited a few minutes for Nightingale to arrive via the stairs. "Car should be waiting for us outside. It's a half-mile walk otherwise, it's hot and I don't want to miss anything."

Nightingale followed Wainwright outside, where a long white limousine was just pulling up. The powerfully built driver might have been a clone of every other chauffeur that Wainwright employed.

"Thank you, Charles," said Wainwright as the man opened the rear door.

It might have been quicker to walk, the Las Vegas strip was packed with traffic. But the air-conditioning in the big car made the trip more comfortable.

"Is it always this busy?" asked Nightingale.

"Pretty much. I guess it's a little quieter in the small hours, but this is a 24-hour city."

"Where are we headed?" asked Nightingale.

"Following your suggestion. Ancient Egypt, my friend."

"Shouldn't you have hired a DeLorean for time travel?"

Wainwright grinned. "No need, in Vegas all kinds of magic is possible, as you're about to see. Here we are at last."

Charles opened the door, from the driver's seat this time, and the two men stepped out. Nightingale gaped at what he saw.

"It's a bloody pyramid. A green pyramid."

"I keep forgetting you're new in town, Welcome to the Luxor Hotel. It was the tallest building on the Strip when it opened. That beam of light going up from its point is the strongest beam on Earth, they reckon planes can see it nearly three hundred miles away."

"I wouldn't like to pay their electricity bill."

"Me either. Come on, let's get inside, show's about to start."

"Which floor?"

"Second, they have to have elevators on an angle to fit the pyramid walls but don't worry, we'll take the escalators. You okay with them?"

"Sure, something goes wrong with an elevator and you're dead, escalators never really break down, if there's a problem, they just become stairs."

The two men walked up to the Atrium level, and Wainwright gave his name at the ticket office. "Helps to have a little pull," said Wainwright, "this show's only on for a few weeks, while the Blue Man Group take a break. Tickets are like gold dust. Valerie had to call in some favours."

Which led Nightingale to assume that Wainwright had planned his trip to Las Vegas long before he'd heard Hart's story. As ever, there was more going on with the Texan billionaire than was apparent.

Nightingale stared up at the poster above the cash desk, into the giant brown, almost black, eyes that seemed to survey everyone from behind the black mask that covered the top half of his face. It was difficult to make out features while craning his neck upwards, but he caught a flash of impossibly white teeth, contrasting with beige complexion, and jet-black hair, worn long over the ears. Behind him stood a Sphinx, and on either side, two golden crocodiles.

"Khamsin, Keeper of the Ancient Secrets," read Nightingale. "Looks to be quite a guy."

"And then some. He's the top banana when it comes to illusionists. Came from nowhere in the last two years."

"I hadn't pegged you as a fan of stage magicians."

"This guy's in a whole different league. I'm surprised you haven't heard of him."

Nightingale flashed him a tight smile. "I don't get much time to read the papers, I'm generally too busy trying not to get killed."

The auditorium was full to capacity, and their two front-row seats were about the last to be filled. Almost as soon as they had sat down, the lights dimmed, and the sound of a woman's voice began.

"From the tombs of Ancient Egypt, the forbidden wisdom and mysteries have been rediscovered and refined. We present the all knowing, the all-seeing, the all-daring, death defying Khamsin, and his assistant Neferu, Princess of the Nile."

As his name was spoken, a figure floated onto the stage. It was smaller than Nightingale had expected. The ankle-length, shimmering white robe gave few clues as to the physique beneath it, and the face was entirely hidden behind a tall mask, gold coloured, except for the downward curving snout and the long ears with squared-off ends, which were all jet black.

"Is that a dog?" asked Nightingale in a whisper.

"No, I think it's what archaeologists call the 'Set animal'. It represents the god Set, but nobody's quite sure what it's meant to be."

The figure continued to float, a foot or so off the ground, then it raised its right hand, which held a long, bronze sword, with a curved blade. The woman's voice came again from off stage.

"Behold. The *khopesh* the traditional sword of Ancient Egypt."

The figure bent at the waist and slashed with the *khopesh* beneath his feet, then straightened up and slashed several times above the head and by his sides, just to convince his audience that there were no wires holding him up, He replaced the weapon in his belt, and lifted up his arms to shoulder level. He rose another ten feet into the air. He slowly pulled his arms into his sides, and began to spin slowly, then with increasing speed, like an ice-skater. He held out his arms again, and the spinning stopped. He lowered his arms slowly, and began to sink down until his feet touched the stage. He gave a small bow, and the audience erupted into applause.

The man bent forward and removed his giant mask, which he handed to a stagehand dressed in black who carried it off into the wings. To Nightingale's surprise, the man still wore a mask, this time made of black cloth, which covered the top part of his face, leaving two holes for the eyes.

"He's a bit shy,"said Nightingale.

"Seems so," whispered Wainwright," or else he's one ugly SOB,"

Again the woman's voice was heard. "The Master Khamsin will now recreate the greatest trick of the Egyptian Magician, Dedi. This is recorded on the famous Westcar Papyrus, written in the eighteenth century BC, and is the oldest record of a magical performance in existence."

Behind Khamsin, a blackout curtain moved aside, and three large black boxes could be seen, each one sitting on a small trestle table. Khamsin walked to each one and opened its front panel. Behind each one were bars. In the first box, sat a white goose, in the second, larger box, a swan. The third box was the largest of all, and contained a flamingo. Khamsin once again drew his khopesh.

"I've got a bad feeling about this," whispered Nightingale.

"Be grateful you ain't a bird."

"Joshua, mate, the clue is in my name.'

Khamsin walked to the goose's cage, pulled the bird's head between the bars, and sliced it off at the neck with his razor-sharp weapon. There was a gasp from the audience, even one or two muffled screams. The bird's head fell to the floor. No blood flowed from its severed neck. Quickly, Khamsin repeated the move with the other two birds. The audience was definitely stirring now, as the woman spoke again. "Any fool may destroy life. It takes a master sorcerer to restore it."

Two burly men, dressed as Egyptian slaves, naked to the waist, carried on a large screen, covered in hieroglyphics, which they placed in front of the cages, hiding them from view. Khamsin took from his robe a curved, flat, ivory wand, which he brandished over the severed heads.

There was another collective gasp, as the three heads glowed green, then slowly floated into the air, and disappeared over the top of the screen. A puff of green smoke rose from behind the screen, and Khamsin gave one more flourish of his wand.

The assistants pulled the screen aside, and there sat the three birds, cackling loudly, the heads re-attached.

"They've got the wrong heads," said Nightingale.

It was true, the swan now had a pink-feathered head, with a long pointed bill. The flamingo was chattering through the goose's shorter beak, and the goose now had the long neck and orange beak of the swan. None of them looked to be at all discomforted by their new body parts.

"It appears something may have been lost in the translation," said the woman, "But, fear not. All shall be as it was."

The slaves reappeared with the screen, Khamsin brandished his wand again, and this time there was a puff of red smoke from the direction of the boxes. The screen was removed, and Khamsin walked over to the three cages, and opened their bars. The three birds, perfectly restored to their original state, hopped down and walked off stage left, to another deafening round of applause.

"Do not be concerned," said the woman's voice. "None of our feathered friends has been harmed in any way."

"Says you," whispered Nightingale. "I'll bet there's at least six dead birds in the wings."

Wainwright grinned. "I find your lack of faith disturbing. Keep watching."

The show progressed at a fast pace, mostly consisting of variations of time-honoured tricks, but given an ancient Egyptian twist. An audience member was placed inside a sarcophagus lined with spikes, which was slammed shut and set alight. When the fire was extinguished by stagehands and the box opened, it contained the magician's woman assistant. It was the audience's first view of her. She was blonde, quite tall, maybe five foot seven, with an extra four inches or so from her gold stilettos which matched her high-cut sparkling gold leotard, and the gold domino mask she wore over her face.

"Nice looking girl, from what I can see," said Wainwright. "All the right parts in all the right places. Wonder why they hide their faces."

A large model of Cleopatra's needle, maybe twenty feet high, was wheeled on stage, fifteen audience members were selected 'at random', and the needle struck with a sword to 'prove' it was solid stone. The audience members formed a circle around it, holding hands, and a curtain was lowered around them. There was a puff of smoke, the curtain rose again to show the circle of people unbroken, but the needle had disappeared Amongst the deafening applause, the curtain came down again, there was another puff of smoke, and it rose. This time, the needle had reappeared, but there was no trace of the fifteen 'volunteers'.

Next, Khamsin demonstrated his hypnotic powers with some more audience volunteers. He put half a dozen or so into a line, and made them stare into a blue scarab, which he dangled on a chain in front of them. Suspiciously quickly, in Nightingale's opinion, they all 'went under' and were given different instructions. One was floated in the air, one chubby woman turned cartwheels on the stage. A man did sit-ups and two men lifted Khamsin above their heads, using only one finger each behind his knees.

Once the audience members had left the stage, the female assistant strapped and chained Khamsin to a wooden table, and a wicked-looking circular saw started to lower itself slowly towards him. A giant clock appeared behind him, with a single hand, counting down from sixty seconds to zero. The illusionist strained and struggled at the straps, and managed to free an arm, but he was working too slowly. The audience gasped as the hand reached ever closer to zero. There was a gust of smoke, a fountain of red liquid and Nightingale could have sworn that the man's body split in two, as the table collapsed, cut in half.

The crowd gasped in horror, but before the first scream had chance to ring out, Khamsin appeared from the wings, holding hands with his assistant, his clothing and his body unmarked.

"Not bad, eh Jack? Or do you think there's two halves of a twin brother in the wings?"

"Nah, he'd need a new one every night. Trick table, probably."

The applause died down. Once again, the woman's voice rang through the auditorium. Nightingale wondered if Khamsin ever spoke for himself. And if not, why not?

"Now, ladies and gentlemen, the ultimate performance of the night, as the Master Khamsin enters the Box of Death."

"Probably easy enough to enter...coming out will be the hard part," whispered Nightingale.

"Keep your eyes on this, Jack, you're not going to believe it."

Pipes, harps and drums played what Nightingale assumed must be an Egyptian tune, As he watched, the entire middle section of the stage opened up, and a glass tank began to rise from below. The tank must have been fifty feet long, and maybe thirty feet wide and perhaps fifteen feet high. As it rose Nightingale could see what looked like astroturf lining the bottom of it, and two long, brown, moving shapes.

"Behold," shouted the woman, "Direct from the land of Egypt. Omari and his mate Akila. Nile crocodiles. The most feared predators in all Africa."

"I hope that glass is bloody strong," said Nightingale. "I wouldn't want one of those monsters joining us in the front row."

"Easy, Jack, I'm guessing nothing short of a tank shell could get through that. I hear the insurance company insists on snipers in the balcony to shoot them in case anything goes wrong."

Nightingale frowned. "What's he doing now...the man must be mad."

Khamsin had removed his robe, and laid it down carefully on the stage by his feet. He wore tight pants of a shiny red material, but nothing above his waist. He raised his arms in front of him, and his body began to lift from the ground, slowly rising until he was above the cage. At this distance, it was hard to make out his features, but his hair and bushy eyebrows were black against the beige of his complexion. As he hovered above the middle of the tank, the two slaves appeared from the wings, each one holding what looked like a raw chicken. Simultaneously they threw the birds over the wall of the tank, and there was a frenzied thrashing as the two giant reptiles scurried towards them, opened their powerful jaws and the food disappeared.

"That's the starter," said Nightingale. "Main course, one magician."

Khamsin began to lower his hands slowly, and he started his descent into the very middle of the tank. He was still three feet from

70

the floor of the box, when the larger of the crocodiles reared up and lunged at him. Khamsin made no attempt to dodge the opening jaws. He just held his hands up in front of him, a strange curved white object in his right hand, and the huge reptile held its position, reared up, with its powerful jaws wide open. The audience gasped, expecting at any moment that the awful teeth would snap shut on the showman.

Khamsin was on the floor of the tank now, his hands still held out in front of him, palms towards the crocodile, which still hadn't moved. There came a flurry of movement, as the smaller crocodile, presumably the female, scurried forward to share in this fresh meal. Keeping his left palm facing the male, Khamsin moved his right hand in a small circle, and held it out to stop the female.

The three figures stood motionless for at least a minute, then the woman on stage started to applaud, and the audience joined in. She spoke again. "And now, Khamsin, Master Magician of the Nile, will place his head in Omari's mouth, holding his jaws apart solely by the power of Set. I must ask for perfect silence during the performance of this feat."

Khamsin lowered his right hand slowly, his eyes never leaving the female crocodile, who lay down at the bottom of the tank, and closed her eyes. Her mate stood still, his huge jaws still open, as Khamsin advanced towards him, placed one hand on the upper jaw, the other on the lower, and then inserted his head between them. The crocodile stayed motionless. It looked to Nightingale as if the animal was straining to close its jaws, but some force, far stronger than human arms, prevented it.

Nobody in the audience made a sound, hardly daring even to breathe, as Khamsin left his head in the animal's mouth for nearly a minute. Finally he stepped back, and brought the palms of his hands together. Omari's jaws snapped shut on empty air, and the man floated up and out of the tank, to rejoin the woman on stage, They bowed, and walked off to deafening applause.

Once the show was over, they went outside and lit up. "So what did you think Jack?" asked Wainwright, once he had got his cigar going.

Nightingale drew on his cigarette and watched the pillar of smoke curl upwards.

"I hope that crocodile had been chewing breath mints."

"Come on, Jack, cut the jokes."

Nightingale shrugged. "It's a very impressive performance. I guess he got the idea for the crocodiles from the two guys who used to have the act with the white lions and tigers."

"Siegfried and Roy? Yeah, they had a good thing going for years."

"Until one of the tigers went berserk and practically bit the guy's head off."

Wainwright shook his head. "No, until the tiger went tiger, and did what you'd expect a tiger to do. Nearly killed the guy. They were finished after that. Both dead now. But let's get back to Khamsin's act. How do you think it's done?"

"The usual stuff, I suppose," said Nightingale. "Misdirection, 'audience members' who really work for him, trick equipment. There was a TV show in Britain before I left, about a magician's assistant, the guy who designed the tricks. I remember him saying that most people watching wouldn't believe the lengths they'd go to to make an illusion work. Maybe there was some wire or something holding the jaws apart."

"So you're saying that everything we saw was an illusion? And that he used stooges?"

"Well, it has to be. We all know that David Copperfield didn't really make the Statue of Liberty disappear, it's not possible, so there has to be another explanation. It's just a case of working out the other possibilities."

"So, when Cleopatra's needle vanished from inside a circle of fifteen people plucked at random from the audience?"

"Who says they were random? Maybe he hired them all to swear they all saw nothing as the needle was winched up. Or lowered through the stage behind that screen."

"What about the hypnotism?"

"Well. First of all we have to assume they're all strangers and not paid-for stooges who have signed non-disclosure agreements. I've seen a British guy, Derren Brown, do some amazing stuff on the stage.

He swears he doesn't use stooges but then he would, wouldn't he? Once you realise that stooges play a big role in his act, everything becomes clear. And even if the Egyptian isn't using stooges, well, we've all seen stage hypnotists. I recall you have a little talent in that respect yourself, you used it in San Francisco."

"True enough," said Wainwright, "but I couldn't put a whole group of strangers under in seconds the way he did."

"Maybe he can, maybe he can't. There'll be some kind of an explanation."

Wainwright tapped the ash off his cigar. "Could be, Jack, could be. But there are two things that don't make sense to me."

Nightingale waited for him to continue.

"First off, why does he keep himself so anonymous? You realise we never once heard him speak, that woman did all the announcements for him. And we never saw his face, he kept that mask on all through the show, except when he put his head in the croc's mouth, and then the angle was all wrong for us to see anything."

"Maybe he's just shy?"

"Maybe he is, at that, but show people generally ain't. And then..."

Another pause.

"Then there's the crocodiles, Jack. You ever met a tame one?"

"No, I met alligators in Louisiana once, at a pretty safe distance, and they didn't seem too friendly. I guess they'd be unpredictable to work with."

"See now, that's where you're wrong. They'd be a hundred percent predictable. A lump of meat walks into their tank, you can bet your ass they'd tear it to pieces, if it were chicken, antelope or human. No doubt at all. You can't train them or domesticate them, even if you raised them from an egg."

"There must be ways of dealing with them. Didn't I read somewhere that if you're attacked by a croc you should play dead?"

"Sure, it'll be good practice for actually being dead, ten seconds later."

Nightingale grimaced. "So what would be your plan?"

"Tell you what, Jack, if we're ever attacked by a croc, we'll just run."

"No use, they're faster than an Olympic sprinter, you'd never outrun one."

"Sure enough, but I'm betting I could outrun *you*."

Nightingale chuckled. "Well, I'm glad I have some use, even if I'm just bait. But let's get back to those two tonight. So what stopped them?"

"You heard. The Power of Set. Maybe it's just another name for some of the demons we know exist, just like some of them have different names in Voodoo."

"So this Khamsin could have made a pact with Set?"

"I'm not saying that, but something was protecting him in the croc tank. You saw it, and I felt it."

"Felt it? How?"

Wainwright shrugged. "I felt the power being used. I wouldn't know how to explain it, any more than you could actually explain how you know you've heard or seen something, but I know it. When he held up his hand to freeze the crocs, I knew he was tapping into some kind of power."

"Okay, maybe that's what he's doing," said Nightingale, "But there's no reason we need to go after Khamsin, even if he's genuinely using Black Magic. He's not doing any harm with it."

"Not in the show. But maybe he's using that power in other ways, ways that aren't so harmless."

"You mean what Paul Hart was talking about? That's quite a leap, Joshua."

"Maybe it is, maybe it isn't. I've had my eye on that Khamsin guy for a while. To do what Paul was talking about, kill from a distance, that would take real power, and that guy has it. I felt it."

"Fair enough, let's tell him what you've deduced and beat a confession from him. Shouldn't take more than ten minutes."

"What if he has real Satanic powers? You go up against that guy on his own turf, and there won't be enough left of you to use as a paperweight. We'll need a better plan."

"I'm all ears."

"I'll get back to you, Jack. Meantime, why not take some of my money, hit the casino, and make a small fortune."

"Can it be done?"

"Sure it can. The secret is to start with a *large* fortune.

CHAPTER 23

Michael Litvinsky was at his desk early to initiate the conference call to his broker. Despite the hour, Nathan Cohen looked immaculate in his dark suit, white shirt and slim red tie. "Nate...give me good news."

"I wish I could, Michael. Old Man Marshall won't budge an inch. You've got all the shares you'd need in theory, but the way the family trust is set up, he has controlling interest, and he's been against it all along."

"Damn it to Hell, Nate, that factory is sitting in the middle of a billion dollar development opportunity for me."

"I know that, Michael, so does he."

"It's hardly breaking even, it'll go under inside a few years. My offer is their last hope."

"Thing is, Michael, he has the idea that as soon as you get your hands on it, it'll be closed down, demolished and the land used for housing. He doesn't want to see his workers thrown on welfare."

Litvinsky was silent, he had no argument against that, as it was entirely true. "So what can we do?" he asked eventually.

"Not much at the moment. Without Marshall I guess his sons would cave in pretty quickly, but the old man could have years left in him."

At that moment, the screen flickered, and Cohen's face was minimised in the lower left corner of the screen. The rest of the screen was filled by the face of an elderly black woman, her hair hidden beneath a green silk turban, her eyes shaded by giant sunglasses.

"What the f..."

"I think we've just been Zoombombed, Nate," said Litvinsky. "Someone's butting in. Who are you? What do you want?"

The woman looked off to the left for a moment, nodded, then began to speak in a flat expressionless tone.

"I represent someone who can help you with your current problem, Mr Litvinsky."

"So put him on, I don't deal with underlings."

Again she paused and looked off screen, as if receiving instructions.

"No, Sir. My principal does not care to make himself known, but he is offering to remove your problem."

"Remove? What does that mean?"

Again the pause before she answered.

"Simply this. You wish to purchase Marshall Manufacturing, At the moment, there is no possibility of your doing so due to the objections of the owner. My principal undertakes to remove that objection, for the sum of five million dollars."

"Not a chance, I wouldn't hand over a quarter to some face on the internet. How gullible do you think I am?"

"We do not think you are gullible at all, Mr Litvinsky and you need take nothing on trust. Inside five days, the objection to your purchase of Marshall Manufacturing will have been removed. Only then will you be asked for payment, if you agree to our terms."

"What do you think, Nate?" asked Litvinsky.

"What do I think to what?"

"What she said?"

"I didn't hear anything, Michael. I can see her lips moving, but I'm getting no sound."

The woman spoke again. "Mr Cohen cannot hear us, it was felt that the proposal should be kept between the two of us, at this stage."

Litvinsky licked his lips, then puffed at his vape. "It's nuts," he said. "There's nothing you can do to change George Marshall's mind.

"I repeat, in five days, the obstacle to your deal will be removed. You have twenty-four hours to come to a decision, you will be contacted again after that time."

The screen flickered again, the old woman was gone, and Nathan Cohen's face was full-size again.

"What was that all about, Michael? What did she want?"

"No idea, just some hacker, I guess, probably trying to get some cash out of me. I cut her off. Nate, keep trying on Marshall. Offer him another ten per cent."

"I will, Michael, but it won't do any good. He's a mule."

"Mules die, just like everything else," muttered Litvinsky to himself.

CHAPTER 24

In the absence of any instructions from Wainwright, Nightingale rose at nine in the morning. He'd ignored Wainwright's suggestion of returning to the casino and slept pretty well, despite the three hour time difference he'd passed through yesterday. He headed down to the Tropicana's main restaurant to take advantage of one of his favourite American traditions - The Breakfast Buffet.

The whole side of the massive room was stacked with pretty much every kind of food that anyone might ever care to eat at breakfast time, with stations for most beverages too. A glance at the heaped plates in front of some of the larger guests confirmed that they regarded "All You Can Eat" as a personal challenge, but Nightingale contented himself with scrambled eggs, some toast, fruit and two cups of coffee. He'd started off with a cigarette in his room before coming down.

After breakfast, Nightingale wandered back through the casino, even this early in the morning, it was doing good business. The high rollers were probably still asleep, but most of the slot machines were in use, often by old ladies, plastic drink cups full of quarters by their sides. They fed their machine, pulled the handle, barely glanced at the reels before repeating the process. Nightingale wondered if their right arms were twice as developed as their left. Then he wondered if there were special machines for left-handers.

He decided a little fresh air might help, so strolled out of the main exit. The heat hit him at once, and he started to sweat. The uniformed doorman smiled at him. "You not used to living in the desert, sir? Fastest warming city in the USA, they say. Gone up six degrees in fifty years. Soon be uninhabitable, they say. That's if we don't run out of water first."

"You work for the Tourist Board?" asked Nightingale.

"No sir, But I'm not telling you anything that isn't generally known. I'd recommend sunscreen and staying indoors as much as possible."

Nightingale looked at the man's badge. "Thank you, Marlon, that's good advice. Perhaps a gentle stroll isn't such a good idea."

"No sir. Head into the hotels, they mostly all join up with each other. Moving walkways. Or you can take the Monorail for five bucks a trip."

Which would have been useful information if Nightingale had anywhere special to go. A leisurely stroll was clearly out, so he thought about the hotel Fitness Centre. After all, he had paid his resort fee. He was saved from making a decision by the sound of his cellphone. There was only one man who knew his latest number. Wainwright.

"Yes?"

"I got a plan, Jack. Whoever this guy is, we need to find some way of flushing him out. Figure out where he's likely to strike next, how he does it, then stop him."

"That took you all night to work out?"

"Not hardly, it's pretty obvious what needs to be done. The how is going to be a lot more difficult."

"You don't say."

"Way I see it, there's only one sure way to know where he's going to strike next."

"Which is?"

"To hire him ourselves."

"And how do you plan to do that? I'm assuming he doesn't advertise."

"Probably not, but he'll need to find his work from somewhere. I've got plenty of connections with people you wouldn't care to meet. How might it be if I put the word out that I'm looking to offer a contract on someone. See if the fish bites."

"Then what?"

"Well. If he takes the bait, I guess you thwart him."

"Thwart? That's not a word you hear a lot."

'It's the right word for this occasion. You thwart him by any means necessary."

"You mean you don't know how?"

"No sense having a hound dog and howling yourself, I got faith in you. You're a resourceful guy, Jack, you'll think of something. You'll have to."

"And if I don't?"

"Well, I'll hate to lose you."

"You don't mean... You can't be serious. Who are you going to put out a contract on?"

"Who else? I'm going to offer a contract on you."

CHAPTER 25

Venetia Curtis shook her head, and the mist finally started to clear from her brain. Where was she? Was she still dreaming? Behind her, the cab pulled away, but she had no memory of getting out of it, being in it or why she had taken it. She almost never took a cab, much preferring her own car. Where was she? On the Strip, near the Bellagio, a hotel she'd never visited. She'd been to shows at the MGM, Caesar's Palace and the Luxor recently, but why would she be here? Oh My God, was this the first sign of advancing dementia? Being somewhere with no memory of how, or why, she'd got there?

Venetia was sixty-seven, retired from her teaching job and a widow. Her children lived out of state, so there was nobody to keep tabs on her, to check that she wasn't having any problems. Sure, she had old friends from her job, but she didn't see them as often as she used to. Could she be losing her grip, without even noticing?

She felt a stirring in her abdomen, and tried to remember when she'd last visited a restroom. She couldn't recall anything after breakfast that morning, but this was no time to hesitate. She headed into the Bellagio and followed signs for the nearest restroom. Once that had been dealt with, she took a look in one of the wash room mirrors, She was fully dressed, a light dusting of foundation on her black skin. But her hair looked like a bird's nest, as if something had been pulled through it. Wherever she'd been, she still had her bag, so she took out a brush and did her best to repair the damage. As she put the brush away, she noticed something soft and green in the bottom of her bag, and pulled it out. A silk turban. What was that doing there? Venetia only wore hats to weddings and funerals, and she'd never owned anything like this. Where had it come from?

She walked to the nearest bar, bought herself a glass of Chablis and sipped it slowly. For sure she hadn't been drunk, she almost never drank, especially since Joseph's death. She wasn't taking any medication which might account for some kind of blackout. She checked her purse. She'd spent a few dollars on the wine, but nothing else was missing. So who had paid the cab?

A ghastly thought occurred to her, she'd read about date rape drugs, could someone have give her a shot of something? No, she hadn't been out at night in a week, and had had no visitors. Besides, nothing had happened in that area, and she felt sure she would have been able to tell.

Venetia never told anyone, family or friends, about her "turn", though she often thought about it and regularly asked herself questions about where she was and what she was doing, just to reassure herself that it wasn't going to happen again, but it never did.

CHAPTER 26

Jack Nightingale didn't scare easily, but he shuddered as Wainwright cut the connection. If the billionaire's plan worked out, then, very soon, someone, or something would be trying to visit death on Nightingale. It could come at any time, and, maybe, over any distance. He'd always known that Wainwright's loyalties were not to him, but he'd never imagined he would be this cold. Running or trying to hide would probably be futile, Wainwright could always find him, and, if he were up against a powerful adversary, there would be no hiding place. On the other hand, sitting in a hotel room waiting to die held no appeal. Nightingale decided he needed help.

He dialled a New Orleans number. The familiar honeyed tones answered on the third ring.

"Hannah Devereaux."

"Hannah, good to hear you. It's Jack, Jack Nightingale."

"Well now, this is an unexpected pleasure. I'm glad to know you're still alive. You never write."

"I...er...sorry, I..."

She laughed. "I'm just joking, Jack, though it really is good to know you're still around, you moved in some pretty nasty circles down here."

"Good thing I'm pure in heart."

"Oh yes, we always thought that of you. Well, I'm doing okay, the Colonel's fine, which takes care of social chit-chat. What is it you need help with?"

"Am I that transparent?"

"You're an easy read. Tell me."

"Well, I'm not sure it makes any sense, but..."

84

Hannah listened without interruption for four minutes as he told her about the convenient deaths. He didn't mention the visit to Khamsin's show, that was too much like guesswork at the moment.

"I see, and you think there might be a Voodoo connection?" she said.

"I have no idea where to start, that's why I called you. Is it possible?"

"It doesn't seem likely, a Voodoo practitioner would need to make a doll, to have access to some personal stuff from the victim. Hair, clothes. And Voodoo curses generally work best against people who are sincere believers. Doesn't sound like that's what you've got here."

"There's a vague idea there might be a connection to ancient Egypt..."

"Vague idea? I wonder where you get that from? That's out of my area of expertise, I'm afraid."

"Do you know anyone I could talk to about it?"

"Well, there's your friend Mrs Steadman back in London."

"I'd rather not involve her at this stage, I'm not sure she'd approve."

"I doubt she would at that. And she's a stickler for the rules. Las Vegas, you say? Let me think. Judy Dubois might be able to help you. She runs the *Crystal Village* on South Decatur Boulevard. She'll put you on the right track, tell her I sent you. She's young, but I think she can be trusted. And next time you're in Louisiana, don't be a stranger."

"I won't" said Nightingale, "thanks."

He had no idea how much time he would be likely to have, but there was no sense in delaying, so he headed for the Tropicana cab-rank.

CHAPTER 27

High above Los Angeles, Wainwright's Gulfstream started its approach towards LAX. Wainwright put down the phone on the last of the calls he had made over the last two hours, and stubbed out his cigar. He had spoken to half a dozen of the worst gangsters who called Las Vegas home. The message had been the same during each call. Wainwright wanted someone killed, but it had to look like natural causes. Of course he didn't actually use the word "killed" but the men he had spoken to had got the message. He had done all that he could, Now it was a question of waiting, to see who might want to pick up the valuable contract offered. Wainwright expected to have his time wasted by any number of local heroes, who'd be happy to put a bullet into someone for a tenth of what was on offer, but had deliberately left his contact details vague. If the killer he was looking for was as good as his reputation, he'd know how to get in touch.

CHAPTER 28

Until a few years ago, Jack Nightingale had no idea that Wiccan stores even existed, much less that every decent-sized city appeared to have several of them. *Crystal Village*, like most American stores to his eyes, was huge, probably five times the size of Mrs Steadman's little shop in Camden. Much better lit too, stocked with pretty much everything a Wiccan practitioner might ever need. Crystal balls, oils, minerals, bracelets, candles, incense sticks, books and shelves full of items Nightingale couldn't identify.

As he walked in a tall, blonde woman in a flowing black dress walked from behind the counter to meet him. She looked to be in her early thirties, her straight blonde hair parted in the centre, and held off her face by a bronze coloured headband, which featured the shape of an eye in the middle of her forehead.

"I'm Judy, you must be Jack Nightingale."

"How..."

"The Inner Eye sees all."

Nightingale's jaw dropped, then he noticed the smile creeping round the corners of her mouth. "Hannah called?"

"Well, yes. She said I'd know you by the shoes. What are they?"

"They're called Hush Puppies. Maybe not as stylish as some, but they're very easy on the feet, and some days I have to do a lot of walking."

"Wow. They look awful. Are they even legal in the USA?"

"Legal? Cheek. They're an American company, based in Michigan."

"Huh. The Midwest? They have some strange people up there."

Which seemed pretty rich, coming from the owner of a Witchcraft store, but Nightingale was diplomatic enough to keep that thought to himself. Judy was wearing long black boots, with silver heels and tips, but he didn't comment on them either. She probably didn't do much walking in a day.

"So, Jack, leaving footwear aside, what is it you think I can help you with? I'm assuming Hannah wouldn't have sent you to me just to buy some incense sticks."

"No, she wouldn't. And that's not what I need. What do you know about killing someone from a distance?"

"I assume you're not talking about a rifle."

"No, maybe a curse of some kind."

"Like Voodoo?"

"Possibly, though Hannah told me it was unlikely."

"And she's pretty well informed about the subject. Well. The short answer is that I don't know anything about it. My practice of Wicca is for purposes of helping and healing only. We mostly don't call down curses on people's heads."

"I know that, but not everyone sticks to the Right-Hand Path."

She raised her eyebrows. "You're quite well informed. Yes, there are rotten apples who use power for evil purposes, but they are very few. What you're talking about would require immense power and knowledge. Ordinary practitioners like myself wouldn't know where to start, even if it were possible."

"Might you know someone who was better informed?"

"Not from a practical point of view, and I wouldn't want to. When it comes to theory, Hannah's the expert on Voodoo. If she says it's not a Voodoo thing, I guess you'd need to do some research on other traditions. Jewish, Egyptian, Norse and so on, to see if they mention anything."

"Egyptian?"

"Well, yes. Their study of the occult goes back thousands of years, I even have some Egyptian wands here."

"Really? Could you show me?"

"Certainly, but bear in mind that these are modern replicas, the originals would be almost impossible to find, and priceless. Come over here."

She led the way to the left of the shop, where there was a case filled with wands of varying lengths, made of different colours of wood. Mostly plain, but some decorated with gold or silver bands, or coloured engraving.

"They don't look very Egyptian," said Nightingale.

"That's because they're not, they're mostly cut from European or American trees. They're a regular seller to what I call the 'Harry Potter Crowd.' People who've read the books and like to pretend."

"I'm surprised you cater for them."

"I don't really, but people who just wander into the store like to find something inexpensive to leave with. Got to keep the cash register moving."

She opened a drawer underneath the case. "This is more the sort of thing you might be looking for."

The items here didn't look anything like Nightingale's idea of a wizard's wand. They were flat and shaped like a crescent. Certainly not made of wood.

"They should be made of ivory," said Judy, "but, of course that's banned these days, so these are ivoroid. Plastic, to be honest."

"Ivory? Did there used to be elephants in Egypt then?"

"Not that I know of, these would have been made from hippo tusks. Hippo ivory is much harder than elephant ivory and it's notoriously difficult to carve. A lot of care went into carving the originals. Take a look ."

The wand was inscribed on one side with figures, most of them with unearthly heads, and carrying curved knives,

"They are deities, and the knives are used to ward off evil spirits," said Judy.

"And the writing on the back? The hieroglyphics?"

"I don't read them myself, but apparently it's a call for protection of a new-born child, son of the woman Sitsobek. It's copied from an original in the Met Museum."

"So that's what they were used for, protection?"

"As far as we know, most of the ones found were meant to protect women and children from evil. Pretty much the opposite of your theory."

"I suppose so. But didn't Egyptian magic have some kind of left-hand path too? I've been told that Wicca is just a source of power, and it can be used for good or evil."

"Well, that's pretty much the limit of my knowledge, I can sell you a copy of this wand for thirty bucks, maybe even get one made to protect your wife or children, but I'm no expert."

"Would you know someone who is an expert?"

"Well, the guy Khamsin who performs at the Luxor is meant to be a powerful Egyptian magician, but I'm told it's pretty much impossible to get anywhere near him. Nobody's even sure what he looks like, he always appears in a mask. "

"Yeah, I've heard of him,"said Nightingale. He thought it best not to reveal that he had already seen the show. "But I'm not really looking for an illusionist. I need someone who knows the history of this stuff, how it works...if it works."

Judy frowned. "I guess there's Dr Mahoub. He used to be an archaeology professor at Las Vegas University, but he's pretty old now."

"There's a University here?"

"Sure there is, we're not just a bunch of casinos."

"How do you know this guy?"

"All the Wicca stores know him, he has an interest in traditional Magic, but he's very enthusiastic about Ancient Egypt. We're meant to call him if anyone offers us anything old and Egyptian."

"Does he buy much?"

"Hardly ever, but then the chances of genuine Egyptian curios showing up here are pretty remote."

"So is he Egyptian?"

"I guess, though I don't think he's allowed back in the country. I think his family had some problems with the authorities. I heard they'll throw him in prison if he sets foot in Egypt again."

"And would he talk to me, do you think??"

"The trick would be to get him to stop talking."

Judy made a call. Dr Mahoub would be delighted to meet with Nightingale, though appointments with his dentist and optician meant he wouldn't be free for another two days.

Nightingale thanked Judy, handed over thirty dollars for a replica Egyptian wand, and left his trusty pink crystal to be recharged. So far so good. Now all he needed to do was to stay alive for two more days.

CHAPTER 29

Nightingale was walking away from the shop when his mobile rang. It was Wainwright. "Jack, I'm back in LA. Paul Hart has been in touch regarding Delia Winston. Her husband just died of a heart attack, remember, after our mysterious killer offering to get rid of her for five million. Paul has come up with an address, so maybe you could go see her. Quite a looker, I'm told, with possibly the best rack in Sin City."

"I will do," said Nightingale. "And while I'm waiting to be killed, I thought I might go and talk to the coroner who did Frankie Marino's autopsy. Maybe any other coroner's too."

"I'll dig out some addresses and send them along with Delia's details. After this, best if we don't have any contact at all for a while. If I manage to get in touch with this presumed killer, he's not likely to take me at face value. He'll get me checked out. If he's powerful enough, might even be able to overlook me."

"What's that?"

"Keep watch on me, or you from afar. Remember back in San Francisco, that woman seemed to know what you were doing before you did it? It takes a powerful practitioner to pull it off, but we don't want to risk our being seen together or talking to each other."

"So, I'm on my own?"

"Safer that way. "

"Safer for whom?" asked Nightingale, but Wainwright had already ended the call.

CHAPTER 30

Nightingale was obliged to agree with Wainwright's assessment of Delia Winston's chest, though he doubted that it was original equipment. From what he'd seen so far, a lot of women in Las Vegas had spent a lot of time and money having themselves surgically enhanced. It went well with the low-cut black dress, which was a little too vampish to constitute mourning. Her eyes showed no signs of recent crying over her loss. Her long blonde hair was either natural, or an immaculate colouring job. Nightingale guessed her age at thirty-four, though she was making plenty of effort to look younger.

"Mrs Winston? Jack Nightingale. Thanks for agreeing to talk to me."

She gave him one of her better smiles, which deepened one or two of the lines round her face and eyes. If she was planning to hook herself another rich man, Nightingale thought she'd better be quick about it. Though from the looks of her penthouse apartment home in an exclusive area of Las Vegas, she wasn't hurting for money at the moment, especially if the rumours of her late husband's wealth were to be believed.

"You were very mysterious when you phoned," she said, her voice low and soft. "Let's just say you piqued my interest. Now, take a seat. Coffee? A glass of wine?"

"Nothing for me thanks."

Nightingale couldn't see any ashtrays, so decided to do without for a little longer. Delia topped up her glass from the bottle in the ice bucket. Genuine Lanson Champagne. The lady did herself well.

"So what is it you want to see me about, Mr Nightingale?" she asked.

"A simple question, Mrs Winston. How much do you owe the people who arranged your husband's death?"

Her eyes and mouth widened in horror and her glass dropped from her fingers, spilling its contents on the thick white rug.

"What? How do you...No, that's ridiculous. My husband died of a heart attack. How dare you suggest..."

Nightingale smiled. "I know that's what the medical report suggests, but we know different, don't we? You were contacted before his death. How much did the woman ask for?"

"It wasn't a wo..." she clapped a hand to her mouth.

"Alright, the man then. How much?" Her eyes darted around the room, then she bent to pick up her glass and slowly refilled it. Her breathing was slowing now, as she composed herself. "I really don't know what you mean, Mr Nightingale. My husband died of a heart attack, and you have no business suggesting otherwise. If you have any evidence, I suggest you contact the police. If you repeat these allegations in public, I'll have you sued for defamation. Now, I'll be grateful if you'd leave my home, and don't come back."

"I think you know what I'm talking about, Mrs Winston. These are dangerous people to be involved with." She picked up the phone. "The door is right behind you. Use it at once, or I'll call the police."

Nightingale knew the signs, she'd decided to hide behind her lie, and would stick to it now, whatever happened. He stood up, leaving a card on the coffee table.

"I'm going. If you change your mind and want to talk to me, here's my number. Take care."

By the time the door had shut behind him, the card was in tiny pieces in the waste basket.

CHAPTER 31

It was less than an hour later that the limousine arrived at Delia Winston's house. The driver carried four pieces of expensive matching luggage to the trunk, then opened the rear door for his client. The drive to Harry Reid International took just thirty minutes, despite the heavy daytime traffic. The driver whistled up a Skycap with a trolley, and Mrs Winston headed for the American Airways first class check-in.

"You're all set ma'am," said the agent. "Your luggage is ticketed through to London. You'll be changing at Chicago. Going to see family?"

"That's right," said Delia. "My sister works over there in London."

Which wasn't true, Delia knew nobody in London, and wasn't planning to stay there for much longer than it took to get a train to Edinburgh. She planned to lose herself in Scotland for a while, let them see if they could find her there. There was no way she was going to pay them, not when Bernie had died of natural causes.

The American Airways Airbus was due to depart on time, and the cabin crew fussed attentively round the first-class passengers. The Supervisor took up her microphone to start the inevitable safety talk, reassuring the passengers that, in the event of the aircraft crashing into the Atlantic at five hundred miles an hour, they would be perfectly safe with their life jacket and whistle. Delia had heard it all before, and paid no attention to the woman, but frowned suddenly as a figure seemed to flit towards her. Was it a man or a dog?

The Cabin Crew Supervisor walked along the cabin, making her usual final check before the plane pushed back from the terminal. One passenger had fallen asleep already, which was a damned nuisance. She put her hand on the woman's shoulder, gave her a little shake.

"Excuse me, Ma'am, sorry to disturb you, I'll have to ask you to fasten your seatbelt for take-off. Ma'am?"

The woman's head lolled limply to one side, The stewardess's eyes widened, but she'd been well trained. She walked forward to the cockpit and knocked.

In the end, the flight to Chicago was delayed by four hours, while the body of Delia Winston was removed and transported to a medical facility.

CHAPTER 32

Major General Zakaria Mustafa still enjoyed using his former rank, though it had been some years since he had retired from Military Intelligence. He had always enjoyed his visits to the United States, and was now making the most of his free time with a stay in Vegas. He had a taste for the finer things in life, and his suite at the Bellagio was one of its most exclusive, complete with steam shower, marble bath with whirlpool tub, mood lighting and climate control.

The Major General was generally considered a good Muslim by his former colleagues and superiors at home, but he subscribed to different standards while travelling. He had developed a taste for Californian champagne, which was regularly delivered to his room, and for American blondes, which Las Vegas was also happy to send to his suite as required. He was a regular visitor to the hotel casino, with roulette and baccarat in the High Limit Lounge his favourite pursuits. Nobody questioned how a former military officer had come to acquire such wealth, many people thought his family had interests in oil companies.

Tonight however, he was unable to indulge in gambling or drinking, the appointment was far too important. He permitted the tall blonde girl to use the shower, the least he could do after the indignities he'd subjected her to, but she had been paid the extra required, so had no grounds for complaint.

He showered and checked himself in the mirror. The short hair was greying now, as was his moustache, and there was just the hint of a double chin. He'd gained a few pounds since his military days, and would need to be careful that he didn't run to fat. The scar across his right cheek had faded over the years, but was still noticeable. He liked people to think it was a relic of some military skirmish, though it had actually been put there by a jealous woman with a knife. She was now dead.

At a few minutes before twelve, he took the elevator down to street level and stood near the famous fountains as he had been instructed.

He was too late to witness the display, which stopped running at midnight. He had time to smoke a cigarette, before the car drew up, an anonymous white Ford Escape. The rear door opened, and he climbed in, nodding silently to the driver, a young man in his twenties, wearing black shirt and pants, who didn't speak for the entire trip.

Twenty minutes later, the vehicle pulled into the underground parking garage of an apartment building well away from the Strip. The driver got out, opened the rear door and walked the Major General to the elevator, where he pressed button 8. Neither man spoke, the doors opened and the driver led the way to apartment C. He knocked, and the door swung open.

Mustafa walked inside, ignoring the attractive blonde woman who held the door for him, and walking over to the rather short, dark-haired man who rose from the sofa to greet him. They exchanged the customary kiss on the cheeks, then Mustafa stood back. "Greetings to you, cousin."

"I return your greetings, cousin. You look well."

"I am well, leaving the military suited me, and this short holiday is refreshing me. Las Vegas has much to offer to a man of taste."

His cousin smiled, but said nothing. Mustafa took one of the chairs opposite the sofa, and turned to the woman.

"Bring me a drink. Whisky."

The woman frowned. "I am not a servant, and there is no drink here, the apartment is borrowed for a few hours only."

Khamsin looked at Mustafa reprovingly. Mustafa swallowed hard, choking back his angry words. On his own territory, such insolence would have merited a beating, but this was not home, he needed the man's goodwill, and it seemed the woman was allowed such liberties. He nodded his head in acknowledgement. "I apologise for my tone," he said, "shall we get to business, cousin?".

"That would be preferable," said Khamsin.

"Our preparations are progressing well. Officers loyal to our Brotherhood are prepared to strike when the time is right."

"You really think you will have enough support?" asked Khamsin.

"I am sure of it, my cousin. With the President dead, and the chain of command in disarray, the chances are very high that the Brotherhood of Canaan will be in control of key positions within a few days. It will be sudden, and there will be no opportunity to coordinate resistance to us. When the dust clears, it will be up to the Brotherhood to choose the new rulers, and our family, the descendants of Bin-Saheed, will once again take their place at the head of our country."

"It may be so," said Khamsin, "but why should an attempted revolution be any more successful now than at any other point in recent history?"

"Because we shall strike at a time of the greatest hope. As you know, the President, along with the Prime Mister of Israel and the head of the Palestinian Authority will be meeting in Washington. If he dies suddenly, while out of the country, chaos will ensue, and out of that chaos will emerge the bright light of a new dawn."

"Very poetic," said Khamsin. "But I am less concerned with poetry and ideology than I am with power and money."

"Your price is known and agreed upon, though there were some who felt that charging such a huge fee was not the action of a patriot."

"I am not concerned with choosing sides."

"Your choice has been made by our ancestors. Do you not wish to see our family restored to power? To reclaim our rightful position?"

Khamsin sucked his teeth, and made no reply. The General continued. "The fee you requested has already been transferred to the account you nominated. You must not fail us, my cousin. I have no understanding of your methods, but you have demonstrated to our satisfaction that they are effective."

"As, yes, the Mossad operative Goldberg," said Khamsin. "It made a pleasant change to rid the world of an enemy of my race, rather than settling scores for criminals, or ex-wives."

"And he will be just the first," said Mustafa. "Once the Brotherhood of Canaan seize power, we will not rest until Israel is destroyed, its inhabitants driven into the sea, and the land returned to its people."

Khamsin smiled. "An ambitious undertaking indeed, I admire your confidence, and hope it is not misplaced."

"It is not, my cousin, I assure you. Everything is in place, we only await the death of the President as the trigger to set it in motion."

"The date in question?"

"The fourteenth. The ideal time would be at eleven am, just as the conference begins."

"And have you brought what I asked for?"

"Of course," said Mustafa, "that is why we had to meet in person."

Mustafa rummaged in his attaché case and produced a plastic bag containing a few locks of hair. "You would not believe the price that his barber charged us for this," he said.

Khamsin took the bag and held it up to the light. "It will be perfectly adequate for my purposes. I give you my guarantee that the President will die at the time you have stated."

"Do not fail us on this, my cousin. There are powerful people within the Brotherhood whom it would not be wise to displease with failure."

Khamsin frowned and half rose from the sofa, then sat down again. His voice was soft and controlled when he spoke. "For a moment there, cousin, it almost seemed as if you were threatening me. I do not like threats."

The General's face grew a little paler, and he held up his hands in apology. "By no means, cousin. I am well aware of your powers, and I meant no threat. I spoke hastily and I apologise. This is of supreme importance to many people, but we have complete faith in you."

"I'm sure you do," said Khamsin, "I just wonder if that faith is shared by others in the Brotherhood. Anyway, we have finished our business here. Ali will return you to your hotel.

Mustafa looked at his Patel Philippe watch. By Las Vegas standards, the night was still young, there would be plenty of time for him to try to win back some of his money in the High Limit Lounge, and, perhaps, another blonde girl before sunrise.

CHAPTER 33

Khamsin turned to his assistant as she shut the door behind the Major General. "And what do you make of him?" he asked.

"A typical pig, used to having his own way and treating people like cattle. I would not care to be in his power. Or his hotel room."

"Certainly he lacks charm," said Khamsin, "but he has access to large sums of money, and still wields considerable influence, even amongst those who are unaware of his connection to the Brotherhood."

She twisted her mouth in contempt. "And what is this precious Brotherhood, except another gang of fanatics, desperate to seize power and oppress those they consider inferior?"

"That probably sums them up nicely. In my opinion their attempt at a revolution will fail. The death of the President will increase their influence for sure, but when the proverbial chips are down, I suspect that individual members will be too frightened for their own skin to rise against the government."

"So you do not intend to complete this mission?"

"On the contrary, I have been paid a very large sum of money and it would be foolish to antagonise them by not earning it. The President shall die, which, in my opinion will be a excellent thing, and let the results of his death be what they may. Perhaps they will favour Mustafa and his Brotherhood, more likely not, but there can be no connection to me Mustafa himself may not survive long."

"So the Messenger of Anubis will be busy."

"Yes, but he does not tire, he does not weaken and he never fails."

CHAPTER 34

The office of the Clark County Coroner and Medical Examiner was a low squat orange building on Pinto Lane, with its name picked out in metal letters on the wall outside. As Nightingale walked in, he was stunned to find that the place had a gift shop.

"Morning, Sir," said the young man behind the counter, whose lapel badge said 'Chad'. "Welcome to the Clark County Coroner gift shop, feel free to take a look around."

There was a wide selection of merchandise. Ballpoint pens bearing the legend *Stolen From Clark County Coroner*, scrub suits with logos, car licence plates and cuff links. Worse yet were the T-shirts, a black one with a slot machine showing three bars and with the slogan *Cashed Out In Las Vegas.* Or a coffee mug saying *Here's Where You're At When The Line Goes Flat.*

"Does nobody find all this a bit macabre,"asked Nightingale.

"Oh yes," replied the young man, "but I guess that's part of the fun. We get lots of visitors here who come just for the gift shop."

Nightingale walked on to the offices. He had been given an appointment with Dr Mary Baker, who had performed the autopsy on the late Francesco Marino. Dr Baker looked around fifty, her greying brown hair tied back in a bun, and she fixed him steadily with her gaze through round, gold-rimmed glasses.

"Mr Nightingale, I've been asked to give you any information you require about the death of Francesco Leonardo Marino. I'm not quite clear what the purpose of that would be, as autopsy results are a matter of public record, you can find all the information you need there."

"Of course, but it tends to be written with a lot of technical terms. Could you explain it simply for a layman like me?"

She sighed. "Very well, to save time, he died because his heart stopped beating."

"Don't we all die that way?"

"It's not always the cause. One of his coronary arteries became blocked, so the blood could not flow, hence he died."

"Did he have heart disease?"

"I think you're aware that he did not. In fact his heart was unusually healthy. There was nothing there to cause a blockage."

"But there still was one."

"Indeed, Completely blocked, almost as if someone had squeezed it shut."

"Is that possible?"

"No, of course not, not without cutting open his rib-cage, and that clearly hadn't happened. I was just trying to use an image to give you the extent of the problem."

"And what could have caused that?"

"I couldn't really tell you. It might have been an hereditary weakness, or a sudden unexpected muscle contraction. You may have heard of the term SADS-Sudden Arrhythmic Death Syndrome, when someone drops dead of a heart attack with no previous symptoms or advance warning. It can be caused by hypertrophic cardiomyopathy, a gradual thickening of the artery. "

"And that had happened in this case?"

"There were no signs of a long-term problem."

"Dr Baker, were you puzzled by this death?"

She took off her glasses and began to polish them with a cloth from her desk. "Not puzzled, Mr Nightingale, the man died of heart failure, but I will say it was a very untypical case."

"Nothing suspicious?"

"I know of no external factor which could have produced such an effect, the police were quite satisfied with the verdict of death from natural causes."

"Thank you, Anything else unusual about the case?"

She hesitated, then put her glasses back on. "Perhaps, but I don't think it's significant. There was an unusual mark on the heart."

"What kind of mark?"

"I'll show you"

She tapped a few buttons on her desktop computer, then swivelled the screen so Nightingale could see it. "It's just a shadow really. Not even a bruise, probably the way that blood pooled on that part of the heart. See?"

Nightingale stared at the screen. Against the pinky surface of the dead man's heart, he could just make out the shadow that she was referring to.

"It's odd," said Dr Baker. "It looks a bit like a dog's head."

CHAPTER 35

Khamsin's hypnosis spot was in full swing. He was able to sense which subjects would go under the most easily, and be easiest to bend to his will. Nobody was near enough to hear the whispered exchanges that took place between them, though they could all hear the instructions he gave them for the purpose of his show.

"What is your name?"

"Yvonne."

"Where do you live?"

"Las Vegas."

"Excellent."

His voice dropped to a whisper. Audible only to the woman.

"Cell number?"

She gave him the number.

"You will come to me when I call you."

"I will."

His voice resumed its normal volume.

Yvonne, you are a circus clown, I want you to walk on your hands across the stage."

The dumpy woman immediately bent low, placed her hands on the stage, lifted her legs into the air and moved a few yards across the stage, a feat she'd last attempted aged ten, and could never have managed in normal circumstances. The crowd erupted in a mixture of applause and laughter.

"What is your name. Sir?"

"Alexander."

"Where are you from?"

"Colorado, in town for my buddy's bachelor party."

"Cell number?" he whispered.

Alexander gave him the number.

"You will come to me when I call you."

"I will."

Alexander was ordered to run round the stage clucking like a chicken.

And you, Sir? What's your name, and where are you from?

"My name is Tommy Chang, I live in Las Vegas."

"Splendid."

Then the whisper again.

"Cellphone number?"

He gave him the number.

"Come to me when I call,"

And then aloud.

"I sense a particularly good subject in Tommy, a man who, before your very eyes, will now defy the law of gravity."

Khamsin waved his hands above the man's head to show there were no hidden wires holding him, then made a series of passes in front of Tommy's face with his fingers spread wide. The audience gasped, as Tommy slowly rose from the stage, until his feet were at least eighteen inches off the floor. Khamsin gave him a little push, and he floated two yards away. A blank expression on his face throughout. Finally Khamsin lowered his hands, and Tommy slowly floated back down. Once his feet were on solid wood, Khamsin clicked his fingers, and the man looked around with a puzzled expression.

The audience erupted.

CHAPTER 36

The taxi rolled to a halt outside the detached house in Southern Terrace, and Nightingale stepped out. By American standards, the home was quite small, probably no more than five bedrooms, with the usual double garage at the front. It was white, looked to have been recently painted, and the lawn and drive were in excellent condition. Either Dr Mahoub worked hard at his property, or he could afford staff.

The man who answered the door was small, probably no more than five foot five, with a pronounced stoop, perhaps from the weight of years, since he looked at least seventy five, maybe closer to eighty. He was thin, the papery skin stretched tight across the bones of his face, his blue eyes watery and tired behind the thick, gold glasses. He was wearing a well-used dark suit, with a white shirt, but no tie. Much to Nightingale's surprise, a black *yarmulke* covered the back of his balding skull. "Mr Nightingale. Come inside, please. We can talk in my study."

The doctor led the way inside. Nightingale stopped to stare at the entrance hall. It was long, painted in light blue and decorated with what looked like Egyptian tomb paintings. Gods, goddesses, farmers, water-carriers, women and children. Mahoub led the way to a door on the right and stepped aside for Nightingale to enter. The room was covered in bookshelves, from floor to ceiling, most of the titles seeming to be in languages Nightingale could not read. There were small tables placed around the room, with a huge array of Egyptian ornaments, mostly of cats, birds, pharaohs and sphinxes, There were two old, green Chesterfield armchairs in front of the mahogany desk and Mahoub waved Nightingale to the one nearer the window. He sank into the other chair, and rang a little bell which stood on the table next to him. The door opened again, and a stout, white-haired woman of similar age to the doctor, dressed in a faded black pant-suit, came in. "My wife, Esther. Mr Nightingale. She is by no means a servant, but the bell saves me from calling to her. My throat is quite weak these days."

The old woman smiled at her husband. "I'm sure Mr Nightingale understands, can I offer you tea or coffee?"

"Not for me, thank you," said Nightingale.

"Might I have an ice tea?" asked Mahoub.

"Of course."

As the door shut behind her, Mahoub gestured at a small wooden box on the occasional table next to Nightingale.

"I observe you are a smoker, sir. Please help yourself. Egyptian cigarettes are one of the few links I keep to the country of my birth."

Nightingale took out his packet of Marlboro. "Thanks, but I'll stick to these."

"As you wish, but I shall trouble you for a light. It must be said that these are not beneficial for my throat, but I am reluctant to give up one of my last pleasures."

Nightingale nodded. Ester Mahoub returned and set the glass of ice tea next to her husband, who took an appreciative sip and nodded his thanks at her as she left. The two men smoked in silence for a while, and Nightingale felt the rheumy eyes of Mahoub studying him, seeming to focus on his throat. Nightingale's hand instinctively fingered the ankh which hung under his shirt.

"I sense you bear powerful protection, Mr Nightingale. Are you in fear for your life?"

Nightingale watched the plume of smoke rise from his cigarette, then took another deep drag. "I don't really feel that way, but maybe I should. I was advised to wear this...protection."

"By someone you trust?"

"No...not entirely. But maybe just enough. How did you know?"

"It is an area I have explored, I am able to sense some things. For example, I can sense that your protection comes from no ordinary source."

"You'd be right there. But I think I'd be best advised not to discuss it."

"And I have no wish to pry into such matters. Let us move on then. I judge from your accent that you are not a native of Las Vegas?"

"No, I'm just in town for a few days, staying at the Tropicana. I'm from England originally. Manchester."

Dr Mahoub nodded. "I have been there some twenty years ago for a conference. As I recall, it rained heavily."

"It generally does," said Nightingale. To his relief, Mahoub didn't make any further enquiries into Nightingale's background.

"You might perhaps find it profitable to learn a little about me, before you decide whether I can help you," said Mahoub.

Nightingale nodded. "Up to you."

"I am sure you noticed my skull cap, it seemed to surprise you that I am a Jew."

"I was told you were an Egyptian."

"The two things are not necessarily mutually exclusive, though very uncommon these days. At the time of my birth, there were many Jews in Egypt, but that changed with the arrival to power of Colonel Nasser in the fifties. He introduced regulations abolishing civil liberties and allowing the state to stage mass arrests without charge and strip away Egyptian citizenship from any group it desired. Prominent amongst whom were the Jews of Egypt. Lawyers, engineers, doctors and teachers were not allowed to work in their professions. Thousands of Jews were arrested and Jewish businesses were seized by the government. Jewish bank accounts were confiscated and many Jews lost their jobs. Those who did not choose to leave of their own volition were expelled, among them my parents, who fled to the United States, with a suitcase each. All their wealth and possessions were confiscated, held to have been 'donated' to the Egyptian state. I was a mere child at the time."

Nightingale said nothing. It was a story as old as the world itself, and was still happening in other countries today.

"My parents were fortunate, they were doctors and had friends in the US who could help them get started. They built a new life here, and I grew up as an American. I have never been able to return to Egypt since."

"But surely, Nasser is long dead?"

"Oh, indeed. But events since have ensured there would be no welcome there for me, or any other Egyptian Jew. My family still has bitter enemies over there. Do you know the population of Egypt, Mr Nightingale?"

"Not offhand," said Nightingale.

"It is a hundred and two million. And how many are Jews? At last count, eighteen, all old women in Alexandria and Cairo. I can never go back. But I have made a study of Egypt, her history and mythology into my life's work, though I have no memory of the country."

"When you say mythology, are you talking about ancient Gods, magic?"

"Such things were very much part of Egypt's history. The myths of their Gods and Goddesses were very well-known, and as for the use of magic, well, it depends what you mean by the words. Many ancient magicians were no more than herbalists, or those with some skill in the limited medical science of the time. But that's not what you want to know, is it?"

CHAPTER 37

Herbert Marshall sat behind his rosewood desk and looked at the email he had just received from his accountant. The old man's face was lined and care-worn, his expression grim. He touched a button on his intercom, and a tall, dark-haired young man entered the room. "You've seen the latest figures, David?"

"Of course, Dad. They don't make pretty reading. We can't go on making losses like this."

"Getting hard to know what to do about it. We've cut expenses to the bone, the market's not going to wear another price increase."

"You know what I think, Dad, and it's beginning to look inevitable."

"There's got to be another way, David. Selling out to Litvinsky would clear our slate, and more besides, but it would mean the end for Marshall Manufacturing. The ink wouldn't be dry on the contract before Litvinsky demolished the factory and sold the site on for redevelopment. I can't be responsible for throwing a hundred long-term workers onto welfare."

"But that's where they're going to end up, if you keep trying to work your way out of this. Litvinsky has offered another twenty percent, you'd be able to pay some redundancy money, help them find work elsewhere."

"In this area? Where do you think the jobs will come from? Unless my boys plan on relocating to China or India. There's nothing for them round here."

"Dad, take the offer. Times have changed, we're not back in your grandfather's day any more."

"I'll be damned if I will, there's just got to be another way."

"There isn't. We've been through this, and we can't afford to sink any more family money into the company."

"Alright David, I know what you think, and Thomas agrees with you, but I'm not going to let it happen. Litvinsky will get this company over my dead body."

It sounded like pure defiance, but neither of them knew it was just a simple prediction, destined to be fulfilled by the end of the week.

CHAPTER 38

"So the average Egyptian 'magician' was just a herbalist, an apothecary," said Nightingale, "and would have had no genuine magical powers?"

Dr Mahoub tilted his head to one side. "Your question contains a very big assumption, Mr Nightingale, that there can be such a thing as "genuine magical powers". Many people think there can not be."

"And what would your opinion be?"

"I am not sure I would care to give one. I am well informed on myths and legends, on the beliefs of Ancient Egypt. I know what they are, but that does not mean I accept them as literal truth. Nor do I dismiss them, I have no proof either way, but I am a sceptic. And you?"

Nightingale shrugged. "Let's just say that these days I don't discount anything."

"Probably wise. There are, of course, stories of powerful magicians who served the Pharaohs, whose abilities were thought to go beyond the mixing of medicines and providing protection from evil for women and children."

"Might their abilities stretch so far as eliminating enemies to order?"

"It would not surprise me. There are many curative herbs and plants, but also many whose effect is, shall we say, not so positive."

"I don't think poisoning quite fits the bill of what I'm interested in."

"So what are you interested in, Mr Nightingale, And why? Have you come to me for advice on committing murder?"

Nightingale lit another cigarette. "In a way. Yes. But not because I plan to kill someone. Quite the opposite, I want to find out how it's done, and stop further deaths."

"Perhaps you should take me into your confidence. You may rely on my discretion."

"Alright, I think I might leave names out of it, if you don't mind, but, essentially, here's the story."

Dr Mahoub listened intently for ten minutes, as Nightingale related his story. At the end of that time, he lit another of his Egyptian cigarettes and held up his index finger, almost reproachfully. "So, really, what you have is a string of coincidences, some seemingly natural deaths, a 'feeling' from someone who claims to be a follower of the left-hand path, and an Egyptian protection amulet which comes to you from someone you claim not to trust entirely, but still seem to believe. Does it not strike you as rather thin?"

Nightingale grinned. "When you put it like that, it does rather. But I've quite often had to start with less. In this job. I'm usually pulling at threads and seeing what unravels."

"And what exactly is, your job, Mr Nightingale. For whom are you working?"

"I hope I'm working for the good guys, trying to stop innocent people getting hurt."

"Hah. A pretty thought indeed. But I fear you delude yourself. Innocent people have been getting hurt since the dawn of time, it is the way of the world."

Nightingale sighed. "I know, but a small difference is still a difference. That's what I'm trying to achieve. Does anything I've told you suggest anything that might help me?"

"One moment."

Mahoub rose from his chair and walked across to the far wall, where he selected a thin volume, bound in gold cloth. The book looked incredibly old. He took it back to his chair, fingered carefully through its pages for a few minutes, then looked up at Nightingale.

"This book is over five hundred years old, but it is still just a copy of an original papyrus, dating back many centuries before the Common Era, or before Christ if you prefer. It is the only copy I know of, and is priceless. I know of at least one billionaire in Texas who would pay me any price I requested for it."

Nightingale tried to show no reaction. Did Dr Mahoub know about Joshua Wainwright, and did he know that Nightingale worked for Wainwright?

"It's a book of stories about magicians in the Ancient Kingdom of Egypt. It duplicates some of the stories found on the famous Westcar Papyrus, including the story of Dedi, who could, apparently, sever and reattach the heads of birds and animals. But there are tales here that appear nowhere else. I think, perhaps, the story that will most interest you is of the magician Baufra."

"I think I've heard of Dedi," said Nightingale.

"Possibly, he was the most famous of Egypt's magicians, but there seems to have been no harm in him. Baufra was quite another matter. Baufra was a magician and advisor to the mighty Pharaoh, Ramesses II, who is thought to have ruled Egypt for over sixty years, and died at the age of 91, both figures were highly unusual for the time. The story in the book tells of how Baufra protected Ramesses with his magic arts against illness and infirmity, and in battle against the Hittites and Nubians. He also protected the Pharaoh's eight Royal wives and his children, which were thought to number over ninety."

"Useful man to have around."

"Of course, there is no evidence that Ramesses's survival and that of his family owed anything to magic. There are two stories about Baufra which may interest you. Let me quote them to you, in translation, of course.

'The priest Nebka discovered that one of his concubines had been having an affair with a young member of his household. He asked Baufra to punish him. Baufra created a wax crocodile which he gave to the priest to drop into the lake where the youth bathed. When this happens, the crocodile came to life and dragged the young man to the bottom. The priest brought his concubine to the lake to see the wonder, Baufra called the crocodile up, and turned it back into a wax figure. The concubine confessed her guilt, and begged for mercy, but the priest gave her none, and the wax figure became a crocodile again and devoured her.'

"Nasty business," said Nightingale, "seems like they took sleeping around pretty seriously in those days."

"Indeed so. Now listen to this second story. In the forty-seventh year of the reign of the great Pharaoh Ramesses, one of his concubines, Nuria, fell in love with a son of the Royal family, Hori, and they plotted together to kill Ramesses and to have Hori installed as Pharaoh. They gathered together many supporters, but their plot was discovered, and they fled to the land of the Hittites. Ramesses could not pursue them there, so he consulted with Baufra, his magician. Baufra used forbidden sorcery, to conjure up a demon, who pursued them across many hundreds of miles and stopped their hearts from beating by the power of the Messenger of Anubis. Ramesses felt that such power should not be used again by mortal man, so he ordered Baufra's purse of forbidden papyri and his magical wands to be removed from human sight, and buried in a chamber of the tomb which awaited his own death. He ordered Baufra to be executed by impalement, saying that no man should possess the secret of such power."

"Poor old Baufra. Sounds a little ungrateful, doesn't it?"

"Indeed it does, but it seems that Ramesses was in fear that the sorcerer might one day use the power against him, so he decided the secret should die with him."

"No good deed goes unpunished."

"I have heard the saying, but I doubt that murder qualifies as a good deed."

"So, the guy could send death by demon, and conjure up crocodiles. A dangerous man. Tell me more about this demon that was conjured up. This Messenger of Anubis."

"I cannot, I have no evidence for any such thing. It sounds reminiscent of the Djinn tradition, but that comes from Arabia."

"Isn't that Islamic?"

"It is certainly spoken of in Islamic tradition, but the legend predates the Prophet."

Nightingale nodded. "Sounds a bit like summoning a Devil in the Western tradition."

"Again, I have no knowledge of such matters. Perhaps you might know more about that than I." There was a twinkle in the doctor's eye, or maybe Nightingale was imagining it. "It would seem that this Messenger of Anubis is perhaps the equivalent of the mythical Angel of Death in the Satanist tradition. Conjured up to visit inevitable destruction on an enemy."

"Maybe. What can you tell me about this Anubis?" asked Nightingale.

"Nothing that you could not find out from an encyclopaedia," said Mahoub. "Anubis was the god of death, mummification, embalming, the afterlife, cemeteries, tombs, and the Underworld. He was generally portrayed with the head of a dog or a jackal. One of his functions was to guide dead souls to the afterlife."

"Any suggestion that he helped them on their way out of this life?"

"You mean by killing them? I have never heard any such story. He was also the weigher of hearts.

Nightingale waited for him to explain.

"A little like the Christian tradition of Judgment Day. By weighing the heart of a deceased person Anubis dictated the fate of souls. Souls heavier than a feather would be devoured by Ammit, a creature part crocodile, part hippo and part lion. Souls lighter than a feather would ascend to a heavenly existence"

"An interesting system," said Nightingale

"Indeed. You have probably never given much thought to the weight of your soul, Mr Nightingale."

"Actually, I think about my soul a lot more often than you might expect."

Again, Mahoub gave a knowing smile.

"Coming back to this idea of conjuring up a demon to kill enemies," said Nightingale, "It seems like the secret died with Baufra. So how could someone be using the same idea today?"

"I see no evidence that they are, though what one man can discover, so, surely can another. It still seems a very unlikely explanation, for which you have no evidence. An ancient myth is proof of nothing."

"True enough. If I hadn't been given a little hint or two, I'd never have made a connection. You say the magician's papyrus was buried?"

"Yes, and his wand and other items used in his work."

"So could someone have dug it up?"

"My dear Mr Nightingale, it's hardly buried treasure. Assuming it ever existed, first of all, the papyrus would probably have rotted to nothing by now. Second, it was buried in the lower reaches of the tomb of Ramesses, twenty years before his death, and would be inaccessible except to a dedicated archaeological team. The *Ramesseum* was extensively excavated in the nineteenth century, but no trace of Baufra's belongings has ever been found. Third, even if it existed, were found, and were miraculously intact, not one person in ten million would have any understanding of what to do with it."

"Yes, I can see why it wouldn't be easy. Shame, as the story fits the bill."

"Maybe so, but after all, it is just a story."

"I suppose. Tell me, what do you know of an illusionist called Khamsin?"

Nightingale was staring at Mahoub's face as he put his question, and couldn't miss the sudden flash of surprise and fear in the old man's expression.

"Khamsin," he muttered. "The Wind of destruction."

"What?" said Nightingale,

"Nothing. I have heard of the man, A highly skilled performer, I am told."

"But you haven't been to see his show?"

"I rarely leave my home these days, much less to visit the casinos and showrooms of Las Vegas."

"So you know nothing of his history?"

Nightingale could have sworn that the old man shuddered.

"No, I do not, and would not wish to. I have enjoyed our discussion, Mr Nightingale, though I fear I have not helped you much.

At my age, I tire easily, so I must beg you to excuse me. Perhaps you will call again soon?"

"I'd like to do that."

"But be aware, Mr Nightingale, if the legend of the purse of Baufra is true, if someone has discovered it, and if they have acquired the knowledge to use it, then it could be one of the most dangerous weapons a man could possess. I hope your protection is adequate."

"Me too," said Nightingale.

Mahoub rang his little bell again, and his wife opened the door, holding it for Nightingale to leave.

Nightingale walked down the path, out into the street and took out his cellphone to call a taxi. As he waited for it to arrive, he thought over what the doctor had said, and perhaps more importantly, what he hadn't said. Nightingale had questioned hundreds of people in his time with the Met and afterwards, and he could often tell when someone was lying He would have bet money that Mahoub had been lying when he'd denied any knowledge of Kahmsin's history.

His phone rang. It was Wainwright.

"Everything good?" asked Wainwright.

"I'm still getting background on Khamsin. Not much progress, to be fair."

"He's obviously hidden his past. But there'll be something out there. There always is." He went quiet for a couple of seconds. "So, I've put the word out."

"My contract you mean?"

"Yeah. I haven't heard anything back yet. But nobody told me I was wasting my time. Look, Jack, I'm going to have to go dark for a while."

"Dark?"

"Low profile. I won't be meeting you or even talking to you. And no calls. Not even texts."

'That sounds a bit dramatic, Joshua."

"We don't know what sort of access this guy has. So as of today. I'm ditching this phone. And we can't meet."

"So how the hell will I know what's going on?"

"I'll text you from a burner."

"That's it? My life is on the line here, Joshua, and you'll be texting me?"

"Jack, calm down. If I put a contract out on you and then he finds out I'm talking to you, what happens then?"

"We had a wife putting a contract out on her husband, I'm assuming they talked right up to the moment it happened."

"This is different. Look, I'll still be watching over you."

"My guardian angel?"

Wainwright ignored the sarcasm. "You'll be fine."

'I wish I had your confidence," said Nightingale. "But then I'm the one with the contract out on his life, so it's not surprising that I haven't."

"I can use intermediaries. Not Valerie, obviously. But I will stay in touch. Just at arm's length."

"Will you be in Vegas?"

Wainwright hesitated. "Probably not," he said.

"So when you say arm's length, we're talking about very long arms, right?"

"It'll be fine. The other victims had no idea what was happening, but you're prepared. You'll see it coming."

"Seeing it coming and stopping it from happening are two different things," said Nightingale.

"You need to thing positively, Jack."

'Easy for you to say." Nightingale gritted his teeth. There was a lot more he wanted to say, but he knew it would be pointless. At the end of the day he was on his own and there was nothing he could do or say that would change that. He felt something hot on his chest and he realised it was the *ankh*. He patted it through his shirt. At least he had one person in his corner. Admittedly she was a demon from hell and he was never sure how much he could trust her, but at the moment she was all he had. "Catch you later," said Nightingale.

'Be caref..." Wainwright began, but Nightingale had already ended the call.

CHAPTER 39

Khamsin sat on his favourite low divan, its firm padding covered in a rich red and gold cloth and inhaled from a shisha pipe, the water bubbling in the bowl with each breath. There were days when the pipe contained hashish, but today concentration was necessary, so it was filled with flavoured tobacco. He took a last sip, then removed the tube from his mouth and returned it to the hook on the side of the pipe. He closed his eyes, breathed in deeply and stroked the small beard at the end of his long chin. He opened his eyes and focused their brown stare on the table in front of him. A crystal ball on a stand lay next to a ball of wax about the size of a baseball. Khamsin reached into the pocket of his midnight-blue silk robe, and took out the pale ivory crescent, the ornate carvings on it still seeming fresh and clear despite its great age.

Khamsin pulled the bell-rope next to the divan, and, in response to a soft, silvery peal, a door opened opposite him, a door so skilfully built and so thickly padded that, when it was closed, gave almost no sign of its presence. The woman who stepped through was tall and blonde with a spectacular figure, which, as Khamsin well knew, owed nothing to any surgeon's skill.

"It is time?" she asked.

"It is, Neferu. Please show our guest in."

The woman closed the door behind her, only to re-open it again a few moments later, as she led a young man into the room. He couldn't have been much more than seventeen, a little short and rather chubby, traces of teenage acne on his face, his eyes unblinking behind his black plastic glasses.

"This is Alexander," she said.

"Ah yes, I remember him from Thursday. He is properly under?"

"Oh yes, he knew he had to come here at this time, though he didn't know why. As soon as he saw me, he fell under."

"I knew at first sight he would be an easy subject. Quite a weak character. Alexander, please sit on this chair."

The boy said nothing, just did as commanded. Khamsin reached for the ball of wax and picked it up. Inside a minute, he had moulded it into the rough shape of a man, with arms, legs and a rudimentary head and face

"The special ingredient, if you please."

Neferu walked across to an ornately carved and inlaid mahogany box which stood on a black lacquered sideboard, opened it, hovered her fingers inside, then brought out a small envelope.

"Hair," she said. "He was followed to the barber last month."

"It is always good to prepare in advance."

Khamsin took the envelope, opened it carefully, then pressed some of the hair into his crude wax doll. He muttered a sentence in a long-dead language, and stroked the figure with his ivory wand.

Alexander, hold this figure, Not too tightly. This is Herbert Marshall. Say his name."

"Herbert Marshall. Herbert Marshall. Herbert Marshall."

"Good, now gaze into the crystal and repeat his name again."

"Herbert Marshall. Herbert Marshall. Herbert Marshall."

"Very good. Now, tell me, what do you see, Alexander?"

"I see him. Herbert Marshall. He is in an office, Sitting behind a desk. Writing something."

"Excellent. Now, take this ivory wand in your right hand, hold the figure in your left. That's right."

The boy sat with his back straight, pointing the wand at the crystal ball.

"Now, repeat these words after me. I call on Kek and Kauket, bringers of darkness and light and on Amit, devourer of souls. Send forth the Messenger of Anubis, to stop the heart of this one. In the name of Set, Lord of Chaos."

The boy repeated the words, in a tone devoid of all expression, his eyes never blinking, the wand never wavering from the crystal. As he said the final word, a green spark shot from the end of the wand into the very heart of the crystal, and, for a fraction of a second, a figure with a strange animal's head seemed to fly towards the ball. The boy's eyes closed, and he fell backwards, as if hit by the recoil of a rifle. The woman bent over him and felt his wrists.

"He will be fine in a moment or two. The force is very powerful."

"As it needs to be. I should not care to endure repeated shocks by using it personally. Also it is necessary to insure against errors by using an intermediary."

The boy was already opening his eyes and starting to stand up.

"Thank you, Alexander. The young lady will show you out, and ensure nobody sees you leave. Find a taxi rank, take the first cab, and ask him to drop you outside the Paris Hotel. You will find forty dollars in your pocket to pay him. When the taxi drives away, you will awaken and go about your life. You will have no memory of your visit, you were never here."

"I understand."

The woman opened the door and led him out. She was back inside two minutes.

"So easy," said Khamsin. "Now, you will need to arrange for another visitor for tomorrow so that Mr Litvinsky can be contacted, and payment arrangements made."

"I shall see to it."

"And there is another matter I wish you to see to. There is in this city a Jew named Mahoub, his family and mine have long been enemies, but I could overlook that. It seems, however that he has been talking about matters which should be kept quiet."

"How do you know this?"

"My crystal and my wand tell me many things. He has lived too long, we must see to his demise."

"Another ritual?"

Khamsin stroked his chin thoughtfully.

"No, I think not, Something more mundane, cruder. That way we will not only rid ourselves of possible interference, it sends a message to those who have contacted him. We may even be able to direct suspicion onto them."

"Shall I send Ali and Salim?"

"No, I trust them, but I feel the fewer people who know about my connection to Mahoub the better."

"Then I shall see to it personally?" she said.

"I think that would be a good idea."

"I should be happy to do so. As you know, my parents were killed by Jews, I welcome the opportunity, in some small way, to even the score."

"Excellent. And perhaps, before he dies, he may be kind enough to give you the name of his recent visitor."

"I shall see to it."

CHAPTER 40

Wainwright was high over the Pacific in his Gulfstream jet when the screen on his laptop flickered, and the list of stocks and shares was replaced by the face of a woman with long, blonde hair, her eyes hidden behind oversized sunglasses. Wainwright said nothing, there could be only one explanation for her sudden appearance.

"Mr Wainwright? My principal has been advised that you may have need of his services."

Wainwright wasted no time on asking for explanations, he was pretty sure they would not be forthcoming.

"It's possible I may," he said. "What services had you in mind?"

There was a short pause, as the woman looked over to her left, then she continued.

"Let us not waste time, Mr Wainwright." It seems that there is someone who is currently inconveniencing certain plans of yours. My principal will undertake to ensure that this person will no longer cause you problems."

"I see. And there's a charge for this service, of course?"

"Naturally. For a fee of five million dollars, we can guarantee no further problems from the individual in question."

"That's a lot of money."

"Not for a man in your position."

"I need to know that I won't be implicated in anything illegal."

"That is also guaranteed, as far as the authorities will be concerned, nothing illegal will have taken place."

"And I don't need to be around when it happens?"

"The further away the better."

"How do I know you won't just take my money and run?"

"Payment will be made upon successful completion of the contract only and via untraceable means. This is the service you are looking for, isn't it?"

"It sounds like it. I'm guessing I don't sign anything."

"Clearly not. My principal merely requires your word, the name of the individual who is causing you problems, and his approximate location."

Wainwright nodded and took a puff of his cigar. "Then I guess it's decision time. How long do I have to think it over?"

"You are not a man who hesitates, Mr Wainwright, make your decision."

"Well, then, I guess I'm in. The subject's name is Jack Nightingale. He's currently staying at the Tropicana Hotel in Las Vegas. You need anything else?"

"No. The matter should be dealt with within a week, at which time payment will be due."

The woman's face vanished, and the list of stocks reappeared.

"Good luck, Jack," muttered Wainwright.

CHAPTER 41

A thousand miles away, Khamsin held up a hand, and the crystal ball on his table clouded over as Wainwright's face vanished. He spoke softly to the woman opposite him, who sat motionless as she listened.

"Thank you, Marion. You will leave us now. Take the first taxi you see, and ask him to drop you outside the MGM Hotel. You will find forty dollars in your purse to pay him. When the taxi drives away, you will awaken and go about your life. You will have no memory of your visit, you were never here. You have never heard of Joshua Wainwright or Jack Nightingale."

The woman made no sound, just rose and followed Neferu to the door. The young woman returned inside a minute. She noticed the frown on Khamsin's brow. "All is not well?"

"I rather think Mr Wainwright is not what he appears to be. His name is known to me, slightly."

"How?"

"I had a contact. A colleague if you wish. A member of the Order of The Nine Angles, a strange and shadowy organisation. She once spoke to me of Wainwright as a possible enemy. He is a man of great wealth, yet seems to do little to earn it. He shuns publicity, yet his name is often spoken of in the circles in which I move. Just now, despite the distance between us, and the use of the intermediary, I felt something, the manifestation of some higher power within him as he spoke to the woman."

"You suspect a trap?"

"I suspect. I am not sure what, but I suspect. Perhaps a little more investigation into Wainwright and this Mister Nightingale might be fruitful."

"Would it not be better just to avoid him? Ignore his contract?"

"Far better to deal with him on my own terms. When one meets a challenge, one may run from it or towards it. Life has been a little easy of late, perhaps this will provide a test of my power. Please prepare a hashish pipe, I have some thinking to do, and plans to make."

"At once. Then I have the other errand to complete."

CHAPTER 42

Esther Mahoub shuffled to the door when the bell rang. She wasn't expecting anyone, but occasionally Aaron forgot to tell her that he had an appointment. She brought one rheumy eye up to the peep-hole and saw a strange woman. Quite young, by the look of her, bright auburn hair peeking out from under her green turban style hat, her face hidden behind large, round sunglasses. Such a pretty face and such a warm smile.

She took off the security chain and opened the door.

"Can I help..."

The blow with the small curved blade of the dagger was vicious and precise, striking straight at the heart. There was almost no blood, and the old woman collapsed backwards into the hallway. The killer stepped over her body and walked down the panelled hallway, her slippered feet making no sound on the carpet. Most of the doors off the hallway were open, showing a lounge, dining room and kitchen, so she knocked on the closed door. A weak, high-pitched voice answered. "Come in my dear."

She walked in, The grey head and black *yamulkah* of the Doctor was inclined downwards, but he looked up as she entered. A puzzled frown came over his face.

"Hello. But where is Esther? Who are you?"

"She had something to do in the kitchen. I'm a friend of the gentleman who called to see you yesterday."

"A friend of Mr Nightingale?"

Her lip curled in contempt. "Too easy, far too easy, you idiotic old fool. This is for my parents."

As he rose from his chair in surprise, she took one quick step forward, and the dagger struck again."

130

CHAPTER 43

Khamsin took one last drag from his hookah as Neferu entered the room, then placed the mouthpiece on the hook of the bowl. Her cheeks were flushed and her eyes sparkled with excitement. "Your errand was successfully accomplished?" he asked.

"But of course. The street was deserted, they were old and unsuspecting. They offered no resistance."

"Excellent. Perhaps news of their fate can be a lesson to others. And did you get a name?"

"Oh I did indeed. He was visited by a Mr Nightingale."

Khamsin smiled and stroked his chin. "Indeed. That is quite a coincidence, since it is also the name of the man that Wainwright claims he wants removed."

"You were right to be suspicious."

He nodded. "I was."

"So will you kill this man Nightingale?"

"I certainly think he needs to die, there are rumours of his interfering with the plans of many people. Mr Wainwright also has lived too long. But let us not be hasty, it might perhaps be expedient to find out a little more information about these two before disposing of them."

"And how would you plan to do that?"

"As always, the best way to defeat an enemy is to use his weaknesses against him. Listen carefully now, we have preparations to make."

CHAPTER 44

Waiting around for something to happen never appealed to Nightingale but at least he had time to eat regularly. After dinner that night, he made his way down to the Tropicana casino for a Corona and a cigarette. He took a stool at the bar, pushed the slice of lime further down into his bottle and took a sip. He fed a dollar into the computerised poker machine embedded in the bar in front of him.

"Pretty small stakes," said a voice behind his right shoulder.

"I'm a small-time operator," said Nightingale, turning slightly to take a look.

She would probably have been a few inches shorter than him if he'd stood up, and was maybe five years younger than him. Her dark hair flowing over her shoulders, and her green eyes flickering at him. He took what he hoped was a subtle look at her figure. Everything looked to be in the right places underneath the dress, which was black with silver trim. Classy, rather than too overt. He knew for a fact that he'd never seen her before, but took a guess at her profession.

"Sorry," he said, "I'm actually waiting for someone."

"You're a very bad liar, Jack Nightingale."

He sat there for a moment, his mouth slightly open.

"You look like a fish," she said. "Joshua said you didn't like surprises."

"Joshua sent you?"

"Either that or I'm very talented at guessing the names of complete strangers."

"Whereas I don't even pretend to be good at it." At least Wainwright hadn't abandoned him completely. That was something. But how much of an asset she would be remained to be seen.

Her smile widened. "Lynsey Lawton. At your service, well, up to certain limits."

"A local girl?"

"I am, these days. Always good to have a guide in a strange town. Let's take a walk."

"Are we going far?"

"Not in these shoes. Let's wander over to a roulette table for a while."

"I don't know about that, as you said, I'm small-time."

"I don't plan to lose much, and Mr W is pretty free with expense money."

He followed her to a nearby table, and they took two vacant seats. Lynsey put twenty on red, but showed no reaction when black turned up.

Nightingale offered his pack of Marlboro.

She shook her head. "Not at the moment, I try not to smoke before eleven at night. It's my way of cutting back."

"How's it working for you?"

"About as well as roulette," she said, as black turned up again and the croupier raked in her next twenty dollars. "So, bring me up to speed."

"A step at a time," said Nightingale. "First, how about a little background on you. I like to know who I'm dealing with"

She wrinkled her nose. "Aren't you the suspicious one. I smell cop."

"Well, if you do, it's a very old smell. Been quite a few years and a few thousand miles away since I answered to that description."

"Detective?"

"Not then. I was a firearms officer and a negotiator. London. Metropolitan Police,"

"Who did you negotiate with? Hostage takers?"

"Very occasionally. Mostly people who were thinking about killing themselves. People in crisis, we call them."

"Yippee."

"What?"

"Red, at last. I win. Were you good at it?"

"Negotiating? I had some successes with hostage situations, maybe talked a few people out of killing themselves. Sometimes not."

"Did you really talk them out of it? Or maybe they just didn't want it enough to go through with it."

"There is that. People who are serious about suicide generally get on and do it, they don't engineer a situation where they can be persuaded not to. So that was me. Now, what about you?"

"Damn, black again. Whatever happened to those 50/50 odds? Well, it's easily summed up. I guess I smell of cop too, if you had a good nose. I was in the LVPD for eight years, spent most of them in vice. Got tired of being a decoy, got tired of seeing girls with no hope trafficked out on the streets time after time. decided to go freelance, almost starved and thought about turning tricks myself. Then I got a break, did a small job for him and did it well and got put on a retainer by your Mr Wainwright."

"Doing what?"

"Pretty much whatever he needs. Background info on companies, checks on people he's thinking of offering work to, assisting people who are in town for some reason or another. Makes a pleasant change from the criminal classes."

Nightingale was well aware that he was not Wainwright's only operative in his shadowy world, though most of the ones he had met appeared ignorant of the young Texan's Satanic connections. He'd met others in New York and New Orleans, and their local knowledge had been invaluable.

"So how much has Wainwright told you?" asked Nightingale.

"Not so much, he said you'd fill me in. Apparently you need some checking done on some guys, without them getting to know about it. Could they be dangerous? Damn."

"What?"

"I lost my last twenty, that's me done. Once I win, or lose, a hundred, I'm finished for the night." She smiled. "Let's go somewhere quieter."

"It's your town, lead on."

"I'm not walking too far tonight. We could try one of the lounges here. I guess you'll prefer a smoking one."

Nightingale would have suggested his room, but didn't want to give the woman the wrong impression, they'd only just met, so they walked across to the Tropicana lounge and sat at one of the tables away from the bar and video screens. Nightingale ordered an orange juice, Lynsey asked for a Cosmopolitan.

"What's in that," asked Nightingale, when the pink drink arrived.

"Vodka, cranberry juice, Cointreau and lime. One a night is my limit."

"You seem to have a lot of rules when it comes to limits."

"Hasn't always been that way, and I've suffered for it. These days I've learned some lessons."

"We all learn lessons as get older, if we survive."

"So far I've survived. Anything else you need to know about me?"

"Nothing I need. I guess I could ask you if you have family?"

"Nothing current. There's an ex-husband, last heard of in New York, but he doesn't occupy my thoughts. You?"

"The question surprised Nightingale, but it was a fair one.

"Me? No, my parents and close relatives are dead. Never married."

Which was all quite true, but glossed over the majority of Nightingale's past life. There were not many who knew the full story, or who would have believed it.

"Wise man. OK, let's say that concludes the social part of the evening. Now, how about you fill me in on what I'm needed for here."

As ever, Nightingale decided to tread carefully. Coming out with a tale of black magic and killer demons would be likely to lose her completely.

"You ever heard of a guy who calls himself Khamsin?"

"The magician at the Luxor? Sure, who hasn't?"

"You ever seen his show?"

"Not really my scene, but I'm told he's pretty good. What about him?"

"Well, Joshua thinks...we think, that he might be mixed up in something pretty nasty. We need to find out more about him."

"Have you tried Wikipedia?" she asked.

"You can't believe anything you read in Wikipedia. I need a source I can rely on, which is where you come in. Would you still have your old police contacts?"

"Not that old chestnut. Surely you'd know that I can't go on using police resources after I leave the Department? I don't have an endless string of favours I can call in, or ex-boyfriends who'll look the other way while I use the police computer."

"Shame," said Nightingale. "So you're saying you can't help?"

She flashed him a tight smile. "No, I'm saying I might not have all the answers for you. I can try, maybe find out a little more than most people."

"Well, that's a start. While you're at it, how about some background on a Mrs Delia Winston, her late husband Jolyon, and a guy named Luca Marino."

"Lucky Marino? I heard his son died."

"He did, I want to know if Marino might have had a reason to want him dead."

She frowned. "You're not thinking he might have had his own son killed for some reason?"

"Who knows?" said Nightingale, "I read somewhere that a fifth of murder victims are killed by a family member."

"Well, it sounds like a snipe hunt to me, but it's Wainwright's money. Here's my cell number, I have yours, I'll get back to you tomorrow with whatever I've managed to get."

"Good. One more thing."

"Yes?"

"Don't put yourself out in the open, if we're right, there may be an element of danger, I wouldn't want you to get hurt."

"Me either. You can take off now, I'll sit and finish my drink, maybe see if anyone follows you."

"Seems unlikely, as far as I'm aware, nobody much knows I'm here."

"Famous last words."

Nightingale walked slowly to the door, then turned around and scanned the room. Nobody appeared to be taking any interest in him or in Lynsey Lawton.

His phone buzzed to let him know that he had received a message. He picked it up and looked at the screen. It was from a phone number he didn't recognise. The message was short and to the point. "GAME ON". Nightingale grimaced. Two words but they changed everything. Wainwright's contract had been picked up, and there was now a big target flashing on Nightingale's back. His life was on the line, and he had no idea how he could defend himself against the attack that was to come.

CHAPTER 45

Tommy Chang's cellphone buzzed just as he was finishing his evening meal - fish-flavoured shredded pork and Yangzhou fried rice. The number was withheld, but he pressed the green button anyway. He didn't speak at first, waiting for the tell-tale clicks that would tell him it was a computerised call, someone trying to sell him something.

"Tommy Chang?"

"Yes."

"You recognise my voice, just answer yes or no."

"Yes."

"You are feeling a little sleepy, Tommy, aren't you?"

"Yes, I am. So sleepy."

"So sleep, Tommy. Sleep, but do not close your eyes. Are you sleeping, Tommy?"

"Yes."

"Good, I have work for you. Would you like to help me, Tommy?"

"Yes, of course."

"Good. Listen closely to my voice. Are you at home?"

"Yes."

"Alone?"

"Yes."

"Excellent. Leave your home, Tommy and go to the nearest taxi rank. Tell him to drop you at this address..."

Tommy Chang left his apartment, rode the elevator to street level and walked to a taxi rank ten minutes away. The taxi dropped him where he had been told to go, and he then walked for another ten minutes, until he came to a detached house on a quiet street, well away from the lights and crowds of the Strip. Someone had clearly been watching for his arrival, as the front door swung open as he walked up the drive. A blonde woman showed him into a spacious but sparsely furnished living-room.

If Tommy had been taking any notice of his surroundings, he might have been surprised at the Egyptian theme to the décor, with an opulent rug on the floor, silk drapes on the walls, a collection of wooden tables dotted with cats, sphinxes and representations of gods and goddesses. As it was, he just sat meekly on the chair to which he was shown, behind a plain wooden desk.

The blonde woman pressed an earpiece into his left ear, and he heard the voice again.

"Thank you for coming, Tommy. I want you to talk to a man named Litvinsky."

The young man sat silent and motionless.

"First, a little concealment."

The woman took a bottle of spirit gum, and an unconvincing black beard, which she fastened to Tommy's chin. Then she put a pair of large round sunglasses on him, and a black fedora, too big for his head, was pulled down low over his brow. None of it looked natural, but his own mother wouldn't have recognised him. Tommy didn't react to any of it. Again the voice came in his ear.

"You will hear my voice in your ear, Tommy. Whatever I say, you will repeat exactly. Do you understand?"

"Yes."

"Excellent."

Khamsin took his ivory wand and brandished it at the laptop computer that faced the young man.

"Michael Litvinsky, Michael Litvinsky," he muttered.

The screen fogged over, and when the mist cleared, the face of Latvisky appeared.

"Good," whispered Khamsin. "Now, Tommy repeat after me, *'Good afternoon, Mr Litvinsky. As agreed, my principal has arranged the removal of the one obstacle to your acquisition of Marshall*

139

Manufacturing. The family will now, doubtless, accept your bid. We now turn to the question of the agreed payment'."

Tommy opened his mouth, and, in a flat tone, repeated what he had been told.

Miles away, Michael Litvinsky listened to his instructions.

CHAPTER 46

Nightingale was lying on his bed trying to blow smoke rings up at the ceiling and wondering what the odds were of an *ankh* forming by chance when there was a rapid knock on the door, followed by an angry man's voice. "Mr Nightingale? Las Vegas Police, could you let us in please."

"What do you want?"

"We want to come in Mr Nightingale."

Nightingale stubbed out his cigarette and walked to the door. He put his eye to the spy-hole. He saw a whole bunch of scratches on the lens and the opposite wall of the corridor. If they were the police, they were wisely standing well away from the door. "Can I see some ID?"

There was a muttering outside the door, and what looked like a police badge was held up to the lens. Nightingale unchained the door, opened the lock, then stood back with his hands in the air. A handgun came through the door, followed by a burly man of forty or so, with dark hair and a grey suit that had probably fitted him better ten pounds previously. A dark-haired younger woman in a navy blue pants suit followed him in, also with gun drawn.

"Your name Nightingale?"

"It is."

"Do you have any weapons in the room?"

"I do not."

"You don't mind if we pat you down?"

"Pat all you want."

The man ran his hands over Nightingale, then stepped back, his posture more relaxed.

"Sorry about that," he said, "standard procedure. I've lost colleagues who went into hotel rooms too quickly."

"Me too," said Nightingale, "always good to meet a professional."

"I'm guessing you weren't an officer with the LVPD," said the woman.

"Metropolitan Police, London. In another life. Now, how can I help you?"

"We need to ask you some questions. We can do it here, or at the precinct. Only trouble is, if we take you to the precinct, we'll have to handcuff you."

"Well, in that case, why don't we do it here? We've got enough chairs." He sat on the bed. The two cops exchanged a look and sat on the small sofa by the window. "It's a smoking room, if you feel the need," he said.

"Not on duty," said the woman, but Nightingale didn't miss the look of disappointment in her partner's eyes. He lit a Marlboro himself, despite her disapproving frown.

The man looked longingly at the lit cigarette, then shook his head. "I'm Sergeant Jose Garcia, this is Detective Camila Martinez. Your name's Jack Nightingale?"

"It is."

"Can we see some ID?

Nightingale got his passport and driver's licence from the nightstand and handed them over. He knew they'd pass muster at this level, though he wasn't sure what would happen if they were checked by the British Consulate or the California DMV. Wainwright's work was usually top-class, but, presumably, even he had limits.

The sergeant took a look and nodded. He handed them back.

"Now, we've done the introductions and pleasantries, suppose you tell me what it's all about?"

"You visited a Doctor Aaron Mahoub and his wife Esther two days ago," said Officer Martinez. "What was the purpose of your visit?"

Nightingale looked up at the ceiling and sighed. "They're dead?"

Sergeant Garcia frowned. "Now how would you know that?"

"Why else would you be here?"

142

"Could be a lot of reasons."

"I can't think of one. Yes, I visited the doctor, and his wife was there too. I arrived about two pm, probably stayed an hour and a half, His wife let me out, she was alive at the time. So was her husband. When were they killed?"

"Yesterday morning. Discovered by the woman who comes in to help with cleaning. As far as we know, you're the last person who saw them alive."

"Not true. That would be whoever killed them."

"Could be one and the same, that's why we're here," said the sergeant. "Now, suppose you tell us why you visited the Mahoubs."

"Sure. I'm doing a little research into Egyptian myths for a client who's writing a book. Doctor Mahoub was something of an expert in that area." He blew smoke at the floor, taking care to keep it away from the detectives. "How did you manage to track me down?" asked Nightingale.

Officer Martinez smiled. "Top class detective work."

The sergeant grinned too. "Doctor Mahoub kept an appointments diary," he said. "Once we had your name it didn't take long to track you to the Tropicana."

"It's not as if I'm hiding, is it? So, am I a suspect?"

They exchanged a glance. "Can't really tie you into it at the moment, but suppose you tell me what you were doing yesterday morning, say between eight and ten," said Garcia.

"Slept till about nine, then the Tropicana breakfast buffet, from about nine thirty to ten thirty."

"Anybody with you?"

"No."

"Remember the name of your server?"

"You don't really get a server at a buffet. Couple of women helping at the omelette station, and a guy offering coffee top-ups, but I didn't get their names."

"So we just have your word for it?" said Martinez, tapping her pen on her notebook.

"I had to sign the bill with my room number. The hotel will still have a copy of that."

"I guess they will," she sounded a little disappointed. "We'll check that out."

Nightingale crushed out his cigarette. "How they were killed?"

The sergeant shook his head. "Nah, we'll reserve that. When you were there, did you notice anything that could be used as a weapon?"

"That's pretty vague," said Nightingale. "I didn't see any firearms, but the place was full of Egyptian curios, some knives in amongst them, plus most kitchens have sharp knives. There were any number of things that could be used to beat someone over the head."

"Did the doctor talk about having any enemies? Did he seem frightened?"

"The enemies he mentioned were all in Egypt, from a long time ago, and I think he'd have been frightened to go back there. But he didn't strike me as a man in fear of his life." Nightingale decided not to mention the shadow of fear that had crossed the old man's face at the mention of Khamsin. It was just a fleeting impression, after all. "Was anything stolen?"

"Beats me," replied the sergeant. "The whole place was crammed full of stuff, like some kind of museum. The cleaning woman says she can't remember anything that isn't there now. She says they didn't keep much money in the house, just enough to pay her every week."

Nightingale shrugged. "I can't think of anything I could tell you that would be helpful. We discussed Egyptian myths for an hour or so, smoked some cigarettes, then I left."

"You planning on staying in Las Vegas a while?" asked Garcia.

"Few more days. My research is done, but I have this infallible roulette system I'm keen to try out."

The sergeant laughed. "Hah, you and every other sucker. Let me know how that works for you. That'll be all for the moment, but we

144

may be back if anything develops. Meanwhile, let us have an address if you leave town."

"Will do," said Nightingale. "I'm sorry about the two of them. I didn't know them at all well, but I thought they were good people. They certainly deserved better than this."

"Damn right," said the sergeant. "I just hope we get the bastard who did this."

CHAPTER 47

Michael Litvinsky sat alone in his office and stared at his laptop screen. The phone call telling him of Herbert Marshall's death from a heart attack had come fifty minutes ago. So far he hadn't made any attempt to contact the old man's heirs. Let them do their grieving, and then they could come to him, desperate to accept his bid. Of course, by then he would be unwilling to pay as much, since the firm's prospects were a lot poorer without their talismanic CEO at the helm. He wondered if he'd ever hear from the old, black woman again. He doubted it, she was probably just some scammer. Though the coincidence in the timings was amazing, and very much in his favour.

The screen sprung into life, though he hadn't touched any part of the keyboard. The face was entirely different this time, a young Asian man, wearing large sunglasses and a ridiculous false black beard.

"Good afternoon, Mr Litvinsky. As agreed, my principal has arranged the removal of the one obstacle to your acquisition of Marshall Manufacturing. The family will now, doubtless, accept your bid."

"Yeah, I heard that Old Man Marshall died, but that was a heart attack. Nobody caused it."

"On the contrary, Mr Litvinsky, my principal arranged it, as promised."

"How the hell did you arrange that?"

There was a short pause before the boy spoke again. "The specifics need not concern you, indeed it is better that you do not know. Now, we turn to the question of payment for this service."

"But the guy had a heart attack, you're not telling me that you caused that? You don't seriously expect me to pay five million dollars to a complete stranger for a heart attack?"

Another pause. "On the contrary, Mr Litvinsky. My principal does expect you to pay, since the obstacle to your financial success has been removed."

"And if I don't?"

Yet another pause. "My principal strongly advises you to pay. He suggests you research the following people. Francesco Marino, Jolyon Winston, Antonio Scarletti and Delia Winston. They were all clients, who declined to conclude the bargain they had made. They are all deceased."

Litvinsky had heard of Francesco Marino and Jolyon Winston's deaths, but not the other two. Still, the list had the desired effect. The defiance on his face folded. "How do I pay?"

"Listen carefully to these instructions, they must be followed exactly." The young man spoke slowly and clearly for a further minute. "Do you understand these instructions, Mr Litvinsky?"

"Yeah, I got it."

"One more thing, you have no information which might be of use to the police, but my principal has no wish for exposure. Any attempt to inform law enforcement, or indeed anyone else, of the details of this agreement will result in your joining the list I gave you, with no further warnings. Understood?"

"Yeah, yeah. Who'd believe me anyway?"

CHAPTER 48

Nightingale's cell phone rang, from a number he didn't recognise. He pressed the green button and waited. "Jack Nightingale?" said the caller.

Nightingale didn't recognise the voice. "Yeah?"

"I met you with our mutual friend in the MGM Grand."

"Okay," said Nightingale. It was Paul Hart, the FBI agent.

"So, our mutual friend asked me to reach out to you. You need to talk to a guy by the name of Michael Litvinsky. Litvinsky has just benefited from the death - by natural causes - of one Herbert Marshall. Mr Litvinsky has been given a number of choices, and the least damaging was to talk to you. So you need to be at Room 303 at Circus Circus in two hours."

"I'll be there."

'Just be careful."

'My middle name is careful."

'Jack Careful Nightingale? Yeah, it has a ring to it. He's expecting you and he'll talk. But don't mention my name or our mutual friend's. He was very clear on that." Hart ended the call.

CHAPTER 49

Nightingale was coming to the conclusion that the whole Las Vegas Strip was just one huge casino and hotel, with different names for the various sections. Circus Circus was, to no great surprise, set up as the world's largest circus. With a big top at the front and a giant sign of a clown, just in case you missed it. The hotel accommodation was in rectangular towers, built on afterwards. Nightingale was no fan of circuses, so avoided the 'midway' section, and stepped out of the way of at least two passing clowns who looked as if they wanted to greet him. He made for the stairs and climbed up to the third floor. As with many of the hotels he'd encountered, the carpet could have done with being replaced, and there was a general stale smell about the place, perhaps a mixture of tobacco, sweat and disinfectant. He knocked on 303.

The room and furniture were pretty standard hotel issue, though it was all a grade or two above the Excalibur. Again, the carpet could have done with a good clean, but neither of them would be staying here long. The man who answered the door was around Nightingale's height, but probably outweighed him by twenty pounds, very little of it muscle. The expensive dark suit he wore did a pretty good job of concealing his paunch, but it wasn't perfect. Either he'd been lucky in keeping all his dark-brown hair into his fifties, or he'd spent a lot of money on his toupée. He waved Nightingale to a seat, and took the one facing it himself. "You FBI?"

"No. Just a concerned citizen. You're Michael Litvinsky?"

"Let's not start using names, okay? I'm not happy about this."

"I'm not overjoyed myself."

"These people, they're dangerous."

Nightingale nodded. "I know."

"You heard what happened to Lucky Marino's boy? Frankie?"

'Yeah. I heard."

"I needed something doing. Now I have to pay, in full. If I don't pay, I was told I'd end up like Frankie Marino."

"You plan to pay?"

"Damn right. There seem to be a lot of coincidental deaths around, what with one thing and another. I don't plan on being the next one. What do you think?"

"I think, if you have the money, you should pay." said Nightingale. "These people seem quite severe about defaulters."

"It's only money. I hate to be taken for a sucker, but I'd hate being dead more."

Nightingale nodded. "You want to tell me about it?"

"Not really. But that bastard FBI agent isn't giving me a choice."

"Let me help you, maybe save you a little time, Someone contacted you, via the internet or TV. Someone you didn't know,"

"Yeah, an old black woman, never seen her before, she was kind of disguised too. Offered to get rid of...an obstacle to a business deal."

"The obstacle was a man? And he's dead now?"

"Yeah...but I never thought he would end up dead. I wanted that deal, but I'm no killer."

"She name a price?"

"Yeah, pretty high, but if the deal went through, it was peanuts."

"You agreed?"

"Why not, she wasn't asking for anything up front, just payment by results."

"And you really had no idea the guy would end up dead?"

The man's eyes flicked around the room and he rubbed his hands together "I swear, I thought maybe she had some way of persuading Mars...the guy. I never meant him any harm."

Nightingale didn't guarantee to be able to tell when someone was lying to him, but this guy was easy to read. Whether or not he really expected his 'obstacle' to die, it was clear he wouldn't be shedding any tears about it. Loathsome as he was, he wasn't the point here, so

Nightingale pressed on. "So when this guy died, and I'll lay ten to one it was a natural death, they came back to you and asked for their money. Same black woman?"

"No, completely different person. Looked like a young Asian guy, dark glasses, fake beard. Nobody I'd ever seen before."

"And he threatened you?" asked Nightingale.

"Sort of. He suggested I pay. He gave me a list of people who hadn't paid and said they were all dead. Frankie Marino was on the list. I know Lucky, we've done business in the past. He pretty much confirmed what I'd been told."

'Who else was on the list?"

"The Winstons, Jolyon and Delia."

"Delia Winston's not dead, I spoke to her yesterday."

"Maybe you should check again. A lot can happen in a day. And some guy called Scarletti. Look, that's all I know, right? I've done what Hart wanted, I've met you. But I've told you all I know. I'll pay what they want and hopefully that'll be the end if it."

Nightingale nodded. "Yeah. Fingers crossed."

CHAPTER 50

Nightingale waited until he was outside the hotel and certain that he wasn't being followed before he called Lynsey Lawton.

"Any news?" she said.

"Some," he said. "Seems like we've got another fish that was hooked."

"Does he have a name?"

"I'd rather keep that to myself."

"Are you any further forward?"

"A little. The weak area in this whole thing is trying to persuade the client to pay up. If these people have a secret way of causing natural-looking deaths, it's kind of hard to claim responsibility for it. It's probably not great for business to keep killing the client, or the client's family, so a few pointed threats might work. You ever hear of a guy called Scarletti?"

"Not that I recall. Is he dead?"

"Could well be. See what you can find. And maybe check on Delia Winston too, she was on the dead list this guy was given. I only spoke to her yesterday, she was pretty alive then."

"I'll get back to you."

She ended the call and he put his phone away. Two men appeared, one either side. The one on his right grabbed his arm, just below the elbow. "Don't do anything stupid," the man growled. He was tall, well over six feet, with dyed blond hair and a square jaw that looked like it could take punches until the cows came home.

"What, like licking an electric socket?" said Nightingale. "Or shaving my pubic hair with a chain saw?"

"What?" said the man.

"You'll need to define stupid, that's all I'm saying."

"Shut the fuck up," said the second man. "And get in the car."

"What car?"

A blue Ford Escape pulled up at the kerb. "That car," said the second heavy. "Mr Marino wants a word with you." If anything he was even bigger than the blond heavy, with a Desperate Dan five o'clock shadow.

"Now you see, that there is a paradox," said Nightingale.

"Para-what?" said Desperate Dan.

"Paradox," said Nightingale. "You said not to do anything stupid. Then you tell me to get into a car with two goons I've never set eyes on before. That's a paradox."

"Can't we just shoot him?" said Blondie, his grip tightening on Nightingale's arm.

"Boss wants to talk to him," said Desperate Dan.

"Lucky me," said Nightingale. "Or is it Lucky him?"

"In the car," said Desperate Dan. He and Blondie pushed Nightingale towards the SUV. Desperate Dan opened the door and shoved Nightingale in. There was a man already sitting in the back. He was in his seventies, wearing a sharp suit and a wide blue silk tie with a gold pin in the middle.

Desperate Dan squeezed in next to Nightingale and slammed the door, while Blondie climbed in next to the driver.

"Mr Marino, I presume," said Nightingale.

"You'll excuse the somewhat anonymous vehicle," said Marino, "I generally travel in a Lincoln or a Hummer, but I didn't want to attract attention today."

"I don't think I'm being followed,"said Nightingale.

"I don't care what you think. Why were you talking to Litvinsky?"

"How do you know I spoke to anyone?"

"Nothing happens in this town without my knowing, Nightingale."

"Look, Mr Marino, I'm not a cop or a Fed, I'm just a concerned citizen."

"Concerned about what?"

"You know what. You know exactly why I wanted to talk to Litvinsky."

"I know the FBI put pressure on him to talk to you, and the FBI has been trying to put me behind bars for years. So until you prove otherwise, that puts you in the FBI camp. And that's not good for you."

"So you've got someone in the FBI working for you?"

"What I've got or haven't got is none of your business."

"You can hear my accent, right?"

"Yeah. Australian?"

"English. And I don't think the FBI employs Brits."

Marino frowned. "So are you British or English?"

"Both," said Nightingale. "But either way, I'm not a Fed. And if you've got someone in the FBI on your payroll, they can sure as shit tell you that I don't work for them. Or for any law enforcement agency for that matter. Look, I'm looking for someone who kills people and makes it look like they died of natural causes. Which is what happened to Frankie, right?"

Marino's eyes hardened. "Right."

"Litvinsky gave me another name. Scarletti."

"Antonio Scarletti?"

"I didn't get a first name."

Another pause. "Perhaps it would fit. Antonio Scarletti was in the importing and distribution business."

Nightingale nodded. He wasn't about to ask what it was that Scarletti imported and distributed.

Marino continued. "Up until a few weeks ago you would say he was one of the two largest 'importers' in the area. His chief rival was a man named Fedorov, a Russian I believe, who had been expanding his business, and was beginning to cause Scarletti's operation some inconvenience. There were one or two minor incidents, resulting in

154

some hospital time for minor operators on both sides. Then Fedorov died."

"Murdered?"

"Apparently not. He died in his bed one night. The police and the coroner found nothing suspicious, and it was put down to natural causes. A heart attack."

"Convenient for Scarletti."

"So it appeared, and it was generally felt that Scarletti's business would expand to fill the space left by Fedorov's organisation, which dwindled in power without its leader."

"But...?"

"Ten days later, Scarletti died too."

"In his bed of a heart attack?"

"No, he crashed his Maserati into a free-way bridge. No other vehicle involved."

"Was he drunk? On drugs?"

"Not that I ever heard, he was a distributor, rather than a user. Perhaps something occurred to make him lose control?"

"Something like a heart attack?" asked Nightingale.

"No way to know, the car caught fire on impact, Scarletti was reduced to ashes."

"Interesting timing,"

"Indeed, though, at the time nobody read anything sinister into the two deaths. Looking at it now, it might fit the pattern, if Scarletti had a hand in Fedorov's death, and then declined to pay."

"It's not much to go on," said Nightingale.

"What can you expect? This person, appears to have a foolproof method of disposing of people, which leaves no trace. Perhaps when we know who, we will understand how. Or vice versa."

"Is there anyone left of Scarletti's organisation who might have any useful information? Maybe someone who might have known about some deal to remove Fedorov?"

Marino paused for half a minute before speaking. "I am not fully informed of the current state of the organisation, let me make some calls. I'll try to get back to you with a name."

"So you'll help me?"

"I want to find out who killed my boy. You might be a means to an end. Conrad, turn right here, and drop the gentleman at the Tropicana Hotel."

"Right, boss," said the driver.

Nightingale smiled as he wondered how Marino knew where he was staying. The man was clearly very well informed about a lot of things.

CHAPTER 51

Nightingale was sitting on the toilet when his phone rang. He looked at the screen. It was Marino. He wasn't sure what the etiquette was for taking a call while evacuating one's bowels, but he took it anyway. "Antonio's cousin is running the show now," said Marino. "His name's Salvatore Romeo."

"Where can I find him?"

"He works out of the Black Diamond Bar, Restaurant and Casino at 2201 East Bonanza Street."

"Thanks, I've got that."

"That's in East Las Vegas, hardly the safest part of town. And Romeo won't take kindly to a stranger asking him about his business, so use my name. That'll get you in to see him, but what happens then is down to you."

"I've been in rough neighbourhoods before, and met a lot of tough guys. I'll be careful."

"Careful might not be enough." Marino ended the call.

Ten minutes later. Nightingale was out on the street and flagging down a taxi. The driver's name was Max and he only agreed to take Nightingale if he paid for a return trip. "Man, you don't want to go out there, there's nothing for tourists there. it's a poor area man, they mug you as soon as look at you. Better you stick to Freemont Street or the Strip, man."

"Thanks, Max, but I hear good things about the Black Diamond."

"Then you listening to the wrong people, man."

As they drove away from the bright lights of the Strip and its tourist traps, Nightingale began to see Max's point. The people here were poorly dressed, some of them clearly homeless, the stores several degrees downscale from the glitzy shopping palaces in the centre. The

Black Diamond looked in need of a coat of paint, and its windows desperately wanted cleaning.

"I'll wait here thirty minutes, man," said Max. "I keep the engine running. Any sign of trouble and I'm gone. If you're not back out in thirty minutes, I'm gone."

"Thanks, Max. This shouldn't take long."

"Sooner you than me, man."

The Black Diamond was larger than most neighbourhood bars that Nightingale had been inside. The bar dominated one side of the long rectangular room, which was packed with tables and chairs for diners, together with roulette and craps tables, tabletop poker machines and the inevitable slots. Nightingale took a stool at the bar. A young black girl in a tight green dress made a move to sit next to him, but the barman shook his head at her, and she scurried away.

The barman looked like a heavyweight wrestler, who'd skipped his training for a year or so. He stood well over six feet, broad shoulders, deep chest and a gut overhanging the waistband of his jeans. His arms and neck were heavily tattooed, the multi-coloured designs all blending into each other. His name badge said *Paco* and he looked at Nightingale with his small brown eyes betraying no warmth.

"What'll it be, Mister?"

"Corona," said Nightingale.

"Coming up."

"And I'd like to talk to Salvatore Romeo."

Paco's face tightened. "Don't believe I've ever heard of the guy." He looked meaningfully at the baseball bat that hung on the wall behind him.

"That's a shame, a friend of mine told me I might find him here. Luca Marino. They call him Lucky."

Paco shook his head. "Don't believe I ever heard that name either. I'll check with one of the other guys."

Nightingale took a sip of beer as he watched Paco disappear through a door at the far end of the bar, to reappear a minute later behind a smaller man, dressed in an immaculate light blue suit and tie with what looked like a brand new white shirt. His hair was slicked back and glistening.

"You were asking abut a Mr Romeo?"

"I was."

"Paco says you mentioned another name too. Some friend of yours."

"Luca Marino. They call him Lucky. Where I come from that's generally a dog's name, but what can you do?"

The man frowned, then gestured at the door. "In here."

Nightingale went through into a windowless room with a desk and a metal filing cabinet. There was a sofa in front of a coffee table and two wooden chairs. Another man with slicked back hair was sitting on the sofa, though his was thinning and chunks of his scalp were visible. He looked big when he was sitting down but when he stood up, Nightingale realised just how big he was, close to seven feet.

"Who are you?" growled the big man.

"Jack. Jack Nightingale."

"You carrying?'

Nightingale shook his head. The big heavy gestured at his companion who proceeded to expertly pat Nightingale down. Once they were satisfied that he was unarmed, the smaller heavy picked up a phone. "There's a guy here to see Antonio. He says Lucky sent him." The heavy listened and nodded. "Nah. He's Australian."

"British," said Nightingale.

"Nah, I could take him with one hand behind my back."

"That's a bit harsh," said Nightingale. "I read a book on Krav Maga once."

The heavy put the phone down. There was another door next to the filing cabinet and he opened it. "This way." He walked down a corridor and Nightingale followed. The big heavy walked two steps behind Nightingale, breathing heavily.

There was another door at the end of the corridor, this one covered by a CCTV camera. The door opened as they approached and

159

Nightingale followed the small heavy into the room. It was larger than the first room and also windowless. There was a red leather Chesterfield against one wall and a bank of six CCTV monitors on another, two of which had views of the Black Diamond. Three heavies were playing cards at a circular table and a fourth man was sitting behind a large desk with three phones in front of him.

The man at the desk was presumably Salvatore Romeo, and at first sight, he was rather unimpressive. Skinny, and no more than five feet six was Nightingale's guess, though the man made no attempt to get up. His brown hair was thinning at the front and flecked with silver. His eyes were an unusually pale blue and he had a pencil moustache above his thin lips. "Your name Nightingale, like the bird?" he asked.

"That's right."

"Never heard of you."

"I'm not from these parts. But Lucky can vouch for me."

"What does he want from me?"

"He doesn't want anything from you. He thought you'd probably refuse to see me, so he said I could use his name. That's all. I just want to ask you a few questions."

"Ha, does this look like *Jeopardy*? You ain't a cop, you ain't a fed. So fuck you and your questions."

"That's right, I'm not a cop, I'm just helping Mr Marino with something. You heard his son died?"

Romeo pushed back his chair, started to get up, then thought better of it. "I had nothing to do with that. Anyway, I heard the kid's heart gave out."

"True enough."

"So how would I know about it?"

"I think what happened to Frankie is connected to what happened to Antonio Scarletti."

"Scarletti? He wrecked his car, that's what happened to him. "

"But there's a why. Let me tell you."

Romeo looked at his watch. "You got a minute."

"Okay. Sometime back when Scarletti was still alive, and having trouble with a guy called Fedorov, he was contacted, probably via the internet or TV by someone he'd never seen. Man or woman, old or young, it doesn't matter. This person claimed to be speaking for someone else, their 'principal'. And offered to remove Fedorov for a large fee. I'm betting Scarletti didn't believe them, thought it was some kind of scam."

Romeo said nothing, but Nightingale was a trained interrogator, he hadn't missed the little nod of the head.

"A week or so later, Fedorov died. Nothing suspicious, heart attack in bed. Scarletti had a free run now. Except, pretty soon, he was contacted again. Different person, but still acting on behalf of this mysterious principal. They wanted the money. Scarletti refused, told them to go to Hell, he wasn't about to pay off on a natural death, however well-timed. They threatened him, he laughed at them. And then he died too. Just like Fedorov, just like Francesco Marino, Just like Enzo Florentino. So, what do you think of my story?"

Romeo stared at Nightingale. "Maybe it would be better as a movie."

"Based on a true story, right? Just the names changed to protect the guilty? Look, all I'm asking is if the same person who killed Marino's son also killed your boss."

Romeo nodded slowly. "First time was a young black guy, second time an old Indian woman. I was in the room both times. Five mil. After Sal died, there was a blonde woman. Said the debt was still due. I paid it. Better safe than sorry, right?"

Nightingale nodded. "That's what they say."

CHAPTER 52

Nightingale phoned Lynsey Lawton and arranged to meet her in his hotel coffee shop. He smoked a cigarette outside while he waited for her, then bought two coffees and sat at a table by the window. "So, are you any further forward after your walk down the mean streets?" she asked as she sat down at the table.

"I'm not sure," said Nightingale. "What they told me ties in with the stories I've had from other sources, but it doesn't point any fingers at anyone in particular. I need some confirmation before I could do anything."

"And if you had it, what would you plan to do? Call the police? Kill the guy?"

"Neither one, I don't think. I can't see any way of getting enough evidence to have anyone arrested, the police don't even think any crimes have been committed. And I'm no assassin. I guess, if I could be sure I'd found the right guy, I would hand it over to Wainwright, who might hand it over to Marino."

Nightingale decided to leave Paul from the FBI out of the discussion.

"Either way, I wouldn't want to be wrong and get an innocent guy killed."

"Here's what I don't understand," she said. "If these deaths aren't natural, how are they being caused? Nobody gets close enough to give them poison, not that there's been any trace of it, and no weapon could cause heart attacks, much less from a distance."

Nightingale nodded. For the moment, he preferred to keep the idea of a lethal demon to himself, it might be too much for Lynsey to swallow. "It's a puzzler, that's for sure. But for me, the bigger mystery is how does the killer get people to act for him. Every time he communicates with a client, it's like he uses somebody different as the conduit. There seems to be an endless supply of them. You'd think that whoever's doing this wouldn't want too large a group knowing about it. From what we've heard, they've never used the same person twice. And such a wide range of people. They've been old, young, middle-aged, male- female, white, black, Asian, Chinese."

"Almost as if they'd been picked at random," she said.

Nightingale sipped his coffee. "Picked at random...now, where would you find a group of such diverse people, with almost nothing in common?"

"Well, for a start, any casino in Vegas."

"Exactly," said Nightingale. "You know, I think I'm going to need to see that show at the Luxor again. What are the chances you can get us tickets for tonight?"

"In theory it's sold out, but in practice, I can get you a ticket, if your budget will stretch to it. But I can't make it tonight, I've got a job on."

"Another one?"

"Sure, I work for Wainwright when he needs me, but it's not an exclusive arrangement. I've got an errant banker's wife to keep tabs on. Girl's got to make a living."

"God, I don't miss my days of divorce work," said Nightingale. "Not to worry, I can handle this on my own."

CHAPTER 53

Lawton managed to get Nightingale a seat in the middle of the fourth row at the illusionist's latest performance. The show didn't vary much from the first one he'd seen, with the various birds having their heads removed and restored, Kahsim levitating himself and other objects, cutting his assistant in half and making people disappear. It was when he called for volunteers from the audience, first to stand around Cleopatra's needle while it 'vanished' and next for the hypnotism, that Nightingale started to pay close attention. He took out his phone, switched to video and zoomed in on the stage. He focused on the magician and concentrated on the man's lips.

He smiled as he saw what was happening, right in front of the audience's eyes. Kahsim would give an order out loud. Then, while the audience's attention was on the new piece of silliness, he would whisper a few quiet words to the next in line, who would reply briefly, and also in a whisper. Not to all of them, it seemed to depend on their answer to his first whispered question. Nightingale could see no system to the choice of audience participants, they came in all ages, colours and sexes.

"A random selection," said Nightingale to himself. That was how he was selecting his helpers. In full view of an enthralled audience.

CHAPTER 54

Khamsin removed his mask, placed it on the dressing room table, and helped himself to a glass of water.

"Did you see him?" asked Neferu, standing at his shoulder and looking at his reflection in the mirror.

"Of course, my dear," said Khamsin, "I see everything I need to. An unprepossessing fellow, in the middle of the fourth row. He paid little attention to my repertoire of illusions, not even bothering with his binoculars for the crocodiles. But when I was conducting the hypnotism session, then I had his full concentration."

"Do you think he has figured it out?"

"I suspect he is very close to the truth. He has the advantage that he has dwelt in our world of the shadows, so his mind is more open to the acceptance of things which the normal mind would reject."

"Does he present a danger?"

"It is possible, though he himself wields no power, he might be able to direct it against us."

"What do you propose to do about it?" Neferu asked.

"Do? Why, fulfil Mr Wainwright's contract first, I think."

"But you felt it was a trap."

"No matter. We shall deal with Mr Nightingale, and then it will be Wainwright's turn."

"I hope I can watch them die."

"It may not be possible my dear. Now, we turn to the question of Mr Romeo. He was instructed to keep quiet, it appears he has disobeyed"

"But he knows nothing useful."

"Not the point, my dear. He has helped our enemies in building their picture of our activities. His death will be a useful example for others."

"Will we use the Messenger of Anubis?"

"I think not, my dear. I think a rather blunter instrument is called for. Send in Ali."

CHAPTER 55

Nightingale had reached the lobby of the Tropicana when the two detectives stopped him. They had been waiting for him, sitting in two armchairs close to the entrance. He had been so caught up in his own thoughts that the first time he noticed them was when Garcia touched him lightly on the shoulder. Nightingale had flinched and his heart had skipped a beat, but he managed to smile and nod.

"We'd like you to come down to Headquarters," said Garcia. "We have some more questions for you."

"But I've told you everything I know. I was nowhere near the Macoub house when they were murdered."

"This is in connection with another matter," said Martinez.

"What? I think I'm entitled to know what's going on otherwise I'm not going anywhere."

"Mr Nightingale, I am thinking of arresting you as a material witness in a murder case," said Garcia. "If you don't want to come with us voluntarily, I have the right to arrest you, and we'll take you down in cuffs."

Nightingale studied Sergeant Garcia's face There was a tiny twitch at the corner of the man's mouth, could it denote a lack of confidence? Or a bluff?

"I'm guessing you're bluffing," said Nightingale "Whatever this is about, you're not sure you have enough to hold me on, and you're hoping I'll come quietly."

Garcia exchanged a look with Martinez. "Maybe. Alright then, how does this sound? We head over to the coffee shop for a cup of coffee, and I'll ask you some questions, which you may, or may not choose to answer. Depending on your answers, if any, I'll still have the right to arrest you as a material witness, and I'll use it if necessary."

Nightingale nodded. "Let's try that way then."

They headed for a secluded table in the lounge. Nightingale ordered coffee and lit a cigarette. The police officers stuck to coffee, though Garcia looked enviously at Nightingale's Marlboro packet.

Garcia nodded at Martinez to start them off. "You went to see a man named Salvatore Romeo yesterday."

Nightingale sipped his coffee and said nothing.

"Yes or no?" she said

"Oh, was that a question? It sounded like a statement."

She sighed and looked at Garcia, who said nothing either. "Okay," she said. "Let's try another way. We have three witnesses who say that a man giving his name as Nightingale and answering your description showed up at a bar run by Salvatore Romeo and asked to speak to him. They particularly noticed the shabby suede shoes."

"They're comfortable," said Nightingale, "in my job I do a lot of walking."

"And what exactly *is* your job?" asked Martinez

"I help people find out things."

"You're a detective?"

"Not exactly."

"Do you hold a Private investigator's Licence in Nevada?"

"No."

"In any state?"

"No. I just gather information and pass it on."

Garcia interrupted. "Let's get back to Salvatore Romeo. Did you visit him yesterday?"

"I did."

"Care to tell us why?"

"Any reason why I should?"

"We're asking nicely."

"I have lots of conversations with lots of people, the police never usually ask me about them. Why is this one important?"

The officers exchanged another look. Garcia nodded at his partner. She continued. "At ten fifteen this morning, Mr Romeo arrived at the Diamond Bar in company with two of his goons. They parked their car opposite and crossed the street. One, maybe two guys in a white panel van fired half a dozen shots, we think from automatic weapons. Four shots hit Mr Romeo and he was pronounced dead at the scene. One of the goons was hit once in the upper arm and is in the hospital, expecting to recover. The other goon was unscathed."

"Really, you call them goons?"

"Goons," said Martinez. "Or hoods. Gangbangers if they're a different complexion. Why what do you call them?"

"Heavies, I suppose. We used to call the top guys Faces."

'Faces?" repeated Martinez.

"Yeah, I guess because they were well known. Celebrities almost. But the heavies, yeah, we'd call them heavies."

Garcia frowned. "I think we're getting off track here," he said. "What did you talk to Romeo about?"

"About his late boss, Scarletti."

"What did you want to know?"

"I wanted to know if someone threatened him before he died. I wanted to know if someone had offered to kill a guy named Fedorov for Scarletti."

"Hold it, now. These guys are hoods, how come an Englishman is involved with them?"

"I'm not involved, I was just asked to make enquiries."

"From what I remember, there's nothing to enquire about. Fedorov died in his sleep, Scarletti crashed his car. Why would you be enquiring into their deaths?"

"I was asked to."

"By whom?"

Nightingale shook his head. "No, I'll keep that to myself. I've done nothing illegal, nobody's suggesting I was in the van, are they? And I'm not American so me getting a gun is problematical at best."

"We have no description, but for the record, where were you?"

"Same answer as last time. Having breakfast. This time I even saved a copy of the bill."

Nightingale opened his wallet and handed over the slip of paper. Garcia looked at it and grunted. "Look, this is twice in two days you go see someone and they end up murdered the next day," he said, giving him back the receipt. "I don't believe in coincidences like that."

"It's a violent city," said Nightingale. "The fact that two murder victims met the same guy doesn't connect me to the killing I have no motive, I had no means. You can't call me a material witness, I was miles away both times."

Garcia sighed. "I got nothing to hold you on, but if anyone else gets hit, and your name comes up, I'm gonna have you in a cell."

Nightingale nodded and stood up, but Garcia raised his hand to stop him. "Just how did you get in to see Romeo? He's not exactly approachable."

"Don't know what you mean," said Nightingale. "I just asked nicely."

CHAPTER 56

Nightingale called Lynsey Lawton's cell, and she answered on the second ring. "Can we meet?" he asked. "I can buy you a coffee in the Tropicana."

"Sure, Jack. But somewhere different this time?"

"Just name it."

"New York, New York. Lobby lounge bar. Thirty minutes."

A quick enquiry of the doorman on the way out informed Nightingale that he could use the walkway to get there, and he was on time. The hotel looked like a miniature version of the New York skyline, complete with small scale versions of the Statue of Liberty, the Empire State Building, the Chrysler building and a selection of other skyscrapers he didn't recognise. The one thing that looked out of place was the giant roller coaster, which snaked in and out of the buildings and rose some sixty metres high. Nightingale shuddered at the thought.

Once inside, the hotel looked pretty similar to all the others, a huge casino ready for its eager punters, signposts to a selection of bars, restaurants and attractions.

Lawton was sitting at a table in the lobby bar, dressed less showily today in denim shorts and a loose white shirt. Nightingale had abandoned his rain coat on the first day, but carried a light jacket, as he needed the pockets. They ordered coffee.

"You want to talk here? I shouldn't think we'll be overheard. Of course, if you want to be really sure, we could ride the roller-coaster together."

"Not in this life," said Nightingale. "It's just an elevator without walls, at ten times the speed."

"And I had you pegged as a thrill-seeker."

"You need new pegs."

171

"Okay. I can give you a resumé of what I've got so far, which to be honest isn't much. Delia Winston. Born in Nebraska, moved out here as a dancer and showgirl, rumour that she was also involved in the 'escort' business, but no real evidence, arrests or convictions. Got herself invited to a lot of parties and met a lot of wealthy men. Finally hooked herself a big fish, Jolyon Winston. Big wheel in the hotel business, and on his third marriage, counting her. Usual story, she behaved herself for a couple years, then started to get itches the old boy couldn't scratch. She was still a looker, and would come with a pile of cash, so she had no shortage of takers Old Man Winston didn't take it too well, and was inclined to be sticky about the divorce settlement. Then he died suddenly, and she cashed in. Much good it did her."

"What do you mean?"

"You didn't know? She's dead too. Taken off an AA flight at Harry Reid before it got chance to take off."

Nightingale frowned. So Michael Litvinsky had been right, Delia Winston was dead. "Let me guess, a sudden heart attack?" he said.

"Sounds a fair guess. At the moment they're calling it "unexplained, but not suspicious.""

"Don't suppose you know where she was headed?"

"Flight was bound for Chicago which is an AA hub. She might have gone on to anywhere from there, and I can't think of a good reason why anyone would want to tell me." He shrugged. "She must have had it in her mind to run out on them when I was there."

"Unless you spooked her. What did you talk about?"

"Her husband's unexpected death."

"That might have done it, if she had some hand in it. Do you think she did?"

"Not in the way you mean. But maybe she had some kind of a conscience."

"'The wicked flee when no man pursueth."

Nightingale frowned. "What? Is that Shakespeare?"

"No, Proverbs. My daddy was a preacherman, some of it stuck."

172

Nightingale grinned. "Sins of the fathers, eh? Well, sounds like she's a dead end...or perhaps confirms some suspicions."

"What suspicions? I'm working in the dark here."

"Me too. Once I find some enlightenment, maybe I can fill you in."

CHAPTER 57

Lawton left after she had finished her coffee. To be honest she hadn't had much information for him that Nightingale didn't know already. He lit a cigarette and had just taken his first drag when his phone rang. The caller was withholding his number so Nightingale was expecting to hear Wainwright's voice. "Is that Jack Nightingale?"

The voice was higher pitched than the Texan's and there was a slight nasal whine to it. Nightingale was sure he'd heard it before but he couldn't place it. "Who wants to know?"

"What?"

"I said who wants to know?"

"Don't fuck around, Nightingale. Is this you or not?"

"Do you know how ridiculous you sound. Look, you called my number, what do you want?"

"Are you always a prick?"

"Sometimes I take the day off, but yeah, I'm generally a prick to people who call me up and withhold their number for no valid reason."

The man cursed under his breath. "This is Silvio. Silvio Balboa."

"Yeah? You related to Rocky?"

"Rocky? Who the fuck is Rocky?"

"Rocky Balboa? The movie. Movies. How many Rocky movies were there?"

"Silvio Balboa. We met today. In Romeo's office. In the Black Diamond."

"So are you the big goon or the small goon?"

"What is your fucking problem, Nightingale? I call to help you and all you do is break my balls."

"Help me, how?"

"I want to talk to you. Soon. Face to face."

"Where and when?" asked Nightingale

"Somewhere that isn't the Black Diamond. Somewhere private. I'm not sure you're a safe guy to be around."

"Well, I wouldn't really want to make a return visit to the Black Diamond anyway. What about somewhere on the Strip?"

"Yeah, somewhere crowded. I got a buddy at the Venetian, meet me at St Mark's Square in an hour. Come alone and don't wear a wire."

"Alright."

"Are the cops interested in you?"

"I don't think so," said Nightingale. "But they know I visited Romeo the day before he was killed."

"Yeah, they asked me all about that," said Balboa. "I was with them the best part of a day. They'd have liked to pin something on me, but there were plenty of witnesses that I was one of the targets, not a shooter. Anyways, make sure you're not followed, what I have to say is for your ears only."

"But you know I had nothing to do with your boss getting killed, don't you?"

"No need to worry, Nightingale. If I was planning on whacking you, you'd be dead by now."

"That's reassuring," said Nightingale, but Balboa had already ended the call.

CHAPTER 58

Khamsin rang the bell for his assistant, and was obliged to wait a little longer than normal. When she arrived finally, she bowed her head to him.

"I am sorry, Khamsin, I had just returned,"

"No matter, my dear, your work is important to me. This man Nightingale is becoming rather a nuisance now, beginning to learn much more than I would wish. It is time to make an end of him, and then, possibly, it will be easier to eliminate Wainwright."

"Should it be done personally?"

"I think not, Nightingale is a capable and resourceful man, a direct approach might fail and also betray our secrecy. Once again, I think, the Messenger of Anubis must strike."

"Very well," said the woman.

"Do we have a suitable intermediary?"

"I will summon one directly."

"Good. And the necessary items?"

"Already obtained."

"Excellent. Then Anubis will soon escort Jack Nightingale to the Underworld."

CHAPTER 59

Nightingale had never been to Venice, or anywhere else in Italy, and was prepared to believe that the Venetian Hotel provided a reasonable facsimile. His cellphone informed him that the original building was designed to look like the city, built in green stone from the Italian Alps, with columns of solid marble in its main colonnade. To either side rose the inevitable modern style tower blocks, containing over four thousand rooms.

The hotel surely was a work of art, with its own versions of famous landmarks such as the Rialto Bridge, the Doge's Palace and the Bell Tower of Saint Mark's Basilica. Just as with the city itself, canals ran through the whole complex, and Nightingale saw several people enjoying a leisurely ride in one of the gondolas that plied their trade there.

There were signs for the *Grand Canal Shoppes* Mall, but Nightingale made his way to the reproduction of Saint Mark's Square. He saw Balboa almost at once, outside one of the restaurants. He was wearing jogging pants and a Las Vegas Aviators baseball jacket with a matching baseball cap pulled low over his eyes. He made a small movement of his hand to tell Nightingale to keep walking, then caught up with him a few moments later.

"Just wanted to check that you're loose," said Balboa, "we ain't doing nothing wrong, but I've answered enough questions from the cops to satisfy me for a while."

"I'm not being followed," said Nightingale. "It does't look like you are either."

"It would take a big team, and they don't have the resources. Let's just be a couple of tourists and take us a gondola ride, My pal Mikey's waiting for us."

He led the way to the gondola station, and made a sign to one of the boatmen, a tall skinny guy in the striped sweater, knee britches and straw hat of the traditional Venetian gondolier.

"Just the two of us, Mikey," said Balboa as they climbed inside. "Take it nice and slow, and you can spare us the song. Hard to talk with you singing *O Sole Mio* at the top of your voice."

Mikey grinned underneath his obviously false moustache. "Whatever you say, but you'll have to pay me, the boss will be watching and making a note of the trip."

Nightingale took out his wallet. "My treat, how much?"

"Hundred and twenty, excluding the tip," said Mikey.

Nightingale was getting used to the idea of Las Vegas prices now. He handed over three fifty dollar bills and gestured to Mikey to keep the change. The man dug his pole in the water and the boat moved off.

The attention to detail with which the designers had recreated the streets of Venice was incredible, even down to the moving clouds of the painted sky, but Nightingale had little opportunity to take it all in, as he was concentrating on what Balboa had to tell him. "It's a damn shame about Sal," said Balboa eventually. "He was a good guy to work for. Better than Scarletti."

"My sympathies," said Nightingale. "You got any idea who was responsible?"

"If I had, he'd be dead. It doesn't make much sense. Since Fedorov died, there's been no organised competition, and nobody inside Sal's organisation had any ideas of promoting themselves to the top job."

"Not even you?"

"I'm no organiser. I wasn't about to try a take-over bid."

"You never got chance to do any shooting when Romeo was killed?"

Balboa grinned ruefully. "Never got a shot off. They hit us from behind, Sal fell on top of me, I never got my gun out."

"Was it the first time he'd been attacked?"

"Yeah, this isn't Chicago in the twenties, in our business settling scores with bullets is pretty rare. There were a few minor skirmishes when Fedorov was trying to grow his business, but nothing since. It makes no sense. Unless..."

He paused, but Nightingale was content to wait.

"The way I see it, everything was quiet after Scarletti died, Sal was running things just fine, nobody looking to make a name for themselves, no serious competition. And then..."

Again Nightingale waited for him.

"And then you show up, asking questions about Scarletti's death. The boss was rattled, I knew him a long time, I could tell It bothered him. Then, the next day, out of nowhere, somebody hits him."

"Could be coincidence," said Nightingale

"Could be, but that's not the way I'd bet. I call cause and effect."

"I told you already, I had nothing to do..."

"Cool it, I don't think you hit him, or had him hit. You wouldn't be here now if you had. But that scenario you laid out for him. It was pretty near the mark."

"And how would you know that?"asked Nightingale.

"Simplest way in the world. He told me. Look, Sal and I were close, a little more than just a working relationship, if you know what I mean."

Nightingale nodded, but said nothing.

"He was in the room when the black guy came on. Scarletti was pissed, couldn't understand how they'd hacked into his computer. He said sure, he'd like Fedorov out of his hair, but never thought some young black kid could do it."

"Black kid?"

"It was a black kid who made the offer."

"And Fedorov died."

"Sure he did, but he died in his sleep, he wasn't hit. Good for Scarletti's business though. Then, apparently, some old Indian woman hacked into his computer."

"When you say Indian..."

"I mean from India, not Pocahontas. Anyway, this old woman came on, told Scarletti her boss had offed Fedorov and it was time to pay up. Scarletti laughed at her. She gave him a week to pay up, or he'd be very sorry. Just about a week later, he was dead."

"In a car crash."

"That's right. That's when Sal Romeo took over, that's when he told me the story."

"Pretty much the story I told him when we met. You were there."

"Yeah, but you don't know the rest of it."

"There's more."

"Sure there is, I was in the office with Sal when some woman in a blonde wig cut in on his computer. She reminded him what had happened to Fedorov and Scarletti. Said that since he'd taken over the business, the debt owing was now on him."

"And how did Romeo react to that.?" asked Nightingale.

"He was scared. He paid up."

"How did he pay?"

"Bitcoin, he told me. I don't understand the stuff myself."

"But if he paid, how come he was killed?"

"Assuming it was the same people, maybe they got wind that you were on to them and getting too close, Tying up loose ends."

"Could be," said Nightingale. "Who else knows about this?"

"Far as I know, just me. Like I said, I was closer to Sal than most people."

"Might be a good idea if you watched your back now, these people might know you were close with Romeo."

"I figured that out for myself. I think maybe I'll take a little holiday, go visit my sister in San Francisco. There's just one more thing."

Nightingale reached for his wallet, but Balboa put a hand on his arm..

"I don't mean that, Nightingale, I don't need a handout. Judging by those shoes, I should be giving you money. Instead I'll give you this."

He handed over a plain white card. Nightingale looked at it.

Amber Diamond, then a telephone number and in pencil underneath, a North 8th Street address.

"What's this, an escort?" asked Nightingale.

"I'm not too sure what she does for a living, but even though she's not a blonde normally, I'd offer three to one that she was the girl who put the screw on Sal. I got a pretty good memory for faces, and I'm pretty sure that was her in a blonde wig and shades that showed up on Sal's computer. Trouble is, there's no way to check it out now, however they hacked the computer left no traces, the message wasn't recorded."

"They'd make sure of that. How do you know this girl?"

"I don't really know her. She tried to pick me up one night at Bally's. About two months before that message came through. I was out with a couple of the guys, her and a friend were working the room. Her hair was darker then."

"You didn't go with her?"

"I don't fuck hookers, but I took her card. You never know when I might have needed to provide entertainment for someone."

Nightingale looked at the card again. "Did she give you her address?"

"Nah, I found that all by myself afterwards." He shrugged. "Not so hard to do if you know the right people."

Nightingale nodded. Back in London he'd known the right people.

"One thing puzzles me," said Nightingale. "If you recognised this girl, how come Sal didn't track her down."

Balboa tugged at his ear and stared off into space. "Because I never told him I'd recognised her."

"Why not," asked Nightingale.

"I told you, I'd offer three to one it was her, but there's no way I could be sure. If I'd told Sal, he'd probably have had her killed, might even have wanted me to do it. If I was wrong, I wouldn't want to have some innocent girl on my conscience. I figured maybe I'd do some

181

nosing around on my own, see if I could connect her to this and then give it to Sal. He could put the squeeze on her. But before that could happen, he was hit."

"And what are you planning to do about it now?"

"Nothing at all," said Balboa. "It's not my fight, and it looks like these people don't play around. I'm just telling you what I know. If you're connected to Luca Marino, maybe you've got the resources to put these guys out of business. I'd like that, for Sal's sake."

"Hey Silvio," said Mikey, "trip's over in about three minutes, unless you want to pay to go round again?"

"No, that's cool," said Balboa, "we're about done here."

The gondola headed back towards dry land and Mikey helped Nightingale out.

"If anyone ever asks, you never got that card from me," said Balboa as they walked away from the gondola. "I'm out of this now, being dead is a lousy career move, I figure I'll look for another line of work."

"Thanks, Silvio," said Nightingale. "I'll do my best to see that Sal's killers get what's coming to them."

"You sound like Jimmy Cagney," said Balboa. "You be careful now." He kept his head down and his hands in his pockets as he walked away.

Nightingale looked at his watch. He needed to see the girl, but he felt it might be better if he didn't go alone. He called Lynsey Lawton and she agreed to meet him in the Tropicana coffee shop in ninety minutes, so it clearly wasn't a rule to keep changing venues. He headed over to a taxi rank.

CHAPTER 60

The taxi stopped outside Crystal Village and Nightingale asked him to wait. Judy was busy with another client, but a tall, dark young girl in a long brown pleated dress came over to him.

"Hello, I'm Aurora. Have you come for your crystal, Mr Nightingale?"

Nightingale frowned. "Well, yes, but how did you know..."

"Oh, Judy described you. Mostly the shoes. They're quite unusual."

"And comfortable."

"They'd have to be." She opened an ornate wooden box. "Here's your crystal." She passed it to him, being very careful to only hold it by the chain.

Nightingale travelled very light as a rule, buying anything he needed in whatever city he found himself. One thing he always carried was the small pink crystal on a silver chain that Mrs Steadman had given him in her *Wicca Woman* shop back in London, in another life. It had several uses, but needed to be cleansed and recharged from time to time, to maintain its energy level and remove unwanted vibrations and contamination that it might have picked up. It was a fairly simple process, but required specific products, so it was easier to let a store handle it for him. Nightingale looked at it, nodded, then put it back into its old, soft leather bag.

"Nice job," he said, "it feels as good as new."

"Can you really feel it?"

Nightingale nodded. "Sometimes."

"Well, it's been soaked in sea-salt and moon-water for over a day, so it should be fully cleansed now."

"That's great."

Judy had finished with her customer and came over to Nightingale. "Did you hear what happened to Doctor Mahoub and his wife?" she asked.

"Yes," said Nightingale. "It's a damned shame, they seemed like a nice couple. Do the police have any leads?"

"Not that I've heard. I think they're working on the theory it was a burglary gone wrong, maybe kids after drug money."

"There's a lot of that around," said Nightingale.

"Well, yes, but the Mahoubs were elderly and pretty weak, they wouldn't have fought, there'd be no need to hurt them."

"People can be pretty vicious."

"True enough. Anyway, hope we'll see you again if there's anything else you need. Give my regards to Mrs Devereaux."

Nightingale nodded, paid Judy for the cleaning and headed back to his waiting taxi.

CHAPTER 61

Nightingale got to the coffee shop first first and had a coffee ready for her. He showed her Amber Diamond's card and he explained how he came to have it.

"That's not her real name, obviously," she said.

"I assume not," said Nightingale. "But you never know."

"And you really think this girl might have something to do with the extortion racket?"

"This guy Balboa said he'd offer three to one it was her."

"That's hardly a cast-iron cert."

"True enough, but it's the only lead I have. Now, we need to think of the best way to approach her. I'm not a policeman any more, and I can't pretend to be one."

"Not with that accent," said Lynsey. "And the shoes, of course."

"I'm English, we don't have an accent, it's the rest of you that can't speak properly. And Hush Puppies are American. Why do I keep having to explain that to people?"

Lynsey forced a smile. "Anyway, prostitution is very illegal in this town, so you don't want to let her smell cop. You could say you're a reporter."

"I thought hooking was legal in Vegas. The clue is in the name, Sin City, right?"

Lynsey shook her head. "The state of Nevada allows counties with a population below 700,000 to offer brothel prostitution, and there are around twenty legal brothels in the state, but none are in Vegas. So she'll clam up if she thinks you're a cop. I'd go for reporter."

"Well, yes," said Nightingale, "but reporting on what? I can't just show up on her doorstep and say I'm working on a story about extortionists and murderers."

She smiled. "I can see where that might put her on her guard." She sipped her coffee.

"So what do we do?"

Lynsey smiled at him. "You're overlooking the obvious. That card tells you how to play it."

"What do you mean?"

"Come on, the girl's a hooker. So, be hooked. Give her a call, tell her you were given her card and a recommendation by a friend, then make yourself a date. Then you can ask your questions, or tell her your theory while you're paying her for her time."

"Paying?"

"Sure, the girl needs to make a living, she won't want to sit and listen to you for free. You're a good looking guy, but still..."

"Okay," said Nightingale. "Er...what's the going rate?"

"What makes you think I'd know," she said, putting on a show of indignation.

"You said you used to work vice."

"Yeah. Well, assuming this girl is hot, she'll probably charge five hundred for an hour, and more if you have special requirements. Of course, your special requirements are just answering questions, but I doubt she has reduced rates for that."

"Cash?"

"Always welcome, but a lot of girls have card readers these days. Or Paypal."

"Isn't technology wonderful? Okay, I'll call her and set up an appointment for us."

"Us? She's going to want more if you bring a friend."

"I was thinking maybe she'd be glad of a chaperone."

She laughed. "Jack, you really don't get out much, do you?"

CHAPTER 62

Getting an appointment with Amber Diamond wasn't difficult, it appeared she was free that evening. The taxi dropped Nightingale and Lynsey outside the apartment block on North 8th Street. It was a four storey complex and looked to be of quite recent construction, grey concrete and white wood framing. Nightingale patted the bundle of notes in his jacket pocket, he'd brought the quoted price, plus the extras that whoever had answered the phone had insisted on since he wanted to use the girl's own apartment. The voice on the phone had sounded older and harsher than he'd expected, but Lynsey told him that was probably a central clearing agency for several girls.

"So how do you want to play this?" asked Lynsey.

"By ear, I guess," said Nightingale. If it was her on that video call, she's not likely to admit it, she'd be an accessory to extortion and possibly murder. I've got a theory as to how this is done, but proving it is not going to be easy."

He pressed the button for Apartment 5A

"Yes?" Amber, assuming it was her, stretched the single syllable over several seconds.

"Jack, I have an appointment with Amber."

"Come on up."

The door lock buzzed and Lynsey pushed it open, The interior of the block was carpeted in grey, and the cream walls looked recently painted and well maintained.

"Nice enough place," said Lynsey.

"Yes, must be doing well for herself."

"There's always a demand."

The block had an elevator, but Nightingale headed for the stairs. Lynsey gave him a quizzical look. "I don't much like elevators," he said.

"You must be fun in high-rise buildings," she said, as she trudged up behind him.

Nightingale knocked on the door of 5A, which opened straight away. His first thought was to wonder whether she'd dyed her hair to match her name, or chosen the name to match her shoulder length flaming red hair. Of course, it could have been fake, her chest certainly didn't look like the original equipment, and her lips had been plumped up with something or other. Her eyes were just a little too vivid a green to be natural. She was tall for a woman, probably just a couple of inches shorter than him. She smiled, showing two rows of dazzling white teeth, but the smile faded as she saw Lynsey. "You didn't say anything about bringing a friend,"she said.

"I thought it wouldn't be a problem, maybe it comes under 'special services'," said Nightingale.

"I guess." She looked over at Lynsey. "Do you plan to watch or participate, honey?"

"Let's just see how the mood takes us," said Lynsey.

"Well, my mood often depends on holding the folding, so perhaps we should get that out the way." She held out her hand. The nails were a glossy bright red and beautifully manicured.

"Where are my manners?" said Nightingale and handed over a bundle of notes.

Amber did a quick count. "Well, that's the price of admission, we can talk about the add-ons in a while. Come on in."

She held the door open for them to walk in. The living room had a sofa and two chairs, a large screen TV hung on the far wall, and there was a coffee table just in front of the sofa. A couple of magazines. An empty ashtray and a laptop computer sat on the table. No trace of books or music. Through the hatchway, Nightingale could see the kitchen, two doors led off the living room. There was a French door leading out onto a balcony. He guessed that the furniture came with the apartment. There was nothing personal about the place, maybe Amber just used it for work purposes and her real home was somewhere else.

"Shower's through there," said Amber, indicating a door on the left, "You'll find towels and a robe. I'll meet you in the bedroom, one or both of you. Anything special you want me to wear?"

Nightingale hoped he wasn't blushing. "I'm not too used to this," he said."How about we just sit down and talk for a while?"

She sighed. "Oh, a talker, eh? Well, honey, it's your dime, but the meter's running anyway."

"I understand, It'll just make me feel more comfortable."

She rolled her eyes and waved them to the sofa. She took one of the chairs. She pulled a pack of cigarettes from her purse, lit one and eased back into the chair. "Excuse me for smoking, if it bothers you, I'll take a breath mint before we get started."

"It doesn't bother me," said Nightingale, taking out his Marlboro pack.

She smiled dreamily. "So, Jack, what you want to talk about?"

"Oh, I don't know, tell me about you. What's it like living and working in Las Vegas?"

Her smile into a sneer. "I get it, you want to know the real woman behind the whore, think it'll make it a better experience for you?" She shook her head and sighed. "Okay, I'll play. I guess turning tricks in Las Vegas is pretty much the same as anywhere else, except the casinos are nicer and the johns are richer. There are worse ways to make a living."

Nightingale decided not to ask what they might be. "What about your free time, what kind of things do you do?"

She laughed. "Free time? Honey, what's that? I'm open all hours, I don't turn down dates."

"But still, you must need a change some time."

"I guess, I like to play roulette and craps a little, but I'm not stupid about it. Now and then I'll go to a show in one of the hotels. I saw Celine Dion, Carrot Top, the Blue Man group. I got a friend or two can sometimes get me cheap tickets if a night isn't sold out."

Nightingale nodded and looked at the end of his cigarette. "You ever see a magician?" he asked.

"Yeah, I saw David Copperfield at the MGM, how does he do all that stuff?"

"Beats me," said Nightingale. "You ever see that new guy, Khamsin or whatever?"

She stared out of the window. "No, I never saw him."

"You know anyone who has?"

Her voice was strangely flat, as if she were reading from a script. "No, I never saw him, I don't know anyone who has."

"I saw him once, he was amazing," said Lynsey.

"If you say so," said Amber.

Nightingale reached into his pocket. "You like jewellery, Amber?"

Her voice had its normal cadence again. "Sure, who doesn't, what you got there?"

"It's not all that valuable, just a beautiful pink crystal. Look."

He took the crystal out of its bag, and held it, swinging by its chain, in front of her face.

"It surely is beautiful," she said.

Nightingale's voice softened, almost to a whisper. "Yes, it is beautiful, Amber. Look at it, really look deep into it. See how it catches the light. Look deeper into it Amber. Really deep. Are you feeling a little tired, Amber?"

Her voice was slow and drowsy. "Yes, tired. Sleepy, so sleepy."

"Go to sleep now, Amber. Go to sleep, but you will keep hearing my voice. Go to sleep."

As they watched, the girl's eyelids closed and she was silent, apart from her regular, even breathing.

"Wow," said Lynsey, blinking and rubbing her nose. "I nearly dropped off myself. Where did you learn to do that?"

"Our mutual friend, Mr Wainwright," said Nightingale, "but he's about ten times better at it than I am, he wouldn't have needed the crystal."

"Do they usually go under that quickly?"

"I don't think so," said Nightingale, "unless they're particularly suggestive, or unless maybe they've been hypnotised before."

"So now what?"

"Now we see if her memory's any better."

CHAPTER 63

Amber Diamond sat back in her chair, her eyes closed, her breathing low and steady. Her arms were at her side, palms open.

"You can open your eyes now, Amber," said Nightingale softly, "but you will stay asleep."

The green eyes opened, but their stare was unfocused.

"Now," said Nightingale, "I want you to think back, to remember. Did you ever go to see the illusionist Khamsin?"

"Yes."

"When?"

"Last month. A friend got me a ticket."

"Did you enjoy the show?"

"Oh yes. It was incredible."

"Did you watch it all?"

"Not all of it, I think. Some of it I can't remember."

"Try to remember it all, Amber. Did you go up on stage at all?"

"Up on stage? Yes, yes I did, he chose me to go up. There were about ten of us."

"And what happened then?"

"He asked me to look at a stone, it was blue, sparkling, pretty. I started to feel sleepy."

"Then what, Amber?"

"He told me I could fly, and I could. It was true. I floated across the stage."

"Then what?"

"I can't say."

"Yes, you can, Amber, you're safe here with us, you can tell me everything he did and everything he said."

"He asked me where I lived, and for my cellphone number."

"And you told him?"

"Of course."

"And then what?"

"Then I went back to my seat, and he brought on those crocodiles."

"Good, well done, Amber. Now, tell me, after the show, after you'd gone home, did you ever hear from Khamsin again."

The girl stared straight past Nightingale and said nothing. Her lips quivered, and a tear ran down her cheek.

Nightingale persisted, his voice still soft and encouraging. "After the show, after you'd gone home, did you ever hear from Khamsin again."

Amber gasped, her eyes closed and she fell forward out of her chair and onto the beige carpet. Lynsey rose to her feet, hurried across and bent over her. "She's fainted, Jack. Get her some water. Come on Amber, it's alright, wake up, you're fine."

Nightingale could hear her soft voice whispering encouragement as he walked to the kitchen, found a glass and filled it with water. By the time he returned, Amber's eyes were open again, and she was getting to her feet. She shook her head as if to clear it. "What happened?" she said. "We were talking about David Copperfield, and the next thing I knew, I was on the floor."

"Looks like you fainted," said Lynsey. "Here. Drink this. Or maybe you've got something stronger?"

"I don't need anything stronger," said Amber, "but it's so hot in here I need some air."

She walked to the glass balcony door and opened it, took a deep breath, then walked outside, placed both hands on the rail and vaulted over.

Lynsey clasped her hand to her mouth in horror, but made no sound. Nightingale strode quickly to the balcony rail and looked down, then turned to block Lynsey's path.

"You don't need to see this."

"I was a police officer, Jack, you don't need to worry about my sensibilities. She's dead?"

"Oh yes, looks like she landed head first and broke her neck."

"But why?"

"Let's talk about that later, it's time we weren't here."

He went to the kitchen and came back with two cloths. "Here, take one and wipe down anything you might have touched The glass, the door, the window handle, the sofa arm. I'd really rather the Police never knew I was here"

Nightingale emptied the contents of the ashtray into a plastic waste bag from the kitchen and folded it into his pocket.

"Done?" he asked.

She nodded.

"Then we're out of here. We'll take the stairs, nice and slowly, and let's hope nobody sees us."

"But that poor girl?"

"I know, but there's nothing we can do for her now, and I don't want to spend time in a police cell trying to convince them she killed herself."

"But I was here, I'll back you up."

"I know, but cops the world over seem to have a way of not believing a word I say these days."

CHAPTER 64

"What the hell was all that about?" asked Lynsey, "one minute she's calmly telling you about the show, next thing she faints and then she takes a flier four floors down. Makes no sense."

They had stopped at the first neighbourhood bar they found and sat at a corner table. Nightingale rarely drank spirits these days, but had ordered himself a Glenlivet, and Lynsey had followed suit. He lit a cigarette and offered the pack across. She reached for it, hesitated, then took one. "I'm sure it's 11pm somewhere in the world," she said. Nightingale lit it for her and they both blew smoke.

"Was it because of something we did?" asked Lynsey. "Was it our fault?"

"Yes and no," said Nightingale. "I mean, we didn't tell her to jump. But we might have triggered it by putting her under." He took another pull on his cigarette. "I saw something similar a few years ago, back in England. You remember I told you I was surprised how quickly Amber went under?"

"Yeah."

"Well, could well be that she was used to being hypnotised, that it had happened to her before, maybe more than once."

"Well, we know about the once, when she was one of Khamsin's volunteers up on stage." She blew smoke up at the ceiling.

"That's right, but I have a theory he contacts them again afterwards, maybe puts them under by phone, and gets them to send out his messages."

"Is that even possible?"

"I think so. You ever see that film 'The Manchurian Candidate'?"

"Wasn't it Denzel Washington?"

"I was thinking of the Frank Sinatra original. The killer gets triggered by a phone call and a deck of cards, so I guess it's possible.

195

Khamsin calls her up, and the sound of his voice puts her under again, so she trots round to help deliver his message."

"That still doesn't explain the skydive off the balcony."

"A friend of mine in England was hypnotised into doing some pretty nasty stuff, and the guy who did it planted a little bomb in her mind. If anyone else hypnotised her and tried to get at the truth, her body was instructed to shut down. Technically she died, but we managed to revive her. I think the same thing happened to Amber. I was getting close, so she lost consciousness, then killed herself to stop me getting at the answers."

"I get it," said Lynsey. "But I'm sure I read that a person can't be hypnotised into doing something that's not in their nature. Does that mean she was already suicidal?"

"Not necessarily," said Nightingale. "I might not be able to persuade you to commit suicide, but what if I could convince you that you could fly like a swan? He'd already done it once, so maybe that's the suggestion he planted in her mind"

Lynsey shivered. "It's horrible. I hate the idea of someone else playing around in my mind."

"Best stay away from Khamsin, it seems he makes a speciality of it."

"But you still don't know for sure that Khamsin brainwashed these people into delivering his messages."

"I can't think of any other reason that she might kill herself." He sighed. "Have you managed to find out anything about this Khamsin character?"

She shifted in her seat, and looked over Nightingale's shoulder. "I'm drawing a blank, Jack. Sorry. I got pretty much nothing on the guy."

"Nothing?"

"Pretty much, except for the stuff written on programmes when he appears, or used to advertise his shows. You know the crap. From the land of the Pharoahs, from a time before recorded history, comes the heir of the great Magicians of Ancient Egypt, with the secrets of

196

Thebes and the Nile at his fingertips. Be astonished by the death-defying, exploits of Khamsin, Lord of the Wind. All that publicity nonsense."

"What about his real name?"

She shrugged. "I guess he must have one, but it's not for public consumption. Here in America, you can call yourself pretty much what you like."

"But he must have a driver's licence, passport, social security number, bank account"?"

"I guess he must, but not in the name of Khamsin, so I've got nothing to go on."

"But it's not possible to live off the grid like that," said Nightingale, though he was pretty sure the current driver's licence he carried had never been legitimately issued. Maybe Khamsin had rich friends too.

"Maybe not, but it'll need someone with much better contacts than mine to trace this guy, and it seems he doesn't want to be traced."

Nightingale exhaled some smoke and thought for a few seconds. "Maybe we could try looking at his assistant."

"Neferu, of the Twelfth Dynasty, Crown Princess of the Nile?"

"Yeah, that's the girl."

"Way ahead of you, but same goes. I can't believe that's her legal name in whatever country she's from, but it's the only one I can find. No records of her under that name either. Chances are she was a showgirl or an out-of-work actress who just had the right figure and looked good being cut in half. But I can't find out anything for sure."

Nightingale forced a smile. "Well, nobody ever said life was easy."

"You want me to keep at it?" she asked.

"Not this way, I don't want them to hear about us asking too many questions. Maybe we can come at it from another direction." Nightingale blew smoke, then continued. "The man's got two giant crocodiles in his act. I don't know much about Nevada law, but I'm betting you'd need some kind of a permit to own those things. And someone must transport them to the theatres for his act. When he's not working, they'll have to stay somewhere, and that glass tank will take up a lot of room. Unless he's got some place where they can roam around until he needs them. It would need to be a big place. And I can't believe it's legal just to buy crocodiles and have them around the place."

Lynsey nodded. "That's a good point," she said. "He must have some kind of special licence. Leave it with me. I'll look into it. So what do we do now?"

"I drop you off wherever you need to be, and head back to the Tropicana for a good night's sleep. Maybe by tomorrow I'll come up with some kind of a plan to put our illusionist friend out of business for good."

CHAPTER 65

Proserpine had forbidden him to summon her, and he dared not go against her command. Wainwright was out of touch and Doctor Mahoub was dead. Nightingale was running out of sources of help and information. He decided to give one more chance to someone who'd never helped him at all in the past.

God.

St Mark's Coptic Church was a sand-coloured brick building, standing at the intersection of two busy suburban roads. It had been built with acutely sloping grey slate roofs and octagonal turrets in three different sizes. Coptic crosses stood on top of each one, their lines each ending in the traditional three points.

Nightingale walked in through the main entrance and took a look around.

The interior was far more lavishly decorated than the average Christian Church he'd been inside, the walls were almost completely covered in pictures of saints, dressed in vivid colours. Separating the nave from the sanctuary was a long wooden screen, also covered in paintings of apostles, flanking a large portrait of Mary in the centre. Nightingale had once been inside an Eastern Orthodox Church in England, where he had learned that the screen was called an *iconostasis* and he should not go past it without being blessed by a priest.

Right on cue, a priest appeared. A tall, thin man who looked to be well over sixty. His white hair was receding over his high forehead, but he had compensated by letting his side-whiskers grow down on either side of his face almost to his collar-bones. He was dressed in a long black robe over a black shirt, and wore a silver Coptic cross on a silver chain, dangling down at belt level. He peered at Nightingale through his black framed spectacles "Good afternoon, and welcome to our church. I am Father David, I don't believe we have met."

"Jack Nightingale, I'm just visiting, wondered if you might be able to help me with a couple of questions I have."

The priest inclined his head. "I should, of course, be pleased to do so. Perhaps you wouldn't mind strolling across the way to my home, and I can offer you refreshment. I must admit, I prefer to conduct conversations sitting down at my age."

"That would be fine."

Nightingale followed the old priest out of the side door and across a courtyard to the door of a small white house. Father David opened the door and ushered him inside, down a short hallway decorated with yet more paintings of saints and apostles and into a study. Plainly furnished with a mahogany desk and leather chair and two old green leather armchairs. The walls were covered with yet more portraits of religious figures in between the bookcases. Many of the books had indecipherable titles in some language Nightingale couldn't read.

"Coffee, tea, sherry or something stronger?" asked Father David, but Nightingale shook his head.

"Not for me thanks."

"Well. I'm sure you'll excuse me if I have my customary sherry at this time."

He filled a small glass from the decanter on his desk, took a sip and smiled "And feel free to smoke, I intend to."

He opened the top drawer, took out a battered pipe and tobacco pouch and started the filling process. Nightingale took out his pack of Marlboro and lighter. The priest said nothing until he'd taken the first puff at his glowing pipe.

"Ah, that's better. Now then, Mr Nightingale, how may I help you? I judge from your face and your accent that you are not an Egyptian copt."

"English agnostic, I'm afraid."

"No matter. So how can I help you?"

"Have you been in Las Vegas long? I take it you're originally from Egypt?"

"I am, but I have no memory of the country. My parents were obliged to flee in the late fifties. It was the time of the Lavon Affair and Suez crisis, and Jews and Coptic Christians were thought of as the enemy within. The Jews were expelled by Nasser, made to sign declarations that they would never return, and the same happened to many Copts, including my parents. Those declarations are still enforced on their families sixty years later, so I have no memory of my homeland."

Nightingale crushed out his latest cigarette. "You know, I heard a very similar story from a Jewish gentleman a few days ago."

The priest looked surprised.

"Really? Would that have been the late Doctor Mahoub?"

Nightingale's eyebrows shot up. "Yes, did you know him?"

"I did indeed," said Father David, "a learned and interesting man. We were of different religions, but our experiences had been very similar. I used to play chess with him, and enjoyed our conversations. I was profoundly sorry to hear of his death, and that of his wife."

"You wouldn't have any idea who might be responsible? Did he have enemies?"

The old priest took a long draw on his pipe and looked up at the ceiling before answering. "Assuming that he did not meet his end at the hands of some street thug or burglar, I can think of nobody in this country who might wish him harm. In Egypt, there might still be those who bear ancient family grudges, and he would not have been permitted to return, but here, he was well liked and well-respected."

"Have you heard of an illusionist from Egypt? His name is Khamsin."

The old priest dropped his pipe, and a look of horror spread over his face. "Khamsin is not a name for a man, it is a harsh and evil wind that sweeps all before it."

"So you have heard of him?"

"I have, but I would prefer not to speak of him, he bears a reputation as poor as the wind from which he takes his name."

"Sorry to press the point, but do you know his real name?"

"I give you a question for a question, do you think he bears some responsibility for the death of Aaron Macoub?"

"Just between us, I do,"said Nightingale. "Problem is, there's no evidence."

"There would not be with that one, he is as cunning as an asp."

"So you know something about him?"

"Most of what I could tell you is the merest rumour. It is said he comes from the Bin-Saheed family, an evil clan from near the Valley of the Kings, renowned for their cruelty and pursuit of power. Nobody seems to know for sure."

"Not one of your flock?"

"As far from it as imaginable. His family have long been followers of Set, or Sutekh, the Lord of all evil, the Egyptian God of Chaos."

"But isn't that a myth from thousands of years ago?"

"Possibly, but then there are some who say that about all religions."

"But we're in the twenty-first century, people don't believe in ancient Egyptian Gods any more."

"Why not? There are plenty of people who believe in the Christian idea of Satan. Do you, Mr Nightingale?"

The sudden question caught Nightingale by surprise. "I don't know, I've never really given it any thought." He didn't like lying, but the truth would mean opening a can of worms that he would rather stay firmly closed.

"Perhaps you should, you know, Sutekh, Satan and Set may just be different names for the same thing. The embodiment of evil, and that has not changed over the centuries and millennia."

"So you are saying that Khamsin comes from a family of Set worshippers?"

"I suspect they do more than worship. His family history is studded with evil committed in Set's name, designed to increase their power. If you are planning to work against this man, Mr Nightingale, I suggest you take the greatest care possible."

Nightingale opened his mouth and was about to say that Careful was his middle name, but he decided that the joke just wasn't funny any more. "I'll do my best," he said.

CHAPTER 66

The woman's name was Yvonne Green, an accountant in her fifties, married with two children, although Khamsin didn't know that. It was unimportant, she was just a tool to be used. Not unattractive, though she could have stood to lose ten pounds, and her roots needed retouching. She sat, silent and motionless in the chair, as Khamsin gave her his instructions. Neferu was standing behind Khamsin, her hands clasped together.

"Yvonne, hold this figure, Not too tightly. This is Jack Nightingale. Say his name."

"Jack Nightingale. Jack Nightingale."

He handed her the roughly modelled clay form of a man, two cigarette butts pressed into the front and back of it.

"Good, now gaze into the crystal and repeat his name again."

"Jack Nightingale. Jack Nightingale ."

He looked across at his assistant.

"When faced with a trap, one may avoid it, or spring it. I choose the latter."

He muttered a sentence in the archaic language, and stroked the figure with his ivory wand. "Very good. Now, tell me, what do you see, Yvonne?"

"I see him. Jack Nightingale. He is in his hotel room. Lying on the bed, smoking a cigarette."

"Excellent. Now, take this ivory wand in your right hand, hold the figure in your left. That's right."

The woman sat there, pointing the wand at the crystal ball.

"Now, repeat these words after me. I call on Kek and Kauket, bringers of darkness and light and on Amit, devourer of souls. Send forth the Messenger of Anubis, to stop the heart of this one. In the name of Set, Lord of Chaos."

The woman repeated the words, her gaze fixed on the crystal, the wand pointing unwaveringly at the image of the man. As she said he final word, a green spark shot from the end of the wand into the very heart of the crystal. A blurred figure seemed to follow it, then was gone.

The crystal clouded and cracked. Almost too quickly for the human eye to follow, a figure with an animal's head sped from the crystal and disappeared into the woman's body. She screamed, her eyes closed, and she fell backwards, as if hit by the recoil of a rifle.

Miles away, Jack Nightingale sat up suddenly, opened his mouth wide, clutched at his chest and rolled back soundless on to the bed. His cigarette fell to the floor.

CHAPTER 67

Neferu stared at the pile of powdered glass where the crystal ball had been. The ivory wand lay on the floor, released from Yvonne's loosened grip. Neferu bent over her, felt for a pulse at the wrist, then put her ear to her chest to listen to the heart. "She's dead," she whispered.

Khamsin nodded. "So it seems. It must be that the man Nightingale has protection, protection stronger than any mortal should know about."

"But you said that there could be no protection against the Messenger of Anubis."

"And, to my knowledge, there can be none. We must be dealing with a force stronger than anything I can direct."

"But why did she die?"

"Once the Messenger of Anubis has been unleashed, it must find a victim. If it is not the intended target, then it will be the one who summoned it."

"Then that is why..."

"Exactly. That is why I have always worked via an unwitting intermediary, so the power can not be reflected back on me. It is regrettable that this woman should die to spring the trap, but preferable to risking my own safety."

Neferu frowned. "Then it was a trap, as you suspected?"

"Possible, though other explanations are possible. For the moment, we have a more pressing problem, a body to dispose of."

"That will not be easy."

"But not too difficult. It could be a little snack for Omari and Akila, they are not particular whether their food is alive or dead. And they would leave very little evidence."

Neferu shuddered. "You would seriously feed her to them?"

"It is an option. Alternatively we could 'help' her into the car, drive her to a secluded patch of desert and leave her to be found by vultures or coyotes. Or, easier yet, just leave her in a quiet street, propped up against a wall. No doubt it will be many hours before someone assumes she is anything other than some drunk, sleeping off her over-indulgence. Anyway, there is no connection between us and this woman, and the police will find no evidence of foul play in her death. There will be no criminal investigation."

"But our activities will need to stop," said Neferu. "The crystal is destroyed."

"It can be replaced, and our activities can continue, but only after we have eliminated the current threat to our operation. It seems that Wainwright has tried to make me expose myself, and has succeeded after a fashion. I doubt this man Nightingale knows much for certain, but it would be foolish to proceed while he is still able to cause us a problem. He must be located and neutralised. And it must be done quickly, the death of the President needs to take place at the agreed time, but I dare not risk unleashing the Messenger of Anubis again until I can be sure it is safe."

"The General will be displeased."

"The General will not need to know, especially if we can remove the problem before the due date."

"And what of Wainwright?"

"Yes, he is the cause of this problem. It is definitely time we met with Mr Wainwright. He has many questions to answer."

"You know where he is?"

Khamsin smiled. "No one can hide from me," he said. "No one."

CHAPTER 68

Jack Nightingale was woken up by the sound of knocking on his hotel room door. He tried to move, but the pain shooting through his chest held him immobile on the bed. He opened his mouth to speak, but that hurt too, and no sound emerged. The last thing he remembered was sitting on the bed, when his eyes had caught the sudden flash of a figure approaching him. A figure that had the head of some animal. A dog maybe. Then the agonising pain.

The knocking was repeated.

"Housekeeping."

He heard the sound of the key-card in the lock, and the door opened. The woman was small, black and was pushing a laundry cart and wearing a hotel cleaner's uniform. She took one look at Nightingale lying on his bed, and her hand shot to her mouth.

"Oh, Sir, excuse me. I didn't know...Are you okay, Sir?"

Nightingale opened his mouth and a weak croak emerged.

"Let me get you some water." The woman hurried into the bathroom and brought out a glass of water. She held it up to Nightingale's lips and he took a couple of weak sips.

"Let me call you a doctor, Sir."

"No," groaned Nightingale, his voice barely audible. "Honestly, I'll be all right, just a little too much to drink last night. Leave the water, maybe fix the room later."

She looked down at him, unsure what to do. "You sure, Sir? You don't smell of drink. Let me fetch that doctor, take a look at you."

Nightingale's voice was stronger this time. "No, honestly. I'll just rest for a while, I'll be fine. Thanks."

He rummaged in his jacket pocket, found a ten dollar bill and pressed it into her hand. The woman slowly backed her cart out of the room and closed the door behind her. He could hear her voice out in the corridor, probably talking to one of the other cleaners. The story would reach the whole hotel staff by the end of the day, no doubt.

Without trying to sit up, Nightingale reached for his pack of Marlboro on the night-stand, got one between his lips, lit it and inhaled deeply. He dropped it on the floor, as a dagger of agony tore through his chest. He swore, and tore open his shirt. He looked down. Over his heart was a dark purple bruise, the size and shape of the *ankh*, almost as if some force had driven it into his body. As he looked at it, the bruise was beginning to fade, and the pain started to recede. Inside another minute, he was able to sit up, retrieve the smouldering cigarette before it had chance to do much damage, and taken another few tentative puffs.

He rubbed his chest gently, and took a look at the ankh. It was still hanging round his neck by its chain, though now the metal of the crosspiece was blackened and twisted. He wasn't sure what had happened, but one thing he knew for sure - Proserpine's gift had saved him. Saved him from what, he wasn't sure, but it had definitely saved him.

He got to his feet and walked across to the minibar. He found a miniature bottle of brandy and gulped it down. That felt a little better. The bruise was continuing to fade, and the pain subsiding to a dull ache. He saw a half-smoked cigarette on the floor. He had been holding it when he'd had the seizure or whatever it was. He picked it up and put it in the ashtray.

He took a shower and changed his clothes, noticing as he did so that the bruise over his heart had almost disappeared. Whatever had caused it had certainly been no normal blow. There was nobody he could call for advice, and he really didn't want to wait around until someone tried again. The *ankh* had taken a battering, and he wasn't convinced it would protect him twice. Of course, that assumed that the mystery killer would know he had failed. How would he know? Perhaps send someone to check?

Nightingale decided he'd be better off elsewhere for a while. Wainwright had probably given the killer his location at the Tropicana, but even Wainwright wouldn't know where to find him if he ran now. It might also mean fewer visits from the local police. His hotel was paid in advance, so he didn't need to show up at reception, he just packed his few clothes into his bag, threw his raincoat over his arm and headed for the emergency stairs. He emerged into the lobby, where nobody seemed to be paying him any attention, and walked on out of the main exit.

He crossed the walkway, then came down to street level a few hundred yards from the Tropicana and found a taxi rank. He looked around again, didn't recognise any faces, nobody was following him. His driver was called Mohammed, according to the licence photo.

"Good morning, Mohammed. I'm new in town, on a bit of a small budget. Can you take me to a cheap hotel, one that doesn't charge a resort fee would be good."

Mohammed nodded enthusiastically. "Apache Hotel. Very cheap, but off-Strip. Near Freemont Street."

"Sounds good to me, hit the gas."

The Apache Hotel at Binnions was the full name of the place, and it was several steps down from the glitz of the large strip hotels. Many dollars cheaper too, not that Nightingale needed to economise. Built in what looked like an art deco style, it reminded Nightingale of the large cinemas in Manchester in his childhood. The outside was a riot of blue flashing lights, with a giant 'B' just above the main entrance. As with many Vegas hotels, a later tower had been added on to it to provide an increased number of guest rooms. Of course, it came fully equipped with a large casino, and a steakhouse to go with the usual selection of bars. He registered with the one driver's licence and credit card that didn't come from Joshua Wainwright, but rather from an old forger he'd helped in Alaska a few months before, so the room was rented to Jay Finch.

The room was functional, but certainly not modern, with furniture which wouldn't have looked out of place in an old lady's house. Dark wood furniture, old-fashioned shaded bed lamps. There were no lace doilies on the night stand, but they would have fitted in just fine. It was clean, and Nightingale had stayed in a lot worse.

With no clear idea of what to do, and no instructions from Wainwright to be expected, Nightingale enjoyed the luxury of a relaxed and leisurely lunch at the hotel steakhouse on the 24th floor. According to the sign, the hotel had Las Vegas's first ever electric elevator, which had been installed in the thirties. Nightingale fervently hoped that it had been serviced regularly since then, but even his hatred of elevators wasn't enough to get him climbing twenty-three flights of stairs.

His waitress recommended the hotel speciality of chicken fried lobster, which was good enough to eat, but probably not repeat. It didn't seem to contain any chicken, but Nightingale couldn't be bothered asking questions. He headed back to the elevator, bound for the casino for a Corona and a cigarette.

He pressed the button for the lobby, the doors slid shut and he closed his eyes tightly, and clenched his fists till the knuckles whitened.

Thirty seconds later, the whole elevator started shaking, there was an appalling noise of gears grinding, and the car ground to a halt. Nightingale opened his eyes, then shut them again as the car dropped like a stone, but fortunately only a few feet. Then it hung motionless. By now he was sweating profusely despite the air conditioning. He pressed the red emergency button on the panel but heard nothing. He stabbed at it again, as the panic in him rose.

"I shouldn't bother with that, Nightingale, you'll break a fingernail.".

He spun round, knowing what he would see. There she stood, this time wearing a plain black T-shirt over a tartan mini-skirt, and what looked like the same black tights and biker boots. Her hair was in a ponytail, the fringe over her eyes tinted pink.

"You're doing this?"

She smiled, which made her look all the more terrifying. "A girl has to have some fun, Nightingale, and scaring you is too easy. You needn't worry you know, elevators are very safe. Fewer than thirty people a year die in elevator accidents, and most of those are repairmen."

"I don't care if it's only one, I don't want it to be me. Now make it work properly."

"Not even a 'please?' You need to mind your manners, Nightingale."

211

"Alright, *please* make it work properly."

"Soon. When it suits me. First you have a little something of mine which I'd like you to return."

She pointed at his neck. He opened his shirt, unfastened the chain and handed her the *ankh.* She held it in the palm of her hand and turned it over a few times.

"Look at the state of it. It's no wonder you can't have nice things if you don't look after them."

"I'll get you another one,"said Nightingale.

"Really. You don't imagine you can just pop into Claire's Accessories and replace it? This was forged for me by Hephaestus, from the same metal that made the chains that bound Prometheus."

"Seriously?"

She gave a sly smile. "Well, truth be told, I did get it in Claire's accessories, I just added a little charm to it before I passed it over. But look at it."

"I didn't do anything to it."

"Somebody did, Nightingale. Somebody who didn't wish you well, by the looks of it. But it worked. Still, it must have hurt."

"Quite a bit actually."

"Be grateful, Nightingale, you'd have been dead without it."

"Then I am grateful. Thank you. But why?"

"Maybe because I really did owe you one. Maybe because I don't want someone else killing you before I get chance to claim your soul. A soul that's rightfully mine."

"Allegedly."

"Don't push me, Nightingale, this elevator has another eighteen floors to fall."

"I'm sorry. Are you going to tell me who wants me dead?"

"Most people who've met you, I should imagine. You have a habit of annoying people."

"I meant on this occasion."

"I'm not omniscient, Nightingale. You're meant to be the detective. Still, I shouldn't imagine you'll need to worry about whoever it was in the future."

"Why not?"

"By the look of my little trinket there, someone unleashed a very powerful force against you. A messenger of death. Once that sort of thing is let loose, it won't go back to Hell empty-handed. If it can't claim its intended target, it will backfire on the one who sent it."

"You mean..."

"I mean that, since you're not dead, Nightingale, whoever tried to kill you, probably will be."

"That's reassuring."

"Reassuring from your point of view, and from mine too. Power like that isn't meant to be exercised by humans, life and death shouldn't be in their gift. Anyway, it should all be sorted out and you should be safe now. Unless..."

"Unless what?"

"No, why cloud the outlook for you? Now, what floor was it you wanted?"

Nightingale turned to look at the buttons on the wall, and the elevator started to glide smoothly downwards again. When he turned his head back, she was gone.

CHAPTER 69

By the time he reached the Apache bar, Nightingale really needed a cigarette and a Corona. He lit up, pushed the lime into the bottle and took a mouthful. He felt better almost at once. Encountering Proserpine always left him shaky, he had to keep reminding himself that, despite the punk exterior, she was a supremely powerful Princess of Hell. Still, if what she said was accurate, it appeared that this case was closed, though he had no idea how he might explain it to Luca Marino, or the FBI man Ward. Still, best to make sure.

He called Lynsey Lawton. "It's Jack Nightingale. Can we meet?"

"Sure."

"I've changed my location, I'm down in the Freemont Street area now."

"Moved downmarket a little, eh? I'm betting you don't want to ride the zip line with me?"

"You win the bet. Somewhere a little less adventurous, with both my feet on the ground."

Maybe the Mob Museum would be more your scene. You look a shifty kind of guy."

"Thanks a lot, where is it?"

"Stewart Avenue, just around from Freemont Street. Give me an hour and a half and I'll meet you outside."

CHAPTER 70

Officer Camila Martinez walked into her sergeant's office, a thick file in her hand. Sergeant Jose Garcia looked up. "You found some stuff?"

She nodded. "Oh, I found some stuff alright."

"Take a seat and talk me through it."

"Alright. Well, to start with, no Jack Nightingale has ever been arrested for a offence in Nevada, much less convicted. No parking fine, speeding ticket, never kept a library book overdue. Nothing."

"You needed a file for that?"

"Not hardly, but then I ran him through the federal computer. Same result, no arrests, no convictions."

"But?"

"But there are plenty of reports of his being around at the time of all kinds of shit. Remember that rush of kids committing suicide in Memphis a while back?"

"I read about it, they never did come up with much of an explanation for it."

"No, it just stopped. But there's a report in the file from a Sergeant Parker of the Memphis PD. Nightingale was on the scene of at least two suicides, and asked a lot of questions about them."

"He was a suspect?"

"Not for more than about two minutes, it was clearly established he had nothing to do with the deaths. But he was there."

"The man has bad timing, to say the least."

"There's plenty more."

She took out the next sheet. "This one was New Orleans. A gangland killing, said to have been carried out by a dead hooker.

215

There's a report from a NOPD detective called Carey Hood, who says Nightingale was around asking questions about the case. Claimed to be working for one of the hooker's families. Hood had his doubts, thought he might be connected with a mob guy called Jefferson. But again, no evidence, he was never arrested or seriously questioned."

"The guy moves around."

"That he does. Here's one from California. Couple of kids kidnapped and some nasty ritual murders."

"I remember that one too. Some big names involved."

"Yeah, most of them got off. The kids were rescued by an Inspector Chen, whose current status is 'missing'. Early on in the case, she'd filed reports about meeting with this Nightingale character, but then he seemed to fade out of that scene."

"How long has that officer been missing?"

"Since a couple months after the case. SFPD have no clues."

"Any more?"

"Well, there was a request from the Sheriff of some one-horse-town in Kansas, Little Bend, for any record on Nightingale, but no reason given."

"Wasn't that the little place they found the dead babies from the old single mothers' home?"

"Yes it was, but that home had closed years before Nightingale showed up."

Garcia patted the pocket of his jacket where he kept his cigarettes, he'd be wanting to go outside pretty soon.

"He turns up like a bad penny. You know, I think it's time someone got to the bottom of this mysterious Mr Nightingale, and it might as well be us. Get a couple of patrolmen to pick him up and bring him down here."

"Do we have a charge?"

"I'm gonna go with material witness. If that won't stick, well, he's not a citizen so let's just check his papers. I want to know more about this guy."

216

CHAPTER 71

The Mob Museum had its name written on black banners hanging from streetlights in front of it. The building itself was a large cuboid of grey brick, with mock Greek columns between each of the six rows of windows at the front, and a pediment with its official name engraved across the top. 'National Museum of Organized Crime and Law Enforcement'. Lynsey was waiting outside, wearing blue jeans and a yellow t-shirt. Her Adidas sneakers were much better suited for walking on hot streets than the shoes she'd worn at the Tropicana.

"It used to be a Post Office and the courthouse," she said. "Then someone had the idea to renovate it and use it to tell the history of organised crime in the United States."

"People were happy with that?"

"Opinions varied. The FBI and Police were all in favour of it, since they came out as the winners. Certain Italian-American families...not so much."

"I'll bet."

"Let's take a look inside. My treat. Well, Mr Wainwright's treat. But then I guess that's true whichever of us pays."

They spent half an hour or so looking at some of the exhibits, from the actual wall in Chicago against which the St Valentine's Day Massacre had taken place, to graphic photos of murdered mobsters and the history of skimming at the local casinos.

"Anyone you recognise?" she asked.

"There was a guy I met in New Orleans, but he doesn't seem to have made the cut yet. I hope they're saving a place for Luca Marino."

"Better not let him hear you say that."

They bypassed the gift shop and headed to the basement where a fully working distillery was installed, and also a replica of a thirties speakeasy, where they sat at a table. It didn't really look all that different from a standard American lounge bar, except for the selection of period photos on the walls. The prices certainly didn't date from the thirties.

Lynsey ordered a glass of moonshine, made on the premises, Nightingale had stuck with coffee.

"Impressed?" she asked.

"I'd like to come again, sometime when I'm not working and take my time over the place. I've seen quite a few cool places in the US, but always on my way to see someone or find something."

"What is this world, if full of care, we have no time to stand and stare?"

"Is that more bible stuff?"

"No, one of your countrymen, a Welsh poet, WH Davies."

Nightingale frowned. "Not really a countryman and I'm no big fan of the Welsh. I've only been there twice, got arrested both times and hit with a truncheon once."

"I assume they had their reasons."

"Allegedly. Anyway, let's bring you up to date. As I said, I've moved, I thought I might be a target for a killer, but I get the feeling I'm not any more. Not immediately, anyway. In fact, I think he tried, but I got away with it."

Lynsey's jaw dropped. "What? You were attacked?"

"Maybe. Probably. I don't know."

"What happened?"

Nightingale shrugged. He didn't want to tell her about Proserpine, or the fact that it was almost certainly Proserpine who had saved him by giving him the *ankh*. And that didn't really give him much to talk about. "There isn't much to say. I had, I don't know what you'd call it. An episode. A seizure. Something. It knocked me for six."

"But you're okay?"

Nightingale held his hands out. "The proof is in the pudding."

"When was this? When did it happen?"

Nightingale frowned. "Why does that matter?"

"Well did something happen to cause it? Did you get a phone call? Did you see someone?"

"I was in my hotel on the bed, smoking a cigarette. I felt a sort of seizure and passed out. The cigarette fell on the floor, I was lucky the bed didn't go up in flames."

'Did you go to the hospital?"

"No need. I was okay when I came around. A bit sore, but…" He left the sentence unfinished. He didn't want to have to explain the burn mark on his chest."

"And you didn't see anything? Nothing touched you?"

"It might have been nothing. It might not even be related to what's happening. Maybe I ate something that disagreed with me."

"Did it feel like heartburn?"

Nightingale shook his head. "Not really. So, any news at your end?"

"Well, Delia Winston's still dead. There's no investigation, they're calling it natural causes."

"Which, I've no doubt it was. Any developments on Khamsin?"

"I was saving that for a punchline. He's gone."

"Gone where?"

"That's the million dollar question. Apparently last night, two trucks turned up at the Luxor in the small hours, loaded all his equipment inside and took off. It was the end of his contract at the Luxor, the Blue Man Group are moving back in. Nobody's seen him or the girl since yesterday's show. "

Nightingale frowned. "Nobody tried to stop them?"

"Why would they, he's not suspected of anything. The cops aren't looking at him. The crew who took away the gear had authorisation, so why would anyone try to interfere?"

"And the crocodiles?"

"They're gone too, but that big glass case they used on stage is still there. Funny thing, nobody claims they saw them leave."

"That's ridiculous, two fully grown crocs can't just walk out of a hotel unnoticed."

"Well, the guy is the world's greatest magician," said Lynsey. "Making things disappear is his speciality."

"I think there are limits, even for a top illusionist. Maybe he bribed a few people to look the other way."

"Maybe he hypnotised them, he's obviously pretty good at that."

"Anyway, they'll have to be somewhere," said Nightingale. "Did you get anywhere on whether he needed a permit for them?"

"Not so much. Nevada's pretty lax about people owning wild animals, but crocodiles are an exception. It's completely illegal to own one, unless..."

"Unless what?"

"Unless you own a zoo, or the animals are used for entertainment performances. Like Siegfried and Roy's big cats."

"So somebody must have okayed those two monsters?"

"I guess, but I can't find any record of it. Maybe some strings were pulled, and some palms greased. Anyway, nobody's talking. And there's nobody else to ask. Khamsin's gone like he was never here."

"Maybe he's dead," said Nightingale.

"Why would you think that? Same tip-off?"

"Could be. I was told the chances were high that he'd unleashed a force which backfired on him. The question is, what am I meant to do now?"

"Ask Mr Wainwright?"

Nightingale shook his head. "He's been out of touch with me for a while, wanted me to work on my own. I guess I could see if Luca Marino is interested in tracking down Khamsin."

"Do you think he would be?"

"I think he'd be very interested in avenging his son's death, but I don't have any evidence to offer him, just a collection of hints and hunches. Besides, if Khamsin isn't already dead, I can't set him up to be killed unless I know for sure he's guilty of something."

"But he ran."

"Maybe, but that's not evidence. I've been known to run myself, from all kinds of people."

"But come on, Jack, if it is this guy Khamsin, why would he need the money? With his act and reputation he could walk into any venue in the world and write his own cheque for as much and as long as he cares to. Why jeopardise all that to run an extortion racket?"

"I really don't know," said Nightingale, "but I do know that even billionaires never get tired of making yet more money. Or maybe he enjoys the power, the thrill of being able to visit life or death on people Tell you what, when we find him, we'll ask him."

"So what's your plan?"

"Well, currently it's to finish this coffee, thank you for your help, and then, pretty much do nothing. Maybe something will turn up soon, or Wainwright will get back in touch with new instructions."

"Or Khamsin will try to kill you again?"

"Nobody ever said my life was boring."

CHAPTER 72

Camila Martinez walked into Garcia's office, a deep frown on her face announcing bad news before she needed to speak.

"He's gone. Nightingale."

Sergeant Garcia hit his desktop with a closed fist and swore. "What do you mean, gone? Checked out of the Tropicana?"

"No, they say he never checked out, but his bag's gone and his bed wasn't slept in."

"Since when?"

"They don't know, he'd hung the *Do Not Disturb* sign, so it was only when our guys went there that they opened up and noticed. His room's paid for the next ten days. So we can't even get him on running out on the bill. You want an APB on him?"

"On what charge? I was pushing my luck to try to get him down here as a material witness, thought maybe I could sweat something out of him. But flag that name on the computer, I'm very interested in Mr Nightingale's career. If he so much as blows his nose in the USA, I want to hear about it."

"Funny you should say that, there's a report just in from the uniforms. Some hooker took an four-floor dive off a balcony up on North 8th Street No sign she was pushed, no evidence of anyone else in the apartment."

"So?" said Garcia

"They found a witness, old lady walking into the building, said she saw a couple walking out. A woman and a man."

"Could she ID them again?" he asked

"She says not, she didn't really look at their faces. But she said the guy was wearing the scruffiest brown suede shoes she'd ever seen."

"Nightingale."

"Not necessarily,"she said, "there's probably hundreds of guys in town with shitty shoes."

"Sure there are," said Garcia, "but I'd love to know where Nightingale was when the girl took her dive. I want him found."

CHAPTER 73

Wainwright's Gulfstream landed on time and taxied to the far end of the private area. Henderson Airport was some thirteen miles south of the city, but Wainwright preferred to use it, as it was quieter and would attract less attention than the International Airport in the city.

Carol, the blonde South African who was duty hostess that day walked back through the cabin, made sure that her boss had everything he needed, as he unfolded his long legs from the white leather seat. She moved to the forward door, disarmed and opened it and stood aside as Wainwright flashed her a grateful smile and walked down the steps.

"See you tomorrow," he said, with a wave.

Carol watched him head to the waiting white limousine, then turned to start tidying up the plane, ready for its next trip.

Wainwright strolled towards the white Lincoln, swinging his black leather attaché case. He gave a puzzled frown as he neared the car. His driver Daniel usually got out to meet him, take his bag and open the rear door, but this time he'd decided to remain in the driver's seat, though Wainwright couldn't see him through the tinted side glass. The rear door sprung open, and Wainwright leaned in. He felt a sharp prick in his arm, and almost immediately he started to lose control of his limbs, collapsing into the seat. The man inside the car pulled the door shut, arranged Wainwright's body in an upright position, then fastened the seatbelt round him.

"My apologies for the drug, Mr Wainwright, but I doubt that I could have made you succumb to my hypnotic abilities."

He pressed the intercom button on his seat. "Start the car, drive. Turn right outside the main entrance."

In the driver's seat, the black man in the chauffeur's uniform stared straight ahead, his eyes blinking very slowly, hearing only the sound of the voice which gave him his orders.

CHAPTER 74

Nightingale placed a twenty dollar chip on black and watched as the cowgirl croupier spun the wheel, then pushed his stake and winnings back towards him. So far he was a hundred and forty up, and following Lynsey Lawton's system, he'd set himself a limit of stopping when he'd won or lost a hundred dollars. Roulette didn't provide a great deal of excitement, but he was running out of ways to kill time here. He was well-fed and rested, had smoked more cigarettes than normal, and was beginning to wonder whether he should have another Corona.

His cell phone had remained silent, the last number he had for Wainwright didn't work, nor did the number that had sent the 'GAME ON' text. Nobody was taking any interest in him at all, much less trying to kill him. If Khamsin was still in this world, he could be anywhere, and Nightingale didn't have the resources to try tracking him down. Or any instructions to do so. He'd had some success in the past using his pink crystal to find people, but never with someone whose real name he didn't even know. And it's not as if he had anything personal of Khamsim's to work with.

He doubled his stake, put it on red this time and won again. The young blonde woman in the tight blue dress walking past the table took a look at him and his pile of chips and sat down next to him. "Hi, you need a little company, maybe bring you some luck?"

Nightingale took a look at her. Pretty enough, nice figure, probably with a little help from a surgeon. It had been a while since he'd enjoyed female company. Quite a few years in fact, and a few thousand miles away, and it wasn't an experience he liked to think about. Still. this girl probably wasn't drawn by his boyish charm, and the memory of Amber Diamond was still a little too fresh in his mind for him to want to think about hookers.

"It's a kind offer, but I don't think my wife would appreciate it. She's upstairs, and I'm just headed back to the room."

She gave him a cold smile, stood up and walked away, in search of other prey. Nightingale looked at the table, he'd managed to win again, and was now a hundred dollars up. He nodded his thanks to the croupier, slid a twenty dollar chip across to her as a tip, stood up and headed to his room. Maybe there'd be something worthwhile on the TV.

He'd barely had time to find the remote when his cellphone rang, from a number that was new to it. He pressed the green circle, but said nothing.

"Jack?"

"Valerie? This isn't your usual number."

"No, and it's not my usual phone either. Mr Wainwright gave orders that you weren't to be contacted, or to be allowed contact until whatever you're working on is finished."

"Well, it might actually be finished. But it's not like you to ignore the boss's instructions."

"It surely isn't, but this isn't a normal situation, and I don't know what I should do."

"You at a loss? I'd better check the weather forecast, see if Hell really has frozen over."

"You know I'm not fond of your humour at the best of times, and this really isn't a good day for it. Mr Wainwright has disappeared. I think he may have been kidnapped."

"Tell me everything you know."

"Trouble is, I don't know much," said Valerie. "His plane landed at Henderson airport on schedule last night, and he was due to be chauffeured out to his house. I called him to confirm some arrangements this morning, but he didn't answer his cell. I called the driver and he's not answering either."

"Is it Joshua's car, or from a service?"

"It's one of his own. He's often in Las Vegas, so keeps one available."

"Who was the driver?"

228

"His name's Daniel Bergeron. He's been with Mr Wainwright for years. Normally, I'd say he's above suspicion."

"Let's hope you're right. Look, Joshua's only really been out of touch for less than a day. Is it possible he had to change his arrangements and forgot to tell you?"

"I guess anything is possible, but it's unheard of. He runs his life very precisely, if he's meant to be somewhere, you can set your watch by him. On the rare occasions that things have needed to be changed, he always keeps me informed."

"It doesn't sound like him. Have you contacted the police?"

"No."

"Any reason why not?"

"Mr Wainwright tends to conduct his life and business in as much privacy as possible. I don't think he'd thank me for getting the police involved."

"They're the people with the organisation and the resources."

"I'm aware of that, but even so. Can't you do anything?"

"Like what? I'm just one guy with a pair of old shoes, there are probably a million places he could be in Las Vegas, and that's assuming he's still in the city. And besides..."

"Besides what?"

"It's none of my business if Joshua chooses to disappear, and I don't think it's any duty of mine to go looking for him. He did me a huge favour a few years back, and he's been using that as a lever ever since to get me to work for him. It might be that we're just about even now, and I don't need to put my head in a noose for him."

"I see."

"Look, there's no sense in my trying to chase after a wild goose. Chances are he'll show up in a day or so."

"And if he doesn't. How do you plan to eat?"

"What do you mean?"

"Well, in Mr Wainwright's absence, he has given me certain decision-making rights if I should need to use them. I can't invest his money, but I could cancel some of his credit cards. Like the ones you use, for example."

"You wouldn't?"

"Well now, I don't know. It might be the responsible thing to do, to make sure Mr Wainwright's money isn't misused in his absence."

"I believe that's what's known as 'playing hardball', Valerie."

"Except I'm not playing. We need to have him found, and I do remember Mr Wainwright telling me that finding people was a particular skill of yours."

"Alright," said Nightingale. "First let's do it the traditional way. Who was he flying out here to meet?"

"I shouldn't really be telling you this, but he was worried about you so wanted to be close by."

"Why didn't he tell me?"

"I think he wanted to play Guardian angel."

"Well that's clearly not gone as planned."

"Can you find him?"

"I'll try."

"Try hard."

"I will. Look, I'm going to need something personal of his."

'Something personal?"

"A lock of his hair would be best. Or something that he kept with him."

"You're going to use DNA to track him down?"

'Something less scientific. What do you have?"

"I could send you an item of clothing. Or a hairbrush. I'll courier it, you should get it tomorrow."

"If he has being taken by somebody, that might be too late," said Nightingale. "I need it now. Does he have a place in Vegas?"

Valerie didn't answer.

"Valerie? You heard me, right?"

'Mr Wainwright is very concerned about his privacy, you know that. There are many parts of his life that he would prefer was not made public."

"Him and me both," said Nightingale. "But I'm not the one who's gone missing. You need to stop pissing around, Valerie, and tell me what I want to know."

She sighed. "Fine. He has a place in Spanish Hills."

"Spanish Hills?"

"It's what they call a guard-gated enclave, a few miles south west of the city. There are something like twelve hundred homes scattered over a hundred acres and the walls are there to keep the locals out. Unless they're maids or gardeners, of course. Mr Wainwright has one of the largest homes on the estate, but like most of his properties it's owned by an offshore shell company. I'll send you the address but please only go on your own and delete the address from your phone and from your memory once you've visited."

"Not a problem."

"I'll text you the address and tell the housekeeper to expect you. His name's Oscar."

"How much does he know about his boss?"

"Just that he's very rich and very secretive. No idle gossip while you're there."

"My lips will be sealed."

"I'm serious, Nightingale."

"My middle name is Serious," said Nightingale, but she had already ended the call. After a couple of minutes his phone beeped as her message arrived.

CHAPTER 75

Khamsin took a long pull on his hookah pipe and felt the smoke from the hashish soothe and relax him. He touched a small bell on the table next to him, and a door at the far end of the room opened. A tall young man, maybe in his early twenties, stood there, dressed in black Levis and a white shirt.

"Ali, bring the driver to me," said Khamsin.

The young man left the room and reappeared two minutes later, with another man, similarly dressed. Between them stood a tall black man in chauffeur's uniform, his wrists handcuffed behind his back, his eyes staring ahead, unfocused.

Khamsin laid down the mouthpiece of his pipe, stood up from his divan and gazed into the sightless eyes.

"I shall count backwards from three," he said."When I click my fingers, you will awaken, with the full knowledge of who you are. You will remember everything. Until you fell asleep in the car. Three, two, one."

The driver shook his head and focused his eyes on what stood in front of him. It made no sense.

"What? Who..."

Khamsin held up a hand to silence him. "What is your name?"

"Daniel."

"And for how long have you worked for Joshua Wainwright?"

"Seven years. Going on eight." He looked fearfully around the room. "What is this? What's happening?"

"I have awoken you only so that you may appreciate what will happen to you. Also, it will be more stimulating for me that you have full consciousness."

The driver looked helplessly around, and strained at the handcuffs, but the two men held him firmly, just above the elbows.

"I bear you no ill-will, but it is necessary to dispose of you. Outside this house, there is a deep pool. It contains two Nile Crocodiles. They have not been fed for several days. I propose to watch them kill and devour you."

"What the fuck? Is this some sick joke?"

"I am not much given to humour, Daniel. Ali, you and Salman take him to the edge of the pool. Please place a divan and my hookah on the balcony, where I shall have a good view of my friends enjoying their lunch. Ah, but first, a little blood, I think."

He drew a curved dagger from his robe, and ran its edge around the driver's arm and his upper thigh. Daniel squealed in pain. Blood started to ooze out through the uniform.

"Excellent. Let us begin."

CHAPTER 76

Nightingale took a cab from outside his hotel. The driver's name was Mykola. He was Ukrainian and had arrived in the country a few months after Putin had invaded his, along with his wife, three children, and his elderly mother. He was in his forties and wore a leather waistcoat over a Bon Jovi t-shirt and had a picture of his family stuck on the dashboard of his Prius. Nightingale wasn't in the mood for conversation and he pretended to study the screen of his phone as he sat in the back, but that didn't deter Mykola. The Ukrainian had opinions on everything and seemed keen to express them to Nightingale, punctuated with glances in his rear-view mirror and "am I right?"

Nightingale just nodded and grunted and that seemed to satisfy Mykola, and he didn't stop talking until they arrived at the gates of Spanish Hills. The barrier stayed down and a broad-shouldered Latino wearing a Spanish Hills t-shirt and black trousers walked up to the car. Mykola wound the window down. "Uber," he said.

The guard peered at Nightingale. "Jack Nightingale," he said. "Here to see Joshua Wainwright."

The guard smiled and nodded. "Let me check," he said, and walked back to the guardhouse.

"Like Russia," said Mykola. "Papers, papers, show me your papers."

"I think the residents pay for privacy," said Nightingale.

"The rich always want the poor to be kept at a distance," said Mykola.

"That is certainly true."

The guard returned, carrying a clipboard. This time he walked to Nightingale's window he wound it down. "Can I see some ID, Mr Nightingale?"

"Sure," said Nightingale. He fished his driving licence out of his wallet. It was one of four that Wainwright had given him, and luckily it was in his own name. The guard took it, wrote down the details and handed it back. "Have you been here before, Mr Nightingale?"

"No, I haven't."

The guard smiled, flashing two gold teeth at the front of his mouth. He scribbled on his clipboard and handed over a printed map of the estate with a plot circled. "First left and then second right," said the guard.

Nightingale thanked him. The guard gave the driver a plastic card and told him to keep it displayed while they were on the estate.

"Bloody Russia," growled Mykola.

"Say what?" said the guard, but Mykola ignored him and wound the window up.

Mykola followed the map and two minutes later they pulled up in front of a huge brick mansion with towering chimneys which presumably were never used. There was a garage at the side with parking for three cars, and a fountain with three entwined dolphins spouting water into the air. Nightingale asked Mykola to wait for him, then he let himself out of the door and walked over to the front door. He pressed a brass button and half a minute later a large black man with a shaved head and a large diamond stud in his left ear opened the door. He was wearing a black suit and a black tie.

"Oscar?" he said, though the man looked nothing like a housekeeper.

"Nightingale?"

Nightingale nodded. "That's me."

Oscar made no move to open the door wider and he stared impassively at Nightingale. "So, Valerie gave me some ground rules."

"Okay."

"I'm to go wherever you go, and I'm to take a picture of anything you touch."

'That's fine."

"And you're not to ask me any questions."

"Not one?'

Oscar shook his head. "Not one."

Nightingale grinned. "See what I did there?"

Oscar's eyes hardened. "No questions."

"Got it."

Oscar stared at him for several seconds, then opened the door. Nightingale stepped into a hall of dazzlingly white marble. A marble staircase curved up around a huge brass and glass chandelier. Oscar closed the door and stood with his arms folded across his barrel-like chest.

"Right, I get the whole 'no questions' thing but I'm going to need your help here," said Nightingale. "I need something intimately connected to Mr Wainwright. Something that means a lot to him, something he would touch often. A favourite piece of clothing would be good, providing it hasn't been washed. A scarf would be good. Or gloves."

"This is Nevada. Not much scarf wearing here. Or gloves."

"Yes, right. Obviously. A watch would work, if he wore it a lot. And the longer he had it, the better."

"Mr Wainwright doesn't keep any watches here."

"Okay."

Oscar frowned. "He has a cigar cutter he always uses."

"Has he had it a long time?"

"I've worked for him for going on six years and he's always had it."

"Sounds perfect," said Nightingale. "Show it to me and I'll get out of your hair." He grinned. "No offence."

Oscar grunted, unfolded his arms and turned and walked down a hallway to an oak door. He opened it and Nightingale followed him into a large study with French windows overlooking a manicured lawn. The walls were lined with books, there were two leather winged

236

armchairs either side of an old oak chest, and a large mahogany desk. Oscar walked over to the desk and reached out a hand. "Please don't touch it," said Nightingale and Oscar pulled back his hand. "Inside the cigar box," he growled.

Nightingale went over to the box. It was a humidor, two feet long and a foot wide, made from a black wood that had been polished to a shine and inlaid with mother of pearl to form a series of Satanic sigils. He looked over at Oscar. Did he understand the significance of the sigils or did he just assume they were for decoration? Nightingale took a quick look at the books on the shelves behind the desk. He knew that Wainwright had one of the largest collections of occult and Satanic literature in the world, but all books he saw were on art and antiques, biographies of political and business leaders, science and religion. So far as he could see, there were no volumes concerning the dark arts. Presumably he had them stored elsewhere, maybe not even in Vegas. He opened the box. Inside were several dozen large cigars, and in a small square wooden section there was a gold cigar cutter. He couldn't tell by looking at it if it was solid gold or gold-plated, but it was clearly beautifully made and obviously an antique.

He took a hotel napkin from his pocket and used it to pick up the cutter.

"Hold it right there," growled Oscar. He fished a smartphone from his pocket. "Hold it out so I can get a picture."

Nightingale held out his hand and Oscar took his picture and then nodded. "Good to go."

Nightingale carefully wrapped the cutter in the napkin. The less physical contact he had with it, the better. He slipped it into his pocket and smiled at Oscar. "Right, that's all I need. Pleasure doing business with you."

Oscar escorted Nightingale to the front door and opened it. "Valerie said to remind you to delete the address from your phone."

"And from my memory. Yeah."

Oscar stared intently at Nightingale until he realised what was expected of him and he took out his phone. Oscar watched as Nightingale deleted the message. "Did the guard give you a map?"

"He did."

Oscar held out his hand and Nightingale gave it to him. "You came in a cab?"

"I assume that's rhetorical because you can see that it's a cab, right? I'm not a fan of driving in the States, for some reason they put the steering wheel on the wrong side."

"If he ever comes back, it's on you," Oscar growled, and shut the door.

Nightingale walked to the taxi and climbed in to the back. "How much do you think the houses cost here?" asked Mykola.

Nightingale shrugged. "I dunno. Millions."

'Two million? Three?"

"Yeah. About that."

"It looks like a luxury prison camp." A golf cart drove slowly by. Two heavily-set men in Spanish Hills t-shirts looked over in their direction. The passenger looked at a clipboard and nodded and the golf cart picked up speed.

"People are happy to pay for security," said Nightingale. "It's America, there are some very dangerous people out there."

"They are paying to be in prison," said Mykola. "Who does that?"

"People who are frightened," said Nightingale. "Hey, can I smoke?"

"Of course you can smoke," said Mykola. "My cab is not a prison. You want me to take you back to the hotel?"

"No, I need you to drop me somewhere else." Nightingale gave him the address.

CHAPTER 77

Nightingale lit a cigarette and watched as Mykola drove away. Nightingale had tipped him handsomely and Mykola had insisted on shaking him by the hand. Nightingale waited until the cab had disappeared into the distance before walking back to the *Crystal Village* shop. He'd picked Mykola at random and he doubted that the Ukrainian had any interest in Nightingale or what he was doing, but it made sense to take basic precautions. He'd avoided one attack but that didn't mean there wouldn't be another, and with Wainwright out of the picture he had no safety net.

Judy was serving two young Goth girls, one of whom was the spitting image of Proserpine and he did a double take when he first saw her. Black motorcycle jacket with a studded pentagram on the back, tight black leggings and high-heeled thigh length boots, her jet black hair was spiky and she had multiple piercings in her ears. She caught him staring at her and she sneered, revealing yellowing teeth and she stuck out her tongue. Nightingale grinned. It was the eyes that gave her away. She had the nervous eyes of a teenage girl playing at being a Goth, whereas Proserpine's eyes were blank, featureless pools of black tar. Nightingale met her stare and after a few seconds she looked away.

The two Goths were buying black candles, seasoned parchment and a number of other items that suggested that the two girls were preparing to cast a Bluen's Satanic death spell. They had almost certainly found the spell on the internet, it was widely known, and as useful as a chocolate teapot. It required a Satanic Bible, which apparently Judy didn't sell, but the Goths had probably already ordered a copy from Amazon. It was a simple enough spell, which is why it was inherently useless. You took a poppet - effectively a simple voodoo doll - and stuffed it with something personal from the victim, ideally nail clippings or hair. The internet said that paper could be used instead of a poppet, all you needed to do was to write down the name of the victim on the paper, or parchment, and say a few words to Satan. Then you divided the poppet- or the paper - into four pieces.

One piece is burned in the flame of a black candle, the second is thrown into a river or the sea, the third is buried in the ground, and the fourth was burned into powder ash and thrown into the air.

It was nonsense, and no serious Satanist would go near the spell. It was the sort of thing that teenagers would get involved with, like playing with an Ouija board. But like Ouija boards, in the wrong hands the spell could turn nasty. The spell itself was useless, but it could act as a flare in the underworld, attracting the attention of a demon from Hell, and that's when amateurs like the two Goth girls could find themselves in big trouble.

If Judy had any inkling as to what the young girls were thinking of doing, she showed no sign of it. Maybe she didn't know. The Bluen's Satanic death spell was from the left path and Judy had made it clear she wanted nothing to do with that.

The girls completed their purchases and left. The girl stuck her tongue out at Nightingale and he grinned. "Stay lucky," he said.

"Eat shit and die," she said, then spoiled the effect by giggling as she followed her companion out of the door.

Nightingale went over to the counter. "And how are you today. Jack?" Judy asked.

"All good. I just need a few things." He knew by heart what he wanted and she had everything in stock. If she knew what he wanted it for, she didn't say.

He paid her in cash and she put everything in a carrier bag with the name of the store on the side. He caught a cab outside the shop and had it take him to his hotel.

He placed his purchases on the bed and phoned Lynsey Lawton. He could do everything on his own but two sets of eyes were always better than one. "Where are you?" he asked.

"I'm about to eat," she said.

"I need your help with something."

"And I need to eat," she said. "I'm in Señor Frog's in the Treasure Island hotel. Any cab will get you here in few minutes."

Nightingale took a cab to the hotel, which looked nothing like an island, consisting of a huge, three-pronged terracotta tower. There were, admittedly a couple of old wooden ships outside, but they looked a little incongruous against the modern architecture.

Señor Frog's had absolutely nothing to do with pirates or treasure, it was a vibrant Mexican restaurant. The place was a riot of colour, with the wooden tables and chairs painted bright green in contrast with the bright orange walls. Giant video screens playing loud music hung at regular intervals round the room and waitresses in skimpy tops juggled large trays of food and drinks.

Nightingale found Lynsey's table and sat down opposite her. She was wearing a blue and white striped top and white jeans and her dark hair was loose around her shoulders.

"So what can I get you?" said the waitress. She was young, blonde, probably a college student, and her name badge said Laura.

Nightingale looked at Lynsey.

"You're the home team," said Nightingale, "what do you recommend? But remember, I've only got a European size appetite."

You ever eaten Mexican before?" asked Lynsey.

"Yeah, whatever you order, it tastes the same, it's just..."

"...folded differently," she said, finishing the old joke "How about we share some wings and poppers, then maybe Mango Tropical Mahi-Mahi?"

"Mahi what?"

"It's fish."

"Fine with me."

"What would you like to drink," asked Laura. "I can recommend our special Yard of Beer."

Nightingale shook his head. "I can't touch alcohol. And I'd rather you didn't."

"Why?"

"I'll explain later." He looked at the waitress. "Coffee. Black. And iced water."

"I'll have a virgin mojito," said Lynsey. "Easy on the virgin."

The waitress laughed but Nightingale shook his head. "Seriously, no alcohol," he said.

"Have those up for you in just a minute," said Laura, as she headed off to place the order.

"So what do you need me for?" asked Lynsey. "I'm guessing the no alcohol means I have to drive you somewhere?"

'When was the last time you spoke to Joshua?"

She shrugged. "Day before yesterday. It's not as if I'm spying on you, I'm just to offer you what help I can."

"He's been kidnapped. Hopefully."

"Hopefully?"

"He got off his plane in Vegas and hasn't been seen since. Valerie is assuming he's been kidnapped. Better kidnapped than dead, right?"

"Valerie?"

Nightingale frowned. "His assistant. Valerie. You don't deal with her?"

"I always call Joshua direct and he calls me."

"Well aren't you the special one?"

"So are you going to call the cops? If Wainwright has been kidnapped, they have experts. Maybe talk to the FBI?"

"The cops and the Feds can't help us, trust me on that score."

"So what are you going to do? You need me to drive you someplace?"

Nightingale shook his head. "No, I need you to come to my hotel room."

She patted her chest. "Why Mr Nightingale, I barely know you."

"It's important. It might be our only chance of finding Joshua."

The drinks and starters arrived very quickly.

"So what are these poppers?" asked Nightingale, looking at his plate.

"Jalapeño peppers, stuffed with cream cheese, breaded and deep fried. You look like a guy who can stand the heat."

Nightingale took a bite of one and nodded his approval.

"Why are we eating and not looking for him right now?" Lynsey asked.

"What I need to do works better on a full stomach, I kid you not."

"And whatever you've got planned, you're sure it'll work?"

Nightingale nodded. "Fairly sure."

"He might be dead already."

Nightingale shook his head. "If they'd wanted him dead, they could just have shot him at the airfield."

"And you think it was this Khamsin guy, and that he also killed those people?"

"Everything points that way."

"But how? He was nowhere near those people when they died."

Nightingale sighed. The time always came in any of his investigations when he had to share what he knew with someone who had no experience of his world, to try to make them believe, ideally without them thinking he was insane. "Khamsin has some system for killing people from a distance and he's hiring himself out. He's killing for money."

"But how does he do it?"

"Lynsey, do you believe in witchcraft? Satanism? The Left-hand path? Voodoo?"

"What? No, of course not. That stuff went out of style centuries ago. Nobody believes that any more." She laughed and shook her head. "Khamsin's show is just a show. Like David Copperfield or Penn and Teller."

"No, magic is still used today, the right-hand path and the left-hand path, and it's as strong as ever. That's what Khamsin is using, an Ancient Egyptian curse that sends a demon to destroy its target."

Lynsey shook her head scornfully. "You quite sure that's just tobacco you've been smoking all these years?"

"I can't say I blame you for feeling doubtful."

"Doubtful? It's TV show stuff."

Nightingale paused, and wondered how he might have felt about the idea a few years ago, back in England, before any of this had happened, back when he was a Police Inspector, believing just the evidence of his own senses, who had never heard of demons, satanists and soul selling. He might have reacted just like Lynsey now. "I know, it's hard to believe, but how else could you explain it?"

"Some kind of poison? Electric shocks down the telephone? Radiation? High frequency sound? Something with a scientific basis. Anything but witchcraft."

They finished their poppers and Laura arrived with their fish. Nightingale wolfed down his food. He was hungry but he knew that the sooner he started looking for Wainwright, the better. Lynsey picked up on his unease and ate quickly.

"Here's what I don't understand," said Lynsey. "If this Khamsin character is the top killer you claim, how come he failed with you?"

"I'm just lucky, I suppose."

"When we were in the Mob Museum, you said you were attacked. Like a seizure, you said."

"Something like that." He waved at Laura the waitress and mouthed "check please."

"So far as we know, everyone that Khamsin targeted ended up dead."

"Well, we only know about the ones where the victim died."

"But you didn't die," said Lynsey.

"Well, obviously."

She shook her head. "Come on now, I'm not buying that, there's got to be more to it . You wearing body armour or something?"

"Let's just say I had protection," said Nightingale.

"What kind of protection?"

"The kind I'm not meant to talk about. Not even to you, I'm afraid."

"Man of mystery."

Nightingale shrugged. "How much do you know about Joshua?"

"I've worked for him for a few years now."

"He's a closed book to most people."

She nodded. "Yeah, I get what you mean. But this isn't about him, is it? It's about you."

"Joshua brought me in on this. And he arranged for Khamsin to attack me."

Lynsey sat back in her seat. "Why would he do that?"

"I was bait. If he attacked me, we stood a good chance of finding out how he was doing it."

"And how did that work out?"

"Not great."

"But if you knew that Khamsin was going to attack you, you must have had something in mind, something that would protect you."

Nightingale grinned. "I had a hunch I'd be okay."

"You risked your life on a hunch?" She shook her head. "I'm sorry, I'm not buying that."

Laura returned with their bill. "I'm not selling it, but I'll pick up the check."

"Damn right you will."

CHAPTER 78

Everything was prepared. Khamsin's divan and hookah had been brought out onto the balcony, which commanded a view of the pool. It was an irregular kidney shape, with an island of concrete topped with earth in the middle. Trees and fresh-water plants grew there and provided shelter from the desert sun. The water was not chlorinated nor regularly cleaned, so had grown dark and muddy. The level of the water was kept well below the edges of the pool, so there would be no danger of the occupants climbing out. A few logs and what looked like logs floated in the water.

The man in the chauffeur's uniform lay by the side of the pool, where he had been placed. The handcuffs had been removed, but his hands and feet were now tied together with strong rope to prevent him moving or struggling. His uniform was matted with blood from the shallow cuts on his arm and leg. The two men in black jeans and shirts stood next to him, but their eyes were on the balcony, awaiting instructions.

Khamsin appeared through the door of the balcony, arranged himself on the divan, and put the tube of his hookah in his mouth. He closed his eyes and inhaled deeply, then opened his eyes and surveyed the scene in front of him. He clicked his fingers, and the two men by the pool sprung to attention.

"Such a spectacle requires a larger audience. Bring him."

The two men walked off in the direction of the old mine, and reappeared five minutes later, pushing a third man between them. His hands were cuffed, and the man called Ali held a shortened broom handle in the crook of the prisoner's elbow, twisting his arm and shoulder, and compelling him to keep moving forward. The three entered the door of the hotel, and arrived on the balcony. The prisoner was put to sit on a wooden chair, his arms handcuffed behind him and to the chair back.

"We can dispense with the gag for a while, I think."

Salman unfastened the straps of the ball gag from the prisoner's mouth, and the two servants returned to the poolside.

"You may now speak, though choose your words carefully. I have heard your voice can be very persuasive, but your skills would be wasted on me. My associates do not have my experience or strength of will, so it was important to protect them."

"The fuck are you and what do you want?"

"I am known as Khamsin, Mr Wainwright, the desert wind. As to what I want, at the moment, I want you to sit quietly and watch the entertainment."

"What entertainment?"

Khamsin stretched out his arm and pointed.

Wainwright's jaw dropped. "What have you done to Daniel?"

"Very little so far, some superficial cuts. My friends in the pool will see to the rest."

"Stop it, " shouted Wainwright "He's just a driver. This has nothing to do with him. Cut him loose. Just tell me what you want."

"You have nothing at all that I could possibly want, Mr Wainwright. I have quite enough money, and many ways of making more. Women can be had for the asking. Your possessions do not interest me. There is nothing you can offer that will deflect me from my chosen course. This man will die because it is expedient, and it will amuse me. Soon, I expect you to follow him."

Wainwright sneered at him. "I'm not afraid of death, I've been prepared for it for many years. But what good will it do you?"

"At the moment, you are but a tethered goat, which I plan to use to catch more important prey. I killed a man at your behest, and yet he still lives. "

"What are you talking about? If you killed him, he must be dead."

"So one would think, And yet he lives. My work is vital, but it cannot continue until I know why, and know that he is really dead."

"And what is your work?"

"Probably the same as yours, Mr Wainwright. The acquisition and use of power."

"That's not what I do."

"Ah, but it is. I have learned a good deal about you in the past few days. You have ridden your luck well and profited from it. You seek to increase your power with more and more knowledge, yes, I know of your book collection. You seek to increase your financial power with your endless stock market dealings. You seek to ensure that others have the use of their power stripped from them by the use of your catspaws, especially the dead man who lives."

"I don't just seek power for its own sake."

"Oh, you do, Mr Wainwright. As do I. We are two faces of the same coin. My methods are just a little more...direct."

Khamsin took another deep draw on his hookah. "But enough of philosophy. It is poor manners to keep a guest waiting." he raised his hand to the two men at the pool. "Proceed."

The men picked up the chauffeur by his shoulders and feet, and swung him into the pool. He landed on his back, creating a heavy splash, and the floating logs started to move nearer him. The water towards the edge of the pool was not deep, and he was able to stand up, the water level reaching just to his chest. He looked up helplessly at the rim of the pool, too far out of reach to permit escape. He looked further up at the balcony, his eyes pleading.

"Mr Wainwright, Sir. Help me. Please."

Wainwright shook his head frantically. "Get him out of there. Get him out. I'll pay anything you ask."

Khamsin smiled. "Nothing you could offer could buy my sense of triumph. The knowledge that you are powerless to help him, while I hold his life in the palm of my hand is an exquisite pleasure."

Wainwright gazed in horror as the twin logs moved ever closer. He could now see the greedy green eyes as they sensed their meal. The larger crocodile opened its jaws to strike, and Khamsin sprung to his feet, his right arm extended, pointing with his curved ivory wand. "Uaf!"

Both crocodiles stopped as if paralysed by the sound of his voice, the larger one with its jaws still wide open.

"Such is my power, Mr Wainwright. Can you match it? By word or deed, can you save this man? Can you? If you can, just speak the word and save him."

"Stop it. Just stop it."

"Hah, you see, you do not have the power. But what is power, unless one uses it?"

Khamsin lowered his wand. "Olfi."

The crocodiles sped forward, the awful jaws snapped shut, there was an appalling scream, the water boiled, bubbled and turned red. Daniel Burgeron disappeared beneath the water, as the two reptiles tore him apart between them.

Wainwright looked down at the ground and tried to blot out the awful sounds.

CHAPTER 79

Nightingale and Lynsey took a cab back to the Apache Hotel. He took her across the reception area to the stairs. "What is it with you and elevators?" she asked.

"I'm not a fan," said Nightingale. "And it's good exercise."

"So you never use elevators?"

"Not unless I have to."

"You are a very strange man, Jack Nightingale."

"You're not the first person to say that. Don't worry, we're on the third floor. Actually, it's the fourth floor for you."

"What?"

'We Brits call the ground floor the ground floor, because it is. You call it the first floor, which it really isn't. So our first floor is your second floor, and so on."

"Are you sure about that?"

"I'm British. I'm sure."

They went up the stairs and along the corridor to Nightingale's room. Nightingale headed to the bathroom. He stripped off his clothes, showered, and used a nailbrush to thoroughly clean his hands and feet. He washed his hair twice, brushed and flossed his teeth, then pulled on a towelling robe. Perfect cleanliness wasn't quite as important here as if he'd been summoning a demon, but it was always best to avoid impurities

Lynsey was examining his purchases when he walked into the bedroom. She raised her eyebrows. "Please don't tell me you're going to go Harvey Weinstein on me," she said.

"Cleanliness is next to Godliness, so they say."

Lynsey gestured at the carrier bag. "What are you planning to do with this?" she said.

"You'll see, soon enough," said Nightingale.

"And why do you need me?"

"A second pair of eyes," he said. "All you have to do is to sit quietly in that chair, and concentrate on the crystal ball. If you see anything in it, anything at all, don't make a noise, just try to figure out what you're seeing, and tell me about it afterwards. Can you do that?"

"Sure, why not? And afterwards, maybe we'll talk again about calling in the police."

Nightingale pointed at an armchair by the window. "Sit."

"Woof," she said, then did as she was told.

Nightingale stood in the middle of the room and started breathing slowly and evenly. It was a ritual he had performed before, but it was important not to overlook anything. Time was of the essence in cases of disappearance or abduction, but a stupid mistake now could render the whole process useless.

He lit the two small blue candles that stood on either side of the solid crystal ball in the middle of the coffee table. He was thankful that he didn't have to try to draw a pentagram on the faded hotel carpet.

He sprinkled herbs from a brass bowl into the flame of each candle, and they burned with blue smoke. He made a small pile of lemon twigs in the bowl, then placed the cigar cutter on it. Nightingale spoke three sentences in a long-dead language. He had learned them by heart years ago in Mrs Steadman's shop, when she had given him the crystal and instructed him in its use. He had no idea what they might mean, but they had always worked for this ritual. Nightingale lit the lemon twigs with his lighter, watching as the flames burned all round the cigar case, without seeming to harm it at all.

Nightingale picked up the brown, leather bag, untied its lace, then took out the pink crystal, the size of a pigeon's egg, which he held by the chain attached to the gold mounting at one end. He lowered it gently, until it was hanging just six inches above the flames. The pink crystal began to glow, as if there were a strong light inside it, almost as if it were a living thing. Nightingale spoke again in the same ancient language. *'Asmla oscsub ascihc odsidrept Joshua Wainwright. Asmla*

251

oscsub ascsihc odsidrept Joshua Wainwright. Asmla oscsub ascsihc odsidrept Joshua Wainwright.'

Nightingale concentrated on projecting an aura of blue light around himself, and on visualising the young Texan billionaire.

The crystal started to swing round slowly, then moved backwards and forwards regularly, towards the south-west;

'Asmla oscsub ascihc odsidrept Joshua Wainwright. Asmla oscsub ascsihc odsidrept Joshua Wainwright. Asmla oscsub ascsihc odsidrept Joshua Wainwright.'

The crystal ball on the table clouded over with a pink mist and Nightingale repeated the incantation for the final time.

The Spell Of Propinquity was complete, and he watched intently as the spell forged a link between the case and its missing owner. The pink stone started to spin on its chain. The mist in the crystal ball began to clear, and wooden buildings came into view. The vision grew still clearer, and Nightingale could pick out the ruins and broken roofs of several buildings, behind them a high red hill, obviously in a desert area somewhere. On the battered, corrugated roof of one of the larger buildings, he could read the wooden sign *Madingly Mining Company*. Further along the street, another large, dilapidated wooden building bore the sign *Hotel*. There were no people, cars, not even horses. It looked like a deserted film set from a Western, but, wherever it was, he felt certain he'd find Joshua Wainwright there.

CHAPTER 80

Khamsin's cell phone buzzed, and he looked at it in irritation. Very few people knew this number, even fewer would dare to ring it. He pressed the green button.

"It is I," announced Major General Mustafa.

"What do you want?"

"You have left Las Vegas?"

"I have. My engagement was finished, there was no reason for me to stay so I am en route to a more permanent home, but at the moment. I am in temporary accommodation, until a small problem is resolved."

"But the President must die in just a few days."

Khamsin sighed. He was not about to confess that he dare not unleash the Messenger of Anubis again until he knew for sure what had caused the failure last time. A few days still remained. "The President will die, as arranged," said Khamsin, "of that you may be sure."

"I hope so. As you know, I have every confidence in you, but some of the Brothers are nervous. What is your present location?"

"It is not necessary for you to know, there is no reason for us to meet again and I value my security. Rest assured, all will proceed as arranged."

"Khamsin, I am concerned by this, I..."

But Khamsin had cut the connection.

CHAPTER 81

The crystal ball had clouded over again, the pink stone hung motionless on its chain. Nightingale snuffed out the candles, poured water on the burning herbs, and lit a cigarette.

"I'll take one of those," said Lynsey. "I guess it must be eleven pm somewhere in the world, and my nerves are shot after that."

He lit it for her, and she took a deep drag. "I've never seen anything like that. What are you, Jack the Vampire Slayer or something, some kind of a magician? Or is it some kind of internet thing?"

"Not really. With a crystal of your own and a few hours of practice, you could do the same. It's a natural force, all you have to do is know how to tune into it. So you saw the image too?"

"I saw something. An old Western town. Like something from a movie. Looked like Clint Eastwood might ride through it any minute."

"Did you recognise it?" asked Nightingale.

"It's nowhere I've ever been. Looked pretty deserted. What was the name of the building we saw?"

"*Madingly Mining Company* wasn't it? Didn't look like a coal mine.

"Too small, and anyway there's no coal worth mining in Nevada, never has been. Far more likely to be gold or silver."

"Really? I thought the gold rush was in California."

"It was, mostly," she said, "but there's plenty of precious metal in Nevada too. Didn't you know it was called the Silver State since its foundation?"

"I'm not from around these parts," said Nightingale.

"You don't say. Let's try tracking this place down."

"How do you plan to do that?"

"Well, let's start with ghost towns near here. There are probably plenty of them. The only one I know of is Calico, just over the border in California. It's set up as a tourist attraction these days, with a campsite and a saloon. Lots of restaurants, you can pan for gold, there's even a little train to ride round in. It's pretty popular."

Nightingale shook his head. "Sounds more like a theme park than an abandoned town. He won't be in a tourist trap. The place in the crystal looked as if nobody had been there in years."

"Let me do some research," she said. She opened her bag, took out a tablet and switched it on.

"Do you need the WiFi password?"

"No, I'm using my phone as a hotspot. I could do this on the phone, but the display's bigger. Let me Google that mining company. *Madingly* wasn't it?" She looked at her tablet and frowned. "Well, there's nothing on Wikipedia."

"What is it with you and Wikipedia? Most of what's on there is written by PR companies or people with axes to grind."

"It's good for the basics," she said. "But if it upsets you that much I'll type a description into Google. Abandoned silver mine, Nevada, ghost town. Oh."

"What?"

"More than six million results."

"Can't you narrow it down?"

"If I type in *Madingly Mining*, I get no results at all. If there's a photo, maybe it's not labeled that way. We'd just have to look through them all."

"Do we have an option?" asked Nightingale.

She shook her head, and started to scroll through the photos. Neither of them was counting, but it was probably a couple of hundred shots later when they both jabbed their finger at the screen together.

"That's the place," said Nightingale. "Different angle, different time of day, but there's the sign. Where's the photograph from?"

Lynsey squinted at the screen. "Taken from some guy's Facebook page, about ten years ago. Tom Langley. He was hiking round there, God knows why."

"Does this place have a name?"

"Medicine Bend," he says. "Abandoned silver mining town. Lots of ghosts here, kind of creepy.'"

"How do I get there?"

She tapped a few more keys on the tablet. "According to Google Maps, we drive about ninety miles south-east of here, out into the middle of nowhere and turn left. You plan on heading out there?"

"Right away."

She nodded. Opened her purse again, took out a small handgun and held it out to him.

Nightingale frowned. "What's that for?"

"I thought maybe you could just shoot yourself now, and save time."

"Why?"

"You seriously plan on driving out into the desert to ask politely if these guys will hand Joshua Wainwright back to you?"

Nightingale grinned. "You're forgetting, I'm a trained negotiator, I can be very persuasive."

"My ass. You'll be dead before you even see Wainwright. And this is all assuming that your Harry Potter stuff actually works."

"Oh, it works. That's where Wainwright is."

"Alive?"

"As of an hour ago, yes. The crystal won't find dead people."

"And you won't call the police? They come out in numbers for a kidnapping, with lots of big guns."

"And what do I tell them? Wainwright seems to have gone missing, but I burnt some incense and saw his hiding place in my crystal ball. Can you see the LVPD turning out in force for that? You don't really believe it, and you saw it with your own eyes."

"So it's just the two of us."

Nightingale shook his head. "No, Lynsey, it's just the one of me. Joshua asked you to help me with information and local knowledge. You've done that. From here on, I work alone"

"Not a chance in Hell. You need me."

"What for?"

"Navigation. Advice. Firepower."

"I could get a gun."

"Could you pass a Nevada background check?"

Nightingale paused. His various IDs from Wainwright had got him through most situations in the USA so far, but he wasn't sure if they would he good enough to get him a gun permit. "Maybe."

"But it's more delay," she said. "And I already have what you'll need. And I have an SUV and your no alcohol policy means that I'm ready to drive."

"No, Lynsey. I'm going alone, it's no..." he bit off the sentence.

"You say 'It's no job for a woman,' and I'll shoot you myself. I'm coming with you."

Nightingale sighed, then gestured at the gun. "Where did you get that from?"

"I'm a Nevada girl. I've got guns."

"Guns plural?"

"Hell yeah. So why don't you get dressed and I'll head off and get what we need to go into the desert. I'll be back here within the hour."

Nightingale looked at her for several seconds, then nodded. "Okay."

She grinned. "You know it makes sense."

CHAPTER 82

Lynsey was back at the Apache within forty-five minutes. She called Nightingale's mobile and he met her in front of the hotel, wearing jeans and a denim shirt. She was at the wheel of a black Jeep Wrangler. She sneered at his Hush Puppies as he climbed in to the passenger seat. "Are they the only shoes you have?" she asked scornfully.

"They're comfortable."

She gestured at the hiking boots that she was wearing. "Comfort might not cut it out where we're going," she said. She gestured at the GPS on the dashboard. "I've programmed in our destination, so we're good to go." She pulled away from the kerb. "The GPS is telling me we'll be arriving in ninety-eight minutes, but I trust GPS the same way you trust Wikipedia."

Nightingale settled back. He looked over his shoulder at a large black nylon holdall on the back seat. "Supplies?"

"Comprehensive first-aid kit, water, energy bars, flashlights, two handguns, both Glocks, hunting knives, an AR-15 and lots of ammunition."

"Is it still legal to own an AR-15? Aren't they what the guy used in that hotel shooting?"

"The Mandalay Bay massacre? I think they were AR-15s, yeah. Sixty dead, four hundred injured."

"But you can still just go into a store and buy them?"

"Yup. Though they did ban bump stocks after that. But we still have the right to bear arms."

"Bump stock? What's a bump stock?"

"They were stocks that helped rapid fire by bumping the trigger against the shooter's finger so that they didn't have to pull the trigger. They were designed mainly for AR-15s and AKs. You could fire between 400 and 800 rounds a minute, depending on the gun. You could get one for as little as a hundred bucks, but, like I said, they're banned now. So what's the plan, Stan? You just going to drive straight into town, horn blasting and calling Wainwright's name?"

"Not exactly,"said Nightingale. "Ideally, I'd have wanted to take a look at the place from the air first, but I can't see a way to do that."

"It's not impossible, though it's way off the route for tourist trips in planes or helicopters. You could probably have chartered an aircraft. Or maybe even hire a drone with a camera."

"Might as well put up a big sign saying 'We're Coming' and have done with it," said Nightingale. "It's so far off the beaten track that anything like that would attract way too much attention."

"You don't think they'll be expecting company?"

"We'd be dead very quickly if we assumed that. They've got to know Wainwright is important, it just depends how much they know about his connections. If they're in the same line as me and him, they'll know all about finding people with crystals. He'll assume that's what I did."

"But look," she said, "if it is this guy from the Luxor, and it seems you've got no hard evidence, then he's just a stage magician. He can't just wave a magic wand and spirit Wainwright away."

"You'd think not, but he does leave a trail of unexplained happenings behind him."

"Well, let's see him explain his way out of a few bullets."

"See now," said Nightingale. "That's what we need to avoid. We don't know how many people are there, if they're well armed or not. We go in with blazing guns, we may find ourselves badly outnumbered. And we don't want the wrong people getting shot."

"We've both had firearms training."

"Yes, but neither of us was trained for a war. Let's take it all very slowly, and keep the gunplay to a minimum."

She took her right hand off the steering wheel, and gave him a mock salute. "Aye, aye, Sir."

"And keep both hands on the wheel. Two o'clock and ten o'clock."

259

She did as she was told. "A lot of things in the world worry you, don't they?" she asked.

"There's a lot to worry about. Okay if I smoke?"

"Go ahead. And light one for me."

"What about your rule about only smoking after eleven pm?"

"I think we're well past the stage of worrying about rules, Jack."

CHAPTER 83

"You should drink some water, Wainwright," said Khamsin. "You need to stay hydrated."

"Fuck you," snarled Wainwright. He was handcuffed to the wooden chair still, but Khamsin's assistants had dragged it inside from the balcony.

"If you continue to use language like that, I will put the ball gag back in. What about some food? We need to keep your energy levels up."

"You really think I could eat after watching what you did to Daniel?"

"I suspect you have seen far worse in your time. No matter, you're unlikely to have enough time left to starve to death. But drink some water."

"Why did you do that? Are you insane? He was just a driver. And you fed him to crocodiles."

Khamsin shrugged. "You wanted to interfere with my business, that was one of the consequences."

"He was a civilian. He was just a fucking driver."

"But his death affected you. Which is what I intended. It gives you some indication of what lies ahead for you. Now, drink some water."

"How do I know it's not drugged?"

"You don't, of course. But if I wanted you dead or unconscious, there would be no need for subterfuge. Another injection would suffice, as it did in the car."

The smaller of the two assistants held the water bottle up to Wainwright's lips, and the young Texan swallowed a few mouthfuls. He had been thirsty, but was determined not to ask. He licked his lips and stared at Khamsin. He had to try to get inside the man's head.

"That wand of yours looks a mighty useful piece of equipment." said Wainwright. "Egyptian, isn't it?"

Khamsin looked at the engraved ivory crescent which now lay on the table in front of him.

"I think you have seen too many movies, Mr Wainwright. Do you think this is the scene where the villain of the piece explains his origins, motives and aims to the helpless hero, for the benefit of the audience? And so the hero, once he has freed himself with one bound will know how to defeat him?"

Wainwright smiled. "Something like that."

"Life is not like the movies, Mr Wainwright. Perhaps, though, I can gratify your curiosity a little. You have heard of the Egyptian magician Baufra?"

Wainwright nodded. "Wasn't he court magician to one of the Pharaohs? Meant to have been very powerful, maybe too powerful."

"Indeed, magician to Ramesses II. As the story runs, in addition to his many other accomplishments, he was adept at controlling crocodiles. But, perhaps his greatest use to the Pharoah was causing his enemies to die at a distance. He learned to control a demon, a messenger of death, if you will. He referred to it as the Messenger Of Anubis."

"And it stopped hearts from beating."

"Indeed, with no trace of violence. But, as is often the case with great leaders, Ramesses grew apprehensive of the sharpness of this weapon, and began to fear that it mights, some day, be used against His answer was typical of the time, he ordered Baufra executed and his materials, including the wand, buried beneath his own tomb."

"Why didn't he just destroy them."

"An unworthy question, Mr Wainwright. I'm sure you know that instruments of power such as this must never be destroyed. Only ill fortune could come to anyone who did such a thing."

"Doesn't sound like Baufra met with much good fortune"

"No, but he overreached himself in allowing the Pharaoh to see the extent of his power."

"It's a cool story, but how do you come by it?"

"As with many stories, it attained the stature of a legend, told by fathers to sons, until it came to the ears of an ancestor of mine, over a hundred years ago, Salman Bin-Saheed. He was a skilled practitioner of the magic arts, and knew the power which could be directed by Baufra's wand and papyri. He studied the legend, until he felt sure he knew of the location where Baufra's magician's purse was buried. It was the time when Egyptian archaeological digs were at their height, directed by Europeans, who came to plunder the country's treasures and history."

Wainwright noticed the gleam in the man's eye. He was clearly no fan of Egyptologists.

"My ancestor offered a large bribe to the peasant boy who carried supplies for the men who excavated the Magician's tomb under the tomb of Ramesses. The boy was able to find and hide the purse of Baufra, and, later, my ancestor took the purse from him."

"And the boy was paid?" Khamsin gave a sardonic smile. "History does not relate the boy's fate. But my ancestor did not long enjoy his new possession, possibly because he had come by it dishonestly. He died a few months later, and the purse was placed among his effects and handed down to his eldest son, who had no knowledge of its contents, and no interest in discovering its secrets. Thus it remained in my family, handed down from one generation to another, awaiting a new owner who could understand its secrets and be worthy of its power."

"And that would be you."

Khamsin inclined his head forward. "From an early age, I interested myself in the Secret Arts of Ancient Egypt, perhaps the spirit of Baufra was guiding me."

"Maybe."

"Do not scoff, Mr Wainwright. I sense that you too have pledged yourself to a higher power. I knew it from our first encounter."

Wainwright said nothing.

"As you wish," said Khamsin. "I know what I know. Soon I shall know even more."

263

"Like what?" asked Wainwright.

"I had assumed my power was without limit, but I used it against one who still lives I must know the source of his protection, and strip him of it, before I continue my work."

"Oh yeah? And do you expect the guy just to tell you what you want to know?"

"Just so, Mr Wainwright. I expect him to arrive soon, and tell me exactly what I want to know."

Wainwright kept smiling but his mind raced. Was he talking about Nightingale? Was Nightingale on his way, hoping to rescue Wainwright? If he was, he was clearly heading into a trap.

CHAPTER 84

Nightingale gestured at the side of the road. "Can you pull over?" There was nothing but desert either side of the highway and it had been at least ten minutes since they had seen another vehicle.

"Rest room break?" said Lynsey. "You can use one of the water bottles."

"My bladder is fine, but we need a plan."

"A plan?"

"Just pull over."

Lynsey did as she was told. "We're still about ten miles away from the mine."

"I know that, but it's time to make a plan."

"I sure hope it's a good one."

"That's the trouble, it isn't."

Lynsey grinned. "And I had such faith in you"

"The impossible we do immediately. Miracles take a little longer."

"Good to know. So what's the plan, Stan?"

"Well, as I see it we have three options. We drive in normally down the main street, we speed through with guns blazing or we circle round the back, park out of sight and earshot, and come in quietly over that hill, and take a good look at the place."

"I vote for the third option."

"Well, so would I, but it won't work."

"Because?"

"Because it's so obviously the only choice. All they need to do is have a guy watching the hill, and the moment he sees movement, he'll raise the alarm. There's no cover up there."

"So you think they'll be expecting company and post a guard?"

"It would be pretty stupid not to, and I don't think Khamsin is a fool."

"So we go in shooting?"

"We do not. For a start, who are we going to shoot at? We don't know how many of them there are, there's plenty of cover, and we can't assume everyone there deserves to die. Plus, when you shoot at people in real life, they tend to shoot back, and all it would take is a bullet wound anywhere on either of us and we'd be done for out here."

"So what's our option then? Just drive straight in and say hello?"

"See now, that's pretty much what I thought I'd do."

She started to laugh and then realised he was serious. "Really?"

Nightingale nodded. "I drive in, on my own. You circle around, on foot."

"From here?"

"A bit closer. Maybe a mile away from the mine."

"On foot? In this heat?"

"Take some water with you. Look, if we turn up with guns, the first thing they'll do is take them off us. Then we're both at their mercy. But if one of us takes the long way around without being seen, we get to keep out firepower. And as I'm the one they'll be expecting, you'll be the ace in the hole."

"You think they're expecting you?"

"I hope not. But if he's a serious Occult practitioner, it's always best to assume the worst. Maybe I'll get there and I'll be able to rescue Wainwright solo, but if not I'd prefer to have you in reserve."

"But how will I know what's going on?"

"I'll call you."

"You'll call me, that's your plan?" She frowned. "What sort of phone have you got?"

'An iPhone 12. One of the small ones."

"Okay, mine's an iPhone, too. Let's set up Find My iPhone and I'll be able to track you."

"I've no idea how to do that."

Lynsey grinned and held out her hand. "Just do the face activation thing and give it to me," she said. Nightingale held his phone to his face and gave it to her. She spent a couple of minutes tapping on his screen and then gave it back to him. "Right, you're good to go."

"I'm going to have to drive," he said.

"Fine."

She climbed out and they swapped seats. "So, we'll drive another mile and then I'll drop you off. How long do you think it'll take you to cover a mile?"

"With my AR-15? Over this terrain?" She shrugged. "Ten minutes."

"Seriously?"

"I'm fitter than I look."

"Well to be fair, you do look fit."

"Thank you, kind sir."

"But really, ten minutes?"

"It's desert but it's flat enough. I can walk a mile on a treadmill in fifteen minutes. Half that time for a jog."

"So we'll call it ten. I'll drop you in a mile, then I'll stay parked up for ten minutes. Then I'll drive to the mine."

"Sounds like a plan, Stan."

CHAPTER 85

Ali knocked on the door of Khamsin's chamber and waited for permission to enter. He put his ear to the wood and heard him say "Come."

The room was decorated with richly embroidered cloth on the walls, and a magnificent Egyptian carpet in shades of red and green wool. I the centre was the silk-covered divan, where Khamsin reclined when smoking his hookah. Around the room, on gold stands were a variety of Egyptian ornaments and curios, including half a dozen statues of Bastet, the cat goddess and Anubis, the jackal-headed god of death. Khamsin himself stood at the window, he had changed his ornate robes for black slacks and a dark blue short-sleeved shirt.

"He comes?" asked Khamsin.

"Yes, Khamsin. We saw the cloud of dust approaching. I estimate he will be here in three minutes."

Khamsin nodded. "He makes no attempt at subterfuge then, he must have realised it would be useless."

He looked out the window, the cloud of dust was quite close now. "I shall go down and greet our guest."

"Is this safe for you?"

"Oh, I think so, it would not advance his cause to shoot me on sight. Still, you and Salim take your rifles and station yourself at the windows. You are not to fire unless I instruct you to, or he fires first."

"Yes Khamsin."

Khamsin drew deeply on his hookah, turned and left the room. He went down the main stairs of the hotel and out of the front door into the street.

CHAPTER 86

Nightingale drove into the old main street of Medicine Bend and slowed down to look at the place. The first construction on the left was the old silver mine, its sign still readable, but its brown varnished timbers cracked and pulling apart from each other. He wouldn't have cared to go down it. Next came a wooden platform with steps leading up to it, and two high upright beams on top. After a little thought, Nightingale realised it was the town gallows.

Next to the gallows was a large black barn, bearing the legend *Thos Appleby Livery Stable*s. There were a couple of long deserted stores - one marked Mercantile the other Dry Goods - and next to them was the Pioneer Saloon, a dirty white shack which didn't look as if it had served a whisky in a century. There was a large water tower next to it, which was a lot less rusty than Nightingale would have expected, perhaps a recent addition. Nightingale braked to a halt outside the hotel, a squat brick building with a grey slate roof, which looked to be in much better state of repair than the rest of the town. Next to the main building was a large pool which was full of water but which didn't look clean enough for swimming.

There was a figure dressed in green, standing in the shadows of the doorway of the hotel, and Nightingale laid both hands on the top of the steering wheel and sat quite still.

"Please get out of the car, but try to keep your hands in sight," said the man. It was Khamsin.

Nightingale obeyed and stood next to the Jeep, his hands at his side.

"Have you brought weapons?"

"There are guns in the Jeep, but I'm not carrying."

"I apologise for doubting your word, but I would prefer to make sure." Khamsin turned to look up at his assistant who was peering

269

through one of the upstairs windows, sighting down a rifle. "Ali, please come and check the gentleman."

Inside a minute, Ali had come down from his window - without the rifle - and began patting him down. He found the Glock in the back of Nightingale's jeans and he pulled it out and held it up so that Khamsin could see it.

"You disappoint me, Mr Nightingale," said Khamsin.

"You can't blame me for trying," said Nightingale.

Ali took out Nightingale's phone, lighter and Marlboro pack. He showed them to Khamsin.

"Take them," said Khamsin.

"I might want to smoke," said Nightingale.

"You lost any good will you might have had when we found the gun," said Khamsin. "Now let us go inside, it is too hot a day for standing in the sun. Follow Ali, please, Mr Nightingale."

Ali took Nightingale inside the hotel. Nightingale wondered if Lynsey was nearby and if she could see where he was going. At least Ali had put Nightingale's phone in his pocket, so as long as Ali was close to Nightingale, Lynsey would be able to find him.

They went in to the reception area. There was a long counter, a scattering of sofas and armchairs and a wide stairway leading to the upper floors. It was much cleaner than Nightingale had expected.

Ali waved with the Glock, indicating that Nightingale should sit on one of the sofas.

Khamsin walked over to stand in front of Nightingale.

"Your name is Jack Nightingale?"

Nightingale nodded. He took his first proper look at Khamsin. He already knew the man was wiry and rather short, no more than five foot six, but this was the first time he had seen the face unmasked. The eyes were dark blue against the beige skin, the lips thin and the dark hair growing over his ears. He was dressed in a green robe and was bare-headed, despite the powerful desert sun.

"I am Khamsin. Lord of the Desert Wind, Master of the Ancient Magics."

"Good to know. I assume you gave yourself the titles. Or did you buy them on the internet? I'm told that these days you can buy a square foot of Scottish turf and call yourself Lord of the Highlands."

Khamsin frowned. "Are you attempting to vex me? There is no point to that, I am a man well used to controlling emotions, and I am unlikely to be goaded into any rash mistakes."

"I suspect you've already made quite a few, or I wouldn't be here."

"You are here because I wished it and arranged it."

Nightingale shrugged. "I know what I had to do to find you, so I know that's not true." He looked around. "Nice place you've got here."

"So glad you approve. It is a mere temporary resting place. I purchased it some time ago and have made a few small improvements to render it habitable. Water for my pets was the major problem, but I do not expect to stay here long. I shall be returning to Las Vegas after your demise."

"I need a cigarette," said Nightingale.

"That does not concern me. And it will be good for you to control your cravings." He nodded at Ali who put the gun into the waistband of his trousers and took a pair of handcuffs from his pocket. He handcuffed Nightingale and stepped back.

"I want to see Wainwright," said Nightingale.

"You shall, all in good time. He has not been harmed yet, I needed him as bait to draw you here. Unfortunately for him, his usefulness to me is now almost ended."

Nightingale kept a smile on his face but his mind was racing. Had it been a trap, right from the start? If so, what did Khamsin want? "Look, Khazi or whatever you call yourself, I'm not much of a conversationalist, so why not get to the point. What do you want from me?"

Khamsin drew in his breath sharply and glared at Nightingale. "My name is Khamsin, as you well know, and you may well die with it on your lips. As for what I want from you, that is very simple. I want you to explain why you are still alive."

"That's easy. I eat well and look both ways before crossing the road."

"English humour? Enjoy it while you may, soon enough you may not find your situation so funny."

"Always look on the bright side of life, that's me."

"I am aware now that you have some knowledge of the dark arts of magic. I sent the Messenger of Anubis to stop your heart, as it has stopped many before you. And yet you live, and the intermediary I used died instead of you. Explain how this is possible."

"Maybe my guardian angel was on the ball that day."

"You persist in your attempts at humour. I must know why I failed, otherwise I will never have the confidence to strike again, and my work depends on my confidence. So I ask again, how did you avoid death at the hands of the demon I sent?"

Nightingale looked at the floor. This man already wielded too much power, which he had misused. Doubt and lack of confidence would set him back for a while. Nightingale couldn't afford to do anything which might increase his power. He was dangerous enough to the world as it was.

"You think silence is your friend?" said Khamsin. "Let me tell you what will happen to you if you refuse my request. Outside, in the pool there are two Nile crocodiles. My control of them is absolute. Killing you would achieve nothing, but a human body can endure much without dying. I would use my control to let them eat, say, part of a leg, and then force them to release you and remove you from the pool."

Nightingale shuddered. "I'd probably die of shock, or bleed to death."

"No, I think you are reasonably resilient. We could cauterise your wound in a bucket of hot tar, there is plenty around, and building a fire to melt it would be easy."

"And being the USA, you'd probably hit me with a huge bill for medical attention."

"Always the cheap humour. Infection would, no doubt, set in, but then your life expectancy would not be long anyway. If you still remained stubborn, there is always the other leg, then an arm or two."

"Whereas, if I tell you what you want to know, you undo the cuffs, give me Joshua Wainwright, and we drive off into the distance, and live happily ever after?"

Khamsin gave a thin smile. "But of course."

"I'm not quite that stupid. Khamsin. Wainwright and I are dead meat, whatever I say or don't say. It just goes a little more slowly one way than the other. I guess it won't be pleasant, but then dying never is. Can't help you. Sorry."

Khamsin walked over to a divan in front of which was a large silver hookah pipe. He took a long pull on the mouthpiece. Nightingale watched him enviously. He needed a cigarette badly.

"You made a request to see Wainwright," said Khamsin. "So you shall, perhaps he can change your mind."

CHAPTER 87

Nightingale followed Khamsin out of the hotel. Ali walking behind him, with the Glock gun trained on Nightingale's back. He stood far enough back that Nightingale would have had no chance of reaching the gun, even if his hands had not been cuffed. Khamsin walked west, past the derelict livery stable and the saloon, and kept going, until they finally reached the elevator tower of the old silver mine.

"The elevator was originally horse powered, but I have installed an electric motor," said Khamsin. "Step onto it please."

As ever, Nightingale was reluctant to stand on an elevator, but Ali shoved him inside, and the rickety wooden box began to descend. It could only have been twenty feet or so before it came to a halt on the dusty floor of the mine. There was a string of small light bulbs running along the roof of the tunnel, providing just enough light to see by. There was another heavy standing there. Nightingale recognised him - he had been one of the assistants on Khamsin's stage show. There was an assault rifle leaning against the tunnel next to him, and a bottle of water.

"How is our guest?" Khamsin asked.

"He wants a cigar."

Khamsin chuckled as he led the way down the tunnel. Nightingale picked his way carefully between the sleepers and rails of the abandoned rail system, Fifty yards further on, they came to a bend in the shaft, where a figure sat, his handcuffs round a long metal staple that had been driven into a wooden sleeper.

Wainwright's expensive dark suit was torn and covered in dust. His black hair was grey with yet more dust, He looked up and smiled at Nightingale."Good to see you, Jack," he said. "I'm hoping you've brought the Seventh Cavalry with you."

"Yeah, they'll be here any minute now, once they've fed the horses. You okay?"

"Nothing broken, nothing hurts, except for where they spiked me with something in the car. I don't suppose you've brought a cigar?"

"Sorry. I don't think our host is too tolerant of his guests smoking."

"Did he tell you why we're here?" asked Wainwright.

"He wants information, wants to know how come his tame demon couldn't kill me."

"You fixing to tell him?"

"Not in this life," said Nightingale.

"Enough of this," snapped Khamsin. "I will have my answers. You seem to have a disregard for your own safety, Nightingale, let's see what you will do to save a friend. Ali, bring Wainwright to the surface, and prepare him for the pool."

"I'm not a great swimmer," said Wainwright.

"Let's see how much you joke when my friends are chewing on your legs," said Khamsin. He glared at Nightingale. "You will talk, Mr Nightingale. Or your friend will die."

Khamsin took Nightingale back to the elevator. "Come with us," he said to the heavy standing there. The man picked up his AR-15 and followed them into the elevator.

They rattled up to the surface and Khamsin took Nightingale along the dusty road to the hotel, but instead of going inside he headed to the pool. A heavy with a rifle followed their progress from one of the hotel's bedroom windows.

They walked to the edge of the pool. The water had turned green and the tiles around the edge were slimy with mould. The two crocodiles were at the far end of the pool, lying parallel to each other.

"So, Mr Nightingale, it will save a lot of time and pain if you tell me what I wish to know."

Nightingale shook his head. "You're not offering me anything, Khamsin. If I don't tell you, your pets get to chew me up a bit at a time. If I do tell you, my money says they get to eat me all in one go. It's not much of a deal"

"You are very blasé about your own survival, Nightingale. What about your friend? Can you stand here and watch him slowly eaten alive, knowing that you could save him?" He turned to look towards the road. Ali was bringing Wainwright along the road towards the hotel.

"You don't have to do this, Khamsin."

"Then tell me what I want to know."

Nightingale watched as Ali poked Wainwright in the back with the Glock. Wainwright stumbled. His hands - like Nightingale's - were cuffed.

The heavy with the AR-15 shouted something to Ali in another language. Arabic maybe, Nightingale wasn't great at languages. Ali shouted back and the heavy laughed. He let the assault rifle swing down so that the barrel was pointing at the tiles. Nightingale knew that he would have only the one chance so he moved quickly. He grabbed the AR-15 with both hands and then kicked the heavy between the legs, hard.

The heavy stumbled backwards, his arms flailing, then he screamed and fell into the pool. He began to splash around as he continued to scream. The two crocodiles began to move towards him.

The handcuffs made holding the weapon difficult, but Nightingale managed to get his finger on the trigger and use his left hand to support the barrel. He aimed at the upstairs window as best he could and fired at the heavy in the window. The shot went high so Nightingale lowered his aim and fired again. The rifle in the window jerked and there was a scream from the room. Nightingale fired three times in quick succession and the rifle disappeared.

The heavy in the pool was trying to climb out, still screaming. The crocodiles were only feet away.

"Help him," Nightingale said to Khamsin.

"Salim can help himself," said Khamsin. He held out his hand. "Or you can give me the weapon and you can help him out."

"Jack, what's happening?" shouted Wainwright from the road.

"Get away from Ali!" Nightingale shouted.

276

Wainwright moved away and Nightingale pointed the gun at Ali. "Drop the gun, Ali, and get over here. Your friend needs help!"

The heavy in the pool was still screaming as he tried to pull himself out of the pool. The crocodiles were moving slowly towards him, their long tails waving from side to side.

Ali pointed his gun at Nightingale but he clearly wasn't used to handling guns and was holding it one handed. Nightingale aimed his A R-15 as best as he could and fired three shots into the road close to Ali's feet. Ali yelped and threw his gun away.

"Get over here now, quickly!" Nightingale shouted. "Your pal's about to be eaten."

Ali obeyed and ran across the road and over to the pool. Nightingale stood back so that he could cover both Khamsin and Ali. Ali knelt down and grabbed the struggling heavy's arms. One of the crocodiles had opened its jaws wide, ready to bite down on the man's legs. Both men were screaming now and as Ali pulled Salim from the water the crocodile snapped its jaws shut, missing by inches. Salim rolled onto the side of the pool, gasping for breath.

"Are you okay, Joshua?" shouted Nightingale, his eyes on the three men in front of him.

"Better than I was," shouted Wainwright.

A shot rang out, the loud crack of an assault rifle. Nightingale flinched and looked up at the hotel but all the windows were empty. He looked around. Lynsey was standing next to Wainwright, her AR-15 across her chest. He grinned. "It's okay, I've got it under control," he said.

"So I see," she said.

"Joshua, I told you the cavalry was on its way." The Glock was lying in the street, a few yards from Wainwright. "Grab the Glock and get up here."

"He's not grabbing anything," said Lynsey. She pointed her weapon at Wainwright's head. "Now give your gun to Khamsin or I will blow his fucking head off."

Nightingale's jaw dropped in amazement. "What?"

"You heard me!"

"What the hell are you playing at?"

Khamsin chuckled. "What took you so long, Neferu?" he shouted.

Nightingale turned to look at him. "Neferu?" he said.

Khamsin's chuckle turned into full blown laughter.

CHAPTER 88

Major General Zakaria Mustafa rolled away from the blonde girl, noticed the bloodstains on the bed sheet and curled his lip in disgust.

"Go on, dress and get out. Take your money and go."

Ordinarily Candy would have asked her client to let her shower before leaving, but every minute she spent with this odious man disgusted and frightened her in equal measure. Sure, he'd paid extra, but the pain told her she wouldn't be able to work again this month. Looking at the wall, fighting back tears, she pulled on her clothes with as much dignity as she could muster, grabbed her bag and fled. At least she could make sure to add his name to the list of past clients with whom her agency would do no further business.

Mustafa got out of bed and lit a cigarette. He picked up the phone on the nightstand and dialled the United reservation number to confirm his flight. He took a long, hot shower, dressed carefully in his best Savile Row suit and called down to reception for the limousine service to the airport.,

Today would mark the start of the crowning achievement of his life, as the Brotherhood of Caanan would be launching their coup, just as soon as the news came through of the President's sad death. His cousin, the one known as Khamsin, had never been known to fail in a task. Mustafa had no idea of the source of his power, he had always lacked the courage to ask, but he knew that Khamsin had a foolproof method of murder, and had proved it on many occasions.

Of course, one of the first acts after the success of the coup, would be to remove Khamsin from the scene, permanently, Such a man would be far too dangerous to be allowed to live.

CHAPTER 89

"What the hell is going on, Jack?" asked Wainwright. He was standing next to Nightingale at the edge of the pool. The crocodiles were in the middle of the pool, their eyes fixed on them. Ali was standing behind them, covering them with an AR-15.

"I screwed up," said Nightingale. "I thought she was working for you."

"Why the hell would you think that?"

The girl was standing next to Khamsin, her AR-15 swinging from her right hand. She grabbed her hair with her left hand, and pulled it away. It was a wig. Underneath her hair was blonde.

"That's Neferu, his assistant,"

"Yes, Joshua, I know that now. She was wearing a mask on stage and she looked taller, and that was a bloody good wig."

"And you brought her here? She was the cavalry?"

"I'm afraid so."

"So you understand now, Nightingale," said Khamsin. "No one is coming to your rescue."

"Tell him what he wants to know, Jack," said Lynsey. "Then you can go."

"He won't let us go, Lynsey," he said. He shook his head. "Neferu, whatever your name is."

"That's not true, Mr Nightingale," said Khamsin. "I am a man of my word. I need to know why my attempt to kill you backfired, so that I can prevent it happening again."

"At which point you'll kill me."

"There would be no point. The contract was from Wainwright. He can pay said contract and the deal is done. You will never see me again." He gestured at the pool. "Or you can go into the pool.

Wainwright first in case you have a change of heart. But if you don't , then the crocodiles can have you."

"And then you'll never find out how I did it."

Khamsin smiled. "So you did do something. I knew it."

"If I did, you'll never know how. The mystery will die with me."

'We'll see about that," said Khamsin. He gestured at the crocodiles. "The second largest reptiles on Earth, surpassed only by the saltwater crocodile. Estimated to kill over four hundred people a year in their natural habitat. They possess the most powerful bite of any animal, once their jaws close on your body nothing could ever pry them open. Once I tell them to attack, you fate is sealed. So, Nightingale, will you tell me what I need to know? Or does Mr Wainwright go for a swim?"

"If I do tell you, what do I get? Another twenty minutes of life? Once you have what you want, neither of us are any use to you except as crocodile food. I'm not going to give you the power you want in exchange for another twenty minutes of life. You might as well get it over with now."

Khamsin gestured at Salim and said something in Arabic. The heavy grabbed Wainwright and pushed him towards the pool. Wainwright struggled but the heavy was stronger. The crocodiles began to move, sensing food was heading their way.

"Sorry about this, Jack," Wainwright grunted. "My bad."

"I screwed up as well," said Nightingale. "I should have brought the cops with me."

"Well we live and learn," said Khamsin. "But not today," obviously.

Wainwright was at the pool's edge now, still struggling but making no headway against the heavy. His left foot skidded off the tiles and hovered above the water. Both crocodiles had their jaws open wide now.

"Okay, okay!" shouted Nightingale. "I'll tell you what you want to know!"

281

Khamsin barked at Salim in Arabic and the heavy released his grip on Wainwright. "We shall go back to the hotel, but if you lie to me again, Mr Nightingale, you will go straight into the pool."

Khamsin took them back to the hotel and sat them on a sofa in reception. "Can I smoke?" asked Nightingale. "Smoking helps me think and what I have to tell you is complicated. I don't want to make any mistakes."

"Give Mr Nightingale his cigarettes," Khamsin said to Ali.

Ali gave Nightingale his pack of Marlboro and his lighter.

"There's a montecristo in my jacket pocket," said Wainwright.

Khamsin spoke to Ali again. Ali went over to Wainwright, took a metal cigar case from his inside pocket, opened it, and gave the cigar to him. Wainwright bit off the end, then Nightingale lit it for him. As Wainwright blew smoke, Nightingale lit a Marlboro.

"Now, for your part of the deal," said Khamsin. "Whence comes the protection that saved your life from my demon?" Khamsin sat on his divan and took a puff from his hookah.

Nightingale blew smoke up at the ceiling. He saw Neferu looking enviously at his cigarette. He smiled and mouthed "screw you" and then looked over at Khamsin. "The reason you couldn't kill me is because someone else has a claim on my soul, and she won't see me dead unless she can redeem her claim first."

"This is nonsense," said Khamsin, his face twisting in anger.

"Any more nonsensical than you using a dead Egyptian wizard's wand to control crocodiles and dispatch demons? We work in the same world, Khamsin, but if you don't want to accept what I say..."

Khamsin took another drag on his hookah, and nodded slowly. "Proceed. Who is this entity that has a claim upon you and affords you protection."

"I don't care to speak her name out loud. She has a dislike for that."

"So, the creature is a woman?"

"Well, I wouldn't go that far, but she always presents in female form. Though I get the impression she has different forms for different audiences."

"What is this creature? A wizard, a demon, a djinn?"

"I rather think she's a Princess of Hell."

"Pah, Christian superstition."

"Whereas you prefer Egyptian superstition. Anubis and Set instead of Lucifer?"

"So this creature is more powerful than the demon I sent to destroy you?"

"So it seems. I think you've just been dealing with minor league stuff. She's the real thing."

Khamsin nodded. "I must meet this Princess of Hell."

"See now, I don't think that's your best idea. She can be a little bit feisty if she's summoned needlessly. You wouldn't like her when she's angry."

"But I have a need. I need to work with her, to add my power to hers. You will show me how to summon her. Remember, I still hold your lives in the palm of my hand."

Nightingale nodded. "Well, don't say I didn't warn you. If you plan on summoning her, you'll need to be prepared to make a deal. She'll want your soul, in exchange for whatever power you want from her."

"And the power is limitless?"

"You can ask for anything you want, except immortality, but I'd advise you to be very careful. If there's a loophole, she'll find it, so read the small print carefully."

Khamsin's eyes were glittering greedily "Tell me how to summon her."

"Well, first of all, I think you're going to need to go shopping."

CHAPTER 90

Once Nightingale had written down everything that they would need for the summoning, Khamsin gave the piece of paper to Neferu.

"Keys," she said to Nightingale, holding out her hand.

"I left them in the Jeep."

"The shop that you went to before, *Crystal Village*, they will have everything we need?" asked Khamsin.

"If they don't they will be able to suggest alternatives."

"Ali, you can go with Neferu."

Ali nodded and followed Neferu outside. After a few seconds they heard the Jeep drive off.

Khamsin took a pull on his hookah, then got to his feet. "I shall rest for a while. I will leave you in the care of Salim. If you make any attempt to get up from that sofa he has instructions to shoot you in the legs and we will then feed you to the crocodiles."

"What if we need a bathroom break?" asked Nightingale.

"I do not find your English humour in any way amusing or endearing," said Khamsin. "And if you continue with it, it could prove to be the death of you." He walked over to the stairs and headed up, his robe whispering on the carpet.

Salim went to stand by the entrance, his AR-15 clasped to his chest.

"Are you okay?" Nightingale asked Wainwright.

Wainwright took a pull on his cigar and blew smoke down at the carpet before answering. "I won't lie, Jack, I've been better." He sighed. "What the hell happened with Neferu? How did you let her get close to you?"

'She turned up and said you'd sent her. You'd just gone dark, remember? No contact. I assumed you'd sent her as back up."

"And you didn't think to check?"

"Check how? You'd said no contact, remember?"

"You could have called Valerie."

"I mentioned Valerie but Lynsey - Neferu - said she always dealt with you direct. Anyway, have I ever checked up on any of the people you've sent to help me?"

"But, Jack, how the hell could she have found out you worked for me?"

Nightingale took a long pull on his cigarette. "Let me think about the timeline here. Whoever killed the Macoubs probably got my name from them, so knew I'd been asking questions, Then, when Khamsin contacted you, my name came up again, and he took that as confirmation that we were working together. It wasn't till after that that she introduced herself to me. "

"You're telling me a girl killed the Macoubs?"

"Why not, they were old and frail, she was young. If she had the right weapon and knew where to strike, nothing easier. How many lethal women have we met in the last few years? Those two killers in San Francisco, the two in New Orleans. I watched Chris Dubois stab someone to death down there. Murder isn't a male preserve."

"So she killed them?"

"Yeah. Come to think of it, it explains Amber Diamond too."

"Who?"

"One of Kahsim's messengers. I managed to hypnotise her, but when I got too close to the truth, she'd been programmed to faint. Lynsey sent me for a glass of water, and while I was gone she was whispering to the woman. Plenty of time to suggest she could fly off the balcony. It was staring me in the face, and I didn't see it."

"She must have been one hell of an actress."

"She surely was. She seemed quite well informed about you, but maybe..."

"Maybe what?"

"Maybe I helped," said Nightingale. "I was expecting you to send someone, so all she really had to do was play along while I filled in the blanks for her. Looks like Proserpine was right."

"How?"

"She often tells me I take people at face value, judge too much by appearances. I can be a lousy judge of character."

Wainwright blew smoke. "If you give Khamsin what he wants, do you think he'll let us go?"

"What do you think?"

"Not a chance in hell."

"Yeah, that's about right. If he does get the power he wants, the first thing he'll want to do is to try it out. On us."

"That's not good," said Wainwright.

"And it'll probably make swimming with the crocs look like a much better option."

"Please tell me you have a plan?"

"I'm working on it, but if you have any ideas I'd love to hear them."

CHAPTER 91

It took Neferu the best part of four fours to drive to Vegas and back. She and Ali carried in their purchases contained in several *Crystal Village* carrier bags and placed them on a sofa. "Where's Khamsin?" she asked.

"He's getting his beauty sleep," said Nightingale. "Look, we need to talk."

"Do we?"

"What Khamsin is planning on doing, it's dangerous. Not just for him, for everyone."

"He knows what he's doing."

"He knows what he's doing in his world, perhaps. The Egyptian occult. But even then, it backfired when he attacked me, didn't it? So he doesn't know everything. When it comes to the occult, a little knowledge can be a dangerous thing. What he wants to do can end very badly. For everyone concerned."

"So what do you want me to do?"

Nightingale looked over at Ali and Salim who were deep in conversation at the hotel entrance, cradling their assault rifles. He leaned towards her and lowered his voice. "Just take off the cuffs and let us go. We'll take you back to Vegas."

"I'll pay you for your trouble," said Wainwright. "I don't know what Khamsin had promised you, but I'll double it."

"He's promised me power."

"I can give you that. But I can show you how to develop and use powers safely."

She looked over at Ali and Salim. "What about them?"

"Up to you," said Nightingale. "We can take them with us, or you can help us overpower them."

She nodded thoughtfully. "And maybe I could give you both blowjobs on the way back to Vegas." She sneered contemptuously. "If you two could hear yourselves," she said. "Like a couple of scared children. You know he's going to kill you when this is done, don't you? No matter what he has promised you, you'll be dead." She grinned and headed up the stairs.

"Well she's a little ray of sunshine, isn't she?" said Nightingale. He took out a cigarette and lit it.

He was just finishing it when Khamsin and Neferu came back downstairs. "So now we will make our preparations," said Khamsin.

Nightingale looked at his watch. "Midnight is the best time for the ritual," he said. "The closer to actual midnight, the better. So you have plenty of time. You need to prepare for this very carefully. First, find yourself a decent sized room and give it a good clean with the mop, brushes and disinfectant."

"Can we do it here, in the lobby?"

"You can, yes. But you should move all the furniture to the side and then take up the carpet. You have to draw the pentagram and it's best to do it on stone or wood."

"Do I have to do that, or can it be done for me?"

"Providing it is done properly, anyone can do it?"

Khamsin nodded. "What else?"

'You also have to be scrupulously clean. Under your nails, behind your ears, all orifices. Clean as a whistle. And any clothing you wear must be spotless. Any impurities will weaken the protective circle."

Khamsin nodded again. "Very well, I shall clean myself now." He looked at Neferu. "Arrange for this place to be cleaned."

He went back upstairs. Neferu called Salim and Ali over. "Get these two to move the furniture away, and pull up the carpet. We need bare floorboards. Then take them to the kitchen and get buckets of water and brushes and have them clean the floor."

"You are kidding me," said Nightingale.

Neferu pulled a gun from her belt and thrust it under his chin. "Or I could just blow your head off right now."

288

Nightingale grinned. "No, that's not going to happen. If you kill me, your boss won't be able to complete the ritual. And I'm sure he won't be happy with you."

She pointed the gun at his right knee. "I could put a bullet in your leg."

"Then I might bleed to death. Plus we're trying to get this place clean and blood spatter isn't going help achieve that objective, is it?"

She took the gun away. "You've got a smart mouth, Nightingale."

Nightingale held up his cuffed wrists. "How about this? You take off the cuffs and Joshua and I will do your cleaning work."

"Jack?" protested Wainwright.

Nightingale looked at him. "What's the choice? We sit here handcuffed and watch them do it? At least we'll have something to do." He stared intently at Wainwright. With the cuffs off, they stood a better chance of grabbing a gun from the heavies.

He wasn't sure if Wainwright got the hint or not, but he nodded. "Okay, fine."

Neferu sighed. "Okay, the cuffs come off. But Salim and Ali will be covering you with their guns. One wrong move..." She left the sentence unfinished.

"Deal," said Nightingale.

Wainwright held out his cuffed hands. "Deal."

CHAPTER 92

It took the best part of half an hour for Nightingale and Wainwright to move all the furniture to the walls and pull back the carpet and underlay. Ali and Salim then took them down the corridor to the kitchen where they filled buckets with water and added disinfectant. They found mops in a storage cupboard and took them and the buckets back to reception. They cleaned the floor, then went back to the kitchen, emptied the buckets and refilled them. They made the journey three times, each time under the watchful eyes of Salim and Ali. Neferu sat on the stairs playing with her phone, her Glock next to her.

Once they had washed the floor, Nightingale and Wainwright used clean towels to rub the wood dry. They were finishing as Khamsin came down the stairs. He had changed into a white robe and his hair was still damp. Neferu put her phone away and walked down the stairs with him.

Khamsin looked at their work and nodded his approval. "Now what?" he asked.

"Now, you're going to need to listen closely, because one mistake and you're toast," said Nightingale.

"I don't expect to make any mistakes."

"Good to know." He took Khamsin over to the reception counter and picked up a pen. Salim kept his AR-15 trained on Nightingale's chest, his finger on the trigger.

Nightingale started to write on a sheet of hotel stationery everything that Khamsin needed to do to complete the ritual. He was working from memory, trying hard to remember every step he had needed to take years ago, the first time he had tried a Summoning. The candles, the chalk, the circle drawn with a birch twig, the goblets of salt were easy enough to remember, but the words of the incantation were much more difficult, He was pretty sure he'd remembered them accurately, but it was difficult, as they were in a long dead language, and he had no references.

"So these are the words I must say," asked Khamsin, looking over his shoulder. "They mean nothing to me."

"Or me," said Nightingale, "but you wouldn't expect them too. Now, don't bother me for ten minutes, I need to do a sketch."

Nightingale's grip tightened on the pen as he cast his mind back to that awful night years ago at Gosling Manor when he had first tried to summon a demon, and nearly lost his life in the process. He forced his memory to show him the drawing. It had to be exact. Finally it was finished and he showed it to Khamsin.

"So what is this?"

"You need to copy this onto the goatskin parchment that Lynsey - Neferu - bought at *Crystal Village*. You need to use the swan quill that she bought."

"Can't you do it?"

Nightingale shook his head. "No, it must be done by the person doing the summoning, and in his own blood. Or you can use the blood of a sea-turtle, but we're a long way from the ocean. That's what that goose feather quill is for. I'm sure you'll have something sharp around here to let some blood out."

Neferu went over to the carrier bags and returned with the parchment and quill. She gave them to Khamsin. He took a crescent shaped knife from inside his robe and ran the blade across the back of his hand. The blood started to flow instantly but he showed no reaction at all. Khamsin dipped his quill into the blood and began to copy Nightingale's drawing. He worked slowly and methodically and showed no sign of discomfort or pain.

"That looks about right," said Nightingale, "but I guess we'll find out soon enough. Now it's time to make the rest of your preparations." He passed the handwritten sheets to Khamsin. "Follow these instructions to the letter."

Khamsin took the sheets and turned to Ali. "Take Mr Nightingale and Mr Wainwright and attach their handcuffs to the balustrade at the top of the stairs. I want them to have a good view of events."

"If it's all the same to you, I'd rather not be here at all," said Nightingale.

"It is *not* all the same to me. I do not have complete trust in you. Whatever happens to me, you shall share my fate."

"I have told you everything you need to know. I have kept my side of the bargain."

"Do as you're told, Nightingale," said Neferu, gesturing with her gun.

Neferu and Ali took Nightingale and Wainwright up the stairs and locked their handcuffs around posts of the balustrade. The wood was old and probably dried out, and Nightingale wondered if he could snap it but decided that the time to try would not be when there were guns trained on him.

Khamsin was right though, they couldn't have had a better view.

Neferu and Ali went halfway down the stairs and sat down, their guns at their side. Salim was standing by the entrance, still cradling his AR-15.

They all watched as Khamsin took consecrated chalk and constructed the pentagram, exactly as he had been instructed, tracing back over the lines with a birch twig., dipped in holy water. He set four large black candles in brass stands at the four corners of the room, and a brass pot at each of the pentagram points. Into these he poured the mixture of herbs which Nightingale had prescribed.

Nightingale strained a little at his handcuffs, and felt the old wood creak. Khamsin moved around the pentagram, lighting the four candles, the northernmost first, and then setting fire to the herbs in the bowls. Thick smoke began to fill the lobby.

"Ali," said Khamsin, "what is the time?"

Ali looked at his wrist. "11.58."

"Count it for me."

Ali stared at his watch. Time seemed to crawl by. "11.59," he said eventually.

Nightingale braced his feet against the wood. The seconds ticked by.

"12.00."

Khamsin began to chant the incantation Nightingale had given him. *"Osurmy delmausan atalsloym chariusihoa..."*

When the incantation was finished, he held the parchment over the candle flame as he had been instructed.

"Come to me, come to me, I summon you."

Upstairs, Nightingale held his breath.

The smoke in the lobby rippled, and began to spin in a vortex, as if a tornado were let loose in the room. A deep booming laugh echoed around the room, the vortex folded itself inside out, and a short squat figure appeared, the large head topped with curly black hair, the body thick and the stumpy legs bowed. He wore a red jacket with gold buttons and epaulettes, black jodhpurs and shiny black boots and carried a vicious looking riding crop.

"Who the fuck is that?" whispered Wainwright.

"Lucifuge Rofocale."

"Oh, shit."

"Yeah."

The dwarf fixed Khamsin with his baleful eyes, his face a mask of fury. "Who dares to summon me? Who dares? On your knees."

Khamsin roared with laughter. "Khamsin kneels to no-one, dwarf. I was told a woman would appear. I summoned her, I want to learn her power. Show her to me. I, Khamsin, Master of the wind, heir to Baufra, command it."

"Bad move," muttered Nightingale.

Despite Nightingale's warning that he should bring nothing into the pentagram that was not necessary, Khamsin reached into the pocket of his robe and produced the wand of Baufra. He held it aloft, threatening the dwarf. "Obey me."

Nightingale couldn't help but smile. "Even worse move," he whispered.

The dwarf's face grew red with fury. "Obey you? Obey you? You gibbering fool. Away with you and your child's toy."

Lucifuge made a slashing motion with his riding crop, and a burst of red flame flew from it, straight at Khamsin's wand. The wand instantly turned to ash, as did the whole of Khamsin's right arm. The screaming was unbearable.

Neferu and Ali stood up. Ali picked up his AR-15 and began to fire at Lucifuge but his shots all went wide. Neferu grabbed her Glock and started firing. Her shots were more accurate, all thudding into Lucifuge's red jacket, but the bullets had absolutely no effect.

Lucifuge glared at them, waved his hand and then pointed, and a blast of black light hit them both and reduced them to ashes. Their weapons thudded onto the stairs.

Khamsin was still screaming in agony, his upper body in flames now. He ran out of the pentagram and pushed his way past Salim then barged out of the hotel, trailing his anguished yelps behind him.

Salim began to fire his AR-15. His aim was better than Ali's and his shots hit Lucifuge in the middle of his back but again they had no effect. Lucifuge turned, waved his hand again, and Salim burst into a shower of ash. His rifle clattered onto the wooden floorboards.

Outside there was a splash, and a horrible thrashing sound, one last, long scream, and then silence.

The dwarf paced the floor and then sniffed the air. He sniffed again, then pronounced a few words. The room seemed to fold in on itself, and he was gone.

Nightingale realised he had been holding his breath, and he sighed. "Well that worked out well, considering," he said.

"That was close," said Wainwright.

'We were lucky he didn't see us," said Nightingale.

"Well I'd like to think I had a hand in that," said Wainwright.

"Really?"

"An invisibility spell. I wasn't sure if it would work on a demon from hell but it seemed to do the trick. Maybe he just didn't see us."

"Either way we were lucky," said Nightingale. He braced his feet against the bottom of the stair rod and pulled with all his strength. The old, dry wood started to splinter, so this time he wriggled onto his back and started kicking at it. The wood gave, and he pulled his handcuffed hands through the break, Coughing from the fumes, he shuffled downstairs to the ashes of Neferu and Ali. He ran his hands through the ashes and found the handcuff key. He used it to open his handcuffs, then went back up the stairs to release Wainwright. "We need to get the hell out of Dodge," said Nightingale.

"I hear you," said Wainwright.

They headed down the stairs and outside. As they passed the pool, they saw that the water was stained red, but there was no sign of the two crocodiles. From the sounds Nightingale had heard, he guessed that Khamsin, driven crazy with pain and fear had run straight into the pool. Without his wand, he would have been dragged to the bottom and drowned, assuming he hadn't died of shock. The crocs were at the bottom, feeding on what was left of their master.

Nightingale shuddered at the thought that it could easily have been him and Wainwright down there.

Wainwright reached the Jeep and pulled open the door. "Keys are in the ignition," he said.

"Finally some good news," said Nightingale. "Are you okay to drive?"

Wainwright grimaced. "It's a stick shift," he said. "I'm not great on stick-shifts."

CHAPTER 93

Medicine Bend was ten minutes behind them before Wainwright spoke again. "So why didn't you just summon Pros...your friend? Wouldn't she have got you out of this?"

"You never can tell with her And she'd given me a direct order not to summon her. She can get a little tetchy when people disobey her."

"So you figured Khamsin would rile up the other guy?"

"I figured it was worth rolling the dice, he was almost as arrogant as Lucifuge, and had way too much confidence in his power. I thought they deserved each other."

"But, one thing I don't get. Khamsin was standing inside a pentagram, In theory Lucifuge shouldn't have been able to harm him. Let alone blast his arm off."

"Yeah, funny thing that. Maybe Khamsin forgot something when he was making his pentagram"

"Like what?"

"I don't remember him putting any cups of holy water at the points of the star."

"Shit, didn't you tell him to do that?"

Nightingale scratched his head. "You know, come to think of it now, I did overlook that. I guess I'd be forgetting my head if it wasn't screwed on."

"You're a mean bastard, Jack."

"Me? I'm not the hired killer around here." He sighed. "At least Khamsin's gone, that wand of his is a pile of ash, and the FBI won't be losing any more witnesses."

"I guess," said Wainwright. " I'll be needing to talk to Luca Marino. Tell him we dealt with the guy who had his son killed."

"I guess someone ought to call the Department of Wildlife and tell them there are two hungry Nile crocodiles looking for a good home."

"Dunno about a good home," said Wainwright, "I'd be happier seeing those two made into luggage. Now, how about you press that gas pedal a little harder and get me to Vegas. I need a shower and a good steak. Not necessarily in that order."

CHAPTER 94

Major General Zakaria Mustafa arrived at Cairo airport on the morning of the peace conference, after a lengthy and tiring journey of nearly twenty-four hours flight via United and Egyptair, changing in Washington. He was dressed immaculately in a dark suit, white shirt and red tie. He planned to go home and change into his old ceremonial uniform, so that he would be ready to appear in public once the news came out.

The plane had not been full, and the first-class passengers were disembarked before the rest, so the line at passport control was a short one. Mustafa handed over his passport, and the young immigration officer passed it under his scanner. His expression never altered as he pressed the silent button under his desk.

Mustafa drummed his fingers on the counter. "Is there some problem?" he asked.

"The computer is running a little slow today," said the officer, but then the two military policemen arrived, and his expression changed to one of relief.

Mustafa felt their presence at his shoulder, before his arms were seized and his wrists handcuffed behind his back. He spluttered indignantly. "What is the meaning of this? This is an outrage. Do you know who I am?"

The policeman on his left spoke. "We know perfectly well who you are, former General Mustafa, we were informed that you would be arriving this morning You are under arrest, on a matter of national security, to answer certain allegations which have been made against you. You will come with us now."

Mustafa was half-dragged away, and the next passengers in line moved forward, as if they had seen nothing.

The trials were held speedily and in camera. Eight members of the Brotherhood of Canaan were sentenced to be shot. Since Mustafa was

no longer a serving officer in the armed forces, his sentence was
hanging. His last words were used to curse the memory of his cousin,
Khamsin.

CHAPTER 95

Nightingale tossed his twenty dollar chip onto red, and watched with no great surprise as black came up on the wheel. He was almost at the loss limit he'd learned from the girl who had called herself Lynsey Lawton, and it was nearly time to be heading back to his room. Tomorrow evening would find him on the opposite coast of the United States, two and a half thousand miles away and three hours ahead. He wasn't looking forward to the four and a half hour flight, and could only hope that Valerie would show her gratitude for rescuing her boss by getting him a decent seat, preferably first class.

He tossed another chip onto black this time, then watched the ball land in a red slot.

"Have you ever considered that you're just a natural loser, Nightingale?" she asked.

He clenched his fists until the knuckles turned white, forced himself to appear calm, took a drag from his latest Marlboro, then turned slowly, knowing what he'd see.

This time she wore a long black T-shirt over her black tights and boots. On the front was a large white skull, in front of four playing cards, all the aces. Underneath the skull were four dice, each showing a six. This time, the tips of her fringe were tinted turquoise, and her impenetrable black eyes were hidden behind small, round, metal-framed sunglasses.

"Just passing the time," said Nightingale. "My last night."

"Off in the morning? Where to?"

"You mean you don't know?"

"Told you before, Nightingale, I'm not omniscient. Maybe this time it'll be our appointment in Samarra. It's overdue. Try twenty six."

Despite himself, Nightingale threw a chip on twenty six.

"Appointment where?"

"Samarra, Nightingale. I would have thought you'd have come across it with all your recent Middle-Eastern research. Look it up, there's a lesson for you there."

The ball landed on twenty six.

"Looks like it's my week for learning lessons."

"I've told you often enough, Nightingale, don't get fooled by appearances. I know one harmless looking dwarf who'd jump at the chance to torture you for eternity."

"It's not like he needed any more reasons to hate me."

"I don't think he appreciated doing your dirty work for you. Any more than I would have. Seventeen, Nightingale, all of it."

"But I didn't summon you."

"No, you didn't. Not like you to follow orders, Nightingale."

"Maybe I wanted to keep you sweet."

Nightingale's eyes opened wide at the pile of chips he'd won on seventeen.

She clicked her fingers and a lit cigarette appeared between her lips. She blew out a smoke ring, which circled his head. "I think I've warned you about trying to flirt with me before, Nightingale. Save your boyish charm for real women, if you can persuade one to stick around long enough. Talking of which, would you like to hear what the lovely Jenny is up to these days? Number four, Nightingale."

"Leave her out of this," snapped Nightingale.

"Temper, temper. I should think I'm due a little gratitude, Nightingale, by rights you should have died this week. I saved your life."

"I'm sure you had your reasons."

"Always. Maybe soon you'll find out what they are."

Nightingale shivered.

"Still, maybe you don't deserve my help," she said.

The wheel spun yet again.

She looked over as the ball rattled to a halt and groaned. "Triple zero, bad luck Nightingale, everyone loses, except the house. Anyway, time for me to pop off now. Don't forget your sunscreen, you can burn quite quickly in Florida."

"Who says I'm going to Florida?"

She grinned and blew him a kiss. Then there was a flash of white light, time and space folded in on itself, and she was gone.

Nightingale couldn't help but smile. She'd be back, he was sure of that. One way or another, she would be back.

THE END

Printed in Great Britain
by Amazon

17577316R00181